BERMAN'S LAMENT

BERMAN'S LAMENT

Mark Kelley

VANTAGE PRESS
New York

FIRST EDITION

Published by Vantage Press, Inc.
516 West 34th Street, New York, New York 10001

Manufactured in the United States of America
ISBN: 0-533-13179-0

Library of Congress Catalog Card No.: 99-93892

0 9 8 7 6 5 4 3 2 1

To Marty, my partner in life

Contents

BERMAN'S LAMENT

One

Suspicions

Berman started out in print, long before he ever thought about TV. He reported for his hometown paper, *The Evening Chronicle*. Classic beginning, obits, police blotter stuff, front page and eventually special features. He won lots of awards, not so much because he was the world's greatest writer, but because he actually cared what happened to people; he was interested in their weird habits and painful experiences. He saw his stories as a way to touch people's lives.

Berman lived by himself in a second floor apartment over the drugstore downtown. He could look out his window and monitor the pulse of Berrington. There wasn't really much to see. Downtown had about twenty fairly large brick buildings, four or five stories each, crowded together in the space of two blocks, as though someone thought they'd need the rest of the space for even more big buildings. But that never happened. Beyond the taller buildings were much smaller brick and block ones, two, maybe three stories, and after about four blocks, old wooden houses, as tall as the smaller businesses, owned by the old families with old money.

Although they'd been built a long time ago, the homes were well kept, the ornate woodwork on many of them had been preserved or replaced. They looked nice. Berman could see the ones on the west side of the street from his window, especially the Wises' house. He plotted the seasons by the changing decorations in the Wises' windows and on their front porch.

It was near Halloween when he first heard about the Spanners. As usual, the little Wises had carved pumpkins and set them out, adding a touch of festivity to their attractive home. The Spanners didn't live in an attractive home. Theirs was little more than a tarpaper shack, on the edge of town near the grain elevators. No fancy woodwork here, just old, fake-brick asphalt siding that looks so worn and dirty as it wears out. It was brown, or had been when it was new. Six kids lived inside with a mom and her live-in boyfriend of the moment. They said every kid had a different father, but no one really knew for sure. The guy living there at the moment swore he wasn't responsible for any of them. He spent little time at home.

What Berman overheard from a couple of secretaries as he copied off the police log at the station was that Ma Spanner was about to lose the kids because someone told Child Welfare she beat them and didn't keep them clean. Berman really didn't know the Spanners, but he jogged by their house every morning and he had the impression Mrs. Spanner did as well as could be expected, under the circumstances. And he'd also heard something else—that the welfare caseworker, Hildy Mazer, was a religious fanatic who found the domestic arrangement in the Spanner home immoral. The two bits of information formed the foundation of what might be a good story. It had plenty of human interest, people tending to feel sorry for the Spanners. And, it had conflict; the secretaries said Mrs. Spanner had heard what Mazer thought of her and didn't appreciate it. The thing was that Charlotte Spanner was essentially defenseless against the system when it showed up in a car driven by Hildy Mazer.

The day after he heard the rumor, Berman took it straight to the source. Hildy Mazer's office was in the next town, Pruitville, which was also the county seat and the location of most county offices. It took about six calls to catch Mazer at her desk, and she didn't sound especially pleased to hear from him when she finally picked up the phone.

"Child Welfare Office, Hildy Mazer. Who's this?"

Berman figured he'd get a lot farther if he turned on the charm. He shifted into his sincere tone of voice.

"Hi, I'm Jed Berman with *The Chronicle*. Do you have a minute to talk?"

Hildy Mazer didn't mince words.

"No, I don't, Mr. Berman. Besides, if you're calling about any of my cases, you already know I am not at liberty to discuss them with you or anyone else outside the courts."

Berman knew this wouldn't be easy. He cranked up the innocence.

"I'm sorry to bother you, Ms. Mazer. Is it Miss or Mrs., by the way?"

"That's definitely not any of your business. What is it you want?"

"O.K., I'll get right to the point. How soon are you going to remove Charlotte Spanner's kids?"

For a moment, Mazer said nothing. Then she started to speak, stopped, started again and stopped again. Finally, the words fell together, slowly.

"I am not at liberty to either confirm or deny the allegations you just mentioned. I have sixty cases to follow and an appointment with one of them in just a few minutes. I really do have to go."

She hung up before Berman could think of a way to keep her on the line. But he thought he'd heard something

3

close to a confirmation. She could have simply rejected what he suggested, but she hadn't. She took the route people often take when you hit the nerve and they don't really know how to hide it: she hung up. He was willing to bet Charlotte Spanner was due for a nasty visit from Mazer and her crew.

But he didn't have much of a story, at this point. He wondered if Charlotte Spanner had heard the rumor. Only one way to find out—ask her. She wasn't listed in the phone book and he drew a blank from directory assistance, so he assumed she didn't have a phone. He grabbed his notebook and headed to his car.

The Chronicle owned one of the big buildings downtown. Foot-tall, green letters above the glass front doors lit up at night to promise: IF IT'S NEWS, YOU'LL KNOW IT. READ THE EVENING CHRONICLE. Berman pushed the door open and headed down the sidewalk to his car. It wasn't much to look at, a 1986 Ford Tempo, red with a gray interior. The paint hadn't so much faded as turned brittle and cracked like mud drying around a waterhole. When he fired the engine up everyone within a block knew his muffler was gone, but his salary didn't allow much pampering of the car or himself.

He banged his way down Main Street toward the grain elevators, which were in full swing with farmers bringing in fall corn for storage. On the downwind side of the elevators, where the grain dust gathered on the bushes, he turned into the gravel lane leading back about three hundred feet to the Spanners' worn out house. As he drove in, he could see three little kids jumping around an obstacle course of broken bicycles and wagons in the front yard. A rusty refrigerator—doorless for safety, he noticed—stood at the corner of the porch. As he got closer, he saw children's toys on the rusted shelves inside the fridge.

He pulled up beside the house, in front of an unpainted garage, and stopped. The kids ignored him; they were playing a strange variety of tag that involved chasing each other with a ripped-up doll, then whacking each other with it before they dropped it and ran in the other direction. They were small and dirty. It was unlikely any of their clothes had been new when they first put them on. Charlotte Spanner, live-in boyfriend or not, just barely squeaked by. No one in this house had anything extra. Everyone knew it, everyone felt pretty badly about it, but no one had figured out how to fix it. The churches pitched in around Christmas and Easter with some presents and food, but the rest of the time Charlotte was condemned to wring everything she could out of her food stamps and welfare check.

Berman stepped onto the porch and knocked on the rusty screen door. At first he heard nothing, then footsteps thumped across the front room and the door swung open. In another lifetime, with better luck, Charlotte Spanner might have had a good time. She had dark brown hair and a pale complexion, with soft blue eyes and a nicely shaped mouth. Given the right clothes, in a different house, she might have turned a few heads. But at thirty-two, with six kids and a hardscrabble existence, the bloom of youth had faded fast. There wasn't much left to look at. Years of neglect had claimed several of her teeth, leaving dark gaps when she tried to smile. Creases furrowed her face, creating the impression she was considerably older than she really was. She knew how she looked, would even cover her mouth to hide the lost teeth, but the grind of daily life had worn her down. She didn't smile much anymore, and if she did, black holes, freely exposed, punctuated her grin.

When Charlotte saw Berman she stepped back quickly. He could tell she hadn't expected to see someone she didn't know. But she didn't close the door.

"Do I know you?" she asked in a tired voice.

Berman spoke gently, trying to ease her obvious discomfort over finding a stranger at her door.

"Hi, my name is Jed Berman. I'm with *The Evening Chronicle*, you know, the newspaper here in town."

She nodded but didn't say anything. He kept talking. At least he was doing better than he had on the phone with Mazer.

"I'm checking out some rumors I heard and I wondered if I could ask you a couple of questions."

"I can't afford the paper, but sometimes my friends bring me theirs. Why do you want to talk to me?"

She had been looking past him all the while at the children in the yard. Now she interrupted the conversation to yell through the screen door in a voice that rang in his ears.

"Amanda Jean! If you dump dirt down your little brother's shirt one more time you're coming in here and getting a licking!" The child in question laughed and ran out of sight. To Berman, Charlotte said, "Why don't you come in for a minute?"

The condition of the children in the yard and the display of parenting skills he'd just witnessed made him wonder if what they said about this woman might be true. Maybe he was wasting his time checking it out. He had come here thinking he might be able to protect an essentially defenseless woman from the Child Welfare Office, an agency he often suspected of acting out of insensitive gestapo-like whims at the expense of families. Charlotte Spanner might not deserve that protection. Then again, maybe she did. He wasn't ready to abandon the idea just yet. He accepted her offer to step inside.

"I didn't mean to interrupt whatever you were doing."

He took a quick look around the sparsely furnished

front room. Two overstuffed chairs, worn bald on the arms; a couch with three badly misshapen, lumpy cushions. An old wooden rocker, with the finish mostly scratched off. A braided rug, faded to an earthy brown, over the center of a hardwood floor. A TV sat on a small bench in the corner, but it was silent and dark. This was definitely the home of a very poor family, but, contrary to the rumors, it was clean. He did not hesitate to sit in one of the overstuffed chairs when Charlotte motioned toward it. She sat on the front edge of the rocker, leaning toward him. She still looked a little bit leery. He was willing to bet she'd never talked directly to a reporter in her life. That always raised a flag in his mind. Chances were he could get her to tell him just about anything he wanted to know, but sometimes it seemed unfair to use his journalistic wiles against someone so uninitiated. He sanctioned it in this case because he was likely to end up on her side, if his suspicions about Mazer turned out to be right. He enjoyed this kind of story, taking on the system.

"What did you want to ask me about?"

Now that he was here facing her, he realized it wouldn't be easy to raise this subject without frightening her. She appeared to have limited strength for dealing with a crisis; the prospect of losing her children due to negligence might be more than she could handle. He decided to approach the topic indirectly.

"Do you know a woman named Hildy Mazer?"

"I'm not sure I do. Does she live here in Berrington?"

"I'm not sure where she lives. But she works out of Pruitville." He paused before adding, "She's with the Child Welfare Office."

Charlotte's hands tightened on the arms of the rocking chair. She didn't speak right away, just nodded slightly. Her face grew taut.

"I think she's been out here before. A woman came here about six months ago, said she heard I don't treat my kids right. Wanted to look around."

"Did you let her?"

"You have to, don't you? She had a policeman with her. I figured I better go along. Besides, I ain't got nothin' to hide."

Berman was compiling mental notes for the article he would write. Charlotte's comments would make clear that she was the intended victim of the system, in the form of Hildy Mazer, and if he could confirm that Mazer was actually using her power for a personal vendetta against this woman, it would be a great story.

"Did she ask you any questions while she was here?"

"Yeah, mostly wanted to know where my husband was."

"Did you answer that?"

"It's a little hard to answer, 'cause I'm not married. I was once, about ten years ago, to the father of my first three kids, but he's long gone. I don't have any idea where he is. Once he saw what raising kids was about, he took off."

"But you have six children, don't you?"

"Yes, I do. But I never married any of the fathers after the first one. Some of my boyfriends used to beat me. I guess I'm sort of a magnet for bad guys. But at least I finally figured out if you don't marry 'em, it's easier to get away."

"Is there a man living with you now?"

"Yeah, Frank. He's the father of number six, Allie. She's two. He don't do a lot for us, but he don't hurt us, either. And once in a while he and I get to laughin' and carryin' on, and he's fun. He don't get rough with us. Says he was whacked a lot when he was a kid, he don't want to see anyone else get it now."

Berman found himself in a situation he had experienced many times before. An ordinary person lets you into her home and quickly opens the floodgates of her personal life, telling you much more than you ever wanted to know. But as he listened, he knew it was good background for his story. If Hildy Mazer intended to break up this woman's home, she'd have to pay a hefty price in the court of public opinion, at least if he had anything to say about it.

"Mrs. Spanner . . ."

"Don't call me Mrs. Spanner, makes me sound even older than I feel. You know, I'm not ancient yet." She swept her hand back over her hair in a dramatic gesture that stopped short of flirting.

Berman smiled. "Okay, Charlotte. What else did the woman who came here say to you?"

"Didn't say hardly anything. Looked in all my rooms, even opened the dresser drawers. Poked around the kids who were here—three of 'em are in school during the day. Then she wagged a finger in my face and said she'd be watching me."

"Is that when she left?"

"Just about. Outside on the porch she turned around and said, 'Are you right with the Lord?' I remember that especially 'cause the way she said it scared me. I'm a believer and all, but I don't go to church. I wasn't sure why someone from the Welfare Department was asking me something like that."

"Did you answer her question?"

"I told her it was none of her business. I said it was between me and the Lord, which is what I believe."

"How'd she take that?"

"Her face got kind of red. She acted like she was going to say something else, but she didn't. Just stomped off the porch and tore out of here and didn't come back."

Berman's feelings about Hildy Mazer were crystalizing

9

into a serious dislike. He decided to let Charlotte in on what he'd heard.

"She may be gone, but I hear she hasn't forgotten you. That's why I came here today."

Charlotte's knuckles turned white as she continued gripping the arms of the chair. "What do you mean?"

"This is just rumor, but I have reason to believe it's pretty reliable. What I heard was that Hildy Mazer wants to take away your kids, because you're not married."

Charlotte leaned toward him, an anguished look on her face.

"She can't do that, can she? I ain't done nothin' wrong! Tell me she can't do that."

"She can try, she's in a position with a lot of power. But I want to help you fight her. That's the kind of reporting I do, sort of a people's advocate. I help protect people from con artists or anyone else who tries to abuse them."

"But if she's so powerful, how can you stop her?"

"My story, if I do it right. But there may be other ways, too. The thing is, it's all rumor right now. I'll keep digging into it, but in the meantime, you'll just have to wait. That's going to be the tough part." He handed her his card. "Call that number if Hildy Mazer contacts you, okay?"

Charlotte nodded. More to herself than Berman she said, "No one can take my kids. I ain't got much else, but at least I got them. And no one is gonna walk in here and take 'em from me. That much I know."

Berman stood up, but Charlotte slid back into her chair and rocked slowly.

"I'll be in touch, Charlotte."

She looked up and nodded again, but remained silent. Berman opened the screen door and walked out. In the yard, the kids still ran in circles, laughing and shouting. They never missed a skip as he drove away.

Two

Fast Pace

Six weeks after Berman left Charlotte Spanner's tired old
house, Hildy Mazer pulled up in a white county car, followed by a deputy in a tan-over-brown cruiser. No lights or
sirens, no SWAT team, but on a mission, nonetheless. And
not far behind was Jed Berman. Charlotte Spanner hadn't
called him, even after she got a letter from Mazer threatening to take her children if this inspection went badly. But
Mazer's police escort had been dispatched by police radio
and Berman just happened to hear the transmission crackling into the newsroom late on this Friday afternoon.

Mazer was already on the porch and brushing past
Charlotte to stomp into the house by the time Berman hit
the driveway. School was out for the weekend, all six kids
sat around the front room, not making a sound. Berman
slammed on his brakes behind the squad car and jumped
out. He ran into the house behind the deputy and saw
Charlotte standing against the open door, a look of terror
on her face. Mazer didn't talk to her; instead she began
examining the children, one at a time, twisting their heads
around so she could see in their ears and down their necks.
The littlest ones had just come in from the front yard,
where they had staged another dirt battle, like the one that
earned Amanda Jean a reprimand the first day Berman was
there.

When she finished with the last child, Mazer picked up

11

the leather case she had brought with her and fished out a document sheathed in the blue paper Berman knew had been stamped in some courtroom in Pruitville. She jabbed it in Charlotte's face and spoke only three words.

"They're mine now!"

Charlotte stood mute against the door, either unable or unwilling to say anything. She made no attempt to follow through on the vow she had uttered under her breath when Berman was with her, the promise that she would allow no one to take her kids. Mazer rounded up the children, ordered them to put on their coats, and herded them out the door. Half of the group she shoved into her car, three across in the backseat; the other three wound up locked in the back of the deputy's car. Strangely, with the exception of the two-year-old, none of them made a sound. Tears rolled silently down their cheeks, and they wore expressions sad enough to break the hardest heart, but they did not speak. As each child passed by her at the door, Charlotte reached out her arms as though she would save them from falling over a cliff, but Mazer stepped in the way and ushered the child through the door and off the porch. In less than five minutes, both cars had circled around through the yard and accelerated toward Main Street.

Charlotte slowly closed the door and collapsed onto the rocking chair where she had comforted each of the children as the traumas of early life washed over them. She buried her face in her hands and wept silently. Across the room, Berman's emotions traveled quickly from embarrassment at having had to witness this scene, uninvited, to an urge to reach out and comfort Charlotte, to anger at Hildy Mazer for pulling off what he believed was a grave injustice. This time the vow was his. To Charlotte, and her kids, and the paper and himself he promised, in George Bush-like syntax, *This will not stand.*

12

He walked to Charlotte's side and put a consoling hand on her shoulder. Her thin body quaked, she was nearly convulsed with sobs.

"We'll get 'em back, Charlotte, I promise you. And it won't take long. And, while we're at it, we'll make sure Hildy Mazer never pulls anything like this again."

Charlotte looked up at him, her face red and wet with tears.

"I hope you're right, Mister, 'cause I ain't got nothin' else in this world worth anything." The tears fell again and she covered her face with her hands.

Berman kicked himself for not staying on top of the story. Maybe he could have prevented this somehow. Now that the courts had ordered the kids removed, it would be tougher to get things back to normal. Charlotte was going to be spending at least a few nights alone with her boyfriend, if he bothered to come home. What did she say his name was? It really didn't matter. He had work to do, and he'd better start doing it.

"Charlotte, may I see the papers Ms. Mazer gave you?"

She pointed to where they had fallen on the floor when she reached out to touch the children. He walked over and scooped up the packet, about four pages, stapled inside an official blue cover, with the county seal at the top of each page.

"May I make a copy of this?"

Charlotte nodded, and he folded the papers and shoved them inside his jacket pocket. Try as he might, the right words for this exit wouldn't come. He finally muttered. "Hang in there. It'll be all right, I promise."

He turned toward the door and pulled it open. Just before he stepped out he looked back at the rocking chair. At that moment, Charlotte raised her head and looked toward him. He had never seen a more sorrowful face in all the sad stories he'd worked. He closed the door behind him and headed back to the office.

*   *   *

Berman knew he should have seen it coming. After all, he'd heard those two women talking about what Mazer was going to do a month and a half ago. Working in a small town police station, they had probably heard a couple of cops gossiping about it. But he never expected Mazer to move so fast. There was no doubt in his mind that Charlotte Spanner was a decent mother. His story would hinge on showing Hildy Mazer for what he suspected she was—a religious zealot who let her personal beliefs cross that important protective line between church and state. He had seen people like her at one of the colleges he'd attended back in the '70s. Fundamentalists! To his mind one of the scariest forms of religious fanatics on the face of the earth. People who had all the answers and couldn't wait to shove them down everyone else's throat. And now, in the days of Pat Robertson, Rush Limbaugh and weird militia groups, that closed-minded approach looked to be on the rise again, at least in some quarters. Most of the people in Berrington didn't seem to be that way; they were mainstream, Lutheran, Methodist, Presbyterian. But in Pruitville, there was a really big "fundy" church, something like the First Official Bible-Thumping-Give-Me-A-Fresh-Dose-Every-Day Church of the Only People on the Face of the Earth Who Really Knew What God Wanted. And he was willing to bet that Hildy Mazer belonged there.

The thought gave birth to another idea—if that was Mazer's church, wouldn't she be ready to crow on Sunday about rescuing those kids from the clutches of their degenerate mother? If he could just get someone close enough to hear what she had to say, it might be all he needed. Berman reached his office and this conclusion at the same time. He yanked open the door and ran for the newsroom, hoping to catch Dee Morgan before she left for the weekend.

She was coming down the stairs as he started up.

"Dee, I gotta talk to you for a minute."

Dee Morgan covered city hall and the county commissioners, but she knew everyone else. Berman figured she knew something was up if he was running into the building rather than out at this hour on Friday afternoon. She stopped three steps from the bottom of the stairs and smiled.

"Why do I think I should keep on walking? What makes me think whatever you have on your mind is going to cost me at least some time and maybe something more precious before it's over?"

She tried to sound irritated, but she wasn't. Berman had worked with Dee for the past five years. She had watched him develop into a top-notch reporter who could generate stories no one else seemed to notice or cared about enough to dig out. The admiration was mutual. Berman considered her the best writer in the shop, next to him. She was the only reporter he confided in, and definitely the only one he'd trust to help him investigate. He sat down on the stairs and pulled her down beside him.

"Hey, you're gonna get my slacks all dirty."

"If I do, I'll pay to clean 'em. This won't take long, Dee. I really need your help this weekend."

She wasn't surprised to hear him say it. She was also curious to know what he was up to.

"What is it? Is this the one that wins the Pulitzer?"

"Just give me two minutes of serious time and I'll let you go. Are you tied up Sunday morning?"

"No, why? And I'm not going back to that motorcycle

gang again. If they want to ride naked through the falling leaves I don't care. I won't pretend to be your 'motorcycle mama' just so you can get the inside scoop on life inside the gang. As I recall, you didn't find all that much inside, anyway."

"Dee! Gimme a break. This has nothing to do with bikers or gurus or anything like that. It has to do with a mother who's lost her six little kids, and I think she's been had by a religious nutcase. I need your help to blow the whistle on her, the nutcase, I mean."

"Are you talking about Charlotte Spanner by any chance? Everybody knows her life is a little close to the edge. Who's the nutcase and how did she get Spanner's kids?"

"Ever hear of a Child Welfare caseworker named Hildy Mazer?"

Morgan pondered the name, but drew a blank.

"Not that I can remember. What's she look like?"

"Short, a little stocky, with long hair wrapped up on top of her head in a bun. Probably about forty."

"Does she work in the county building in Pruitville?"

"Yes, she does."

"Was she the one who marched around the courthouse that day with people who didn't think the caseworkers deserved a raise?"

Berman hadn't thought about that for a long time, but it was, in fact, the first time he'd seen Hildy Mazer. Her demonstration helped drive a wedge through the Child Welfare Office that remained to this day.

"Bingo! That's the one. Dresses a little old-fashioned, skirts that always look too long. She's not exactly a trend-setter."

"So how'd she get Charlotte Spanner's kids?"

"I think she trumped up a case against Charlotte

16

because she doesn't approve of her lifestyle—Charlotte has a boyfriend living with her, he's the father of her sixth child."

"Sounds possible. So what's this have to do with me?"

"I'm playing a hunch here, but I'm willing to bet Mazer belongs to that big Bible-thumper church in Pruitville, you know, the Church of I'm Gonna Get to Heaven Before You Do and I'm Not Gonna Let You In."

Morgan laughed. She always enjoyed Berman's forays into irreverence.

"Yeah, I know the church you mean. What do you want me to do?"

"Well, here's the slightly tricky part. I want you to go to that church this Sunday and, if Mazer is there, I want you to stay close to her and take notes on her conversations. If she's as big a nut as I think she is, she's gotta tell somebody what she's done. I'm betting she thinks it was her religious duty. And if she ripped Charlotte Spanner's family apart for that reason, without any real evidence of abuse or neglect, then I'm going to expose it and get those kids back where they belong, with their mother."

"How sure are you that Mazer is wrong?"

"I've been to Spanner's house twice in the past month and a half; the second time was this afternoon when Mazer brought a cop and grabbed the kids. It's not an exciting place, but she keeps it neat and the kids don't look any dirtier than most kids. I'm gonna try to dig around Mazer's office to be sure there isn't a smoking gun somewhere that Spanner forgot to tell me about. And then I'm going to put it all together in a prize-winning article exposing the over-zealousness of this little…"

Morgan cut him off mid-sentence.

"Whoa, buddy! One step at a time. I'll check out the church and you check out Mazer's office. I'll let you know what I find out on Monday. Is that soon enough? You can't get into her office before then anyway, can you?"

"No, I can't. And I feel badly about that. I saw this coming and I intended to put the story together sooner, but I got distracted, plus, I didn't expect Mazer to move so fast. Now, those kids have to spend a lot of time away from their mother, so we gotta work as fast as we can. If you can get me Mazer's testimony in church on Sunday, I'll do the rest."

Morgan stood up and patted Berman on the shoulder.

"I'll do my part. See ya Monday. Have a good weekend."

He watched her walk toward the front door.

"You have a good weekend, too. See ya Monday. And thanks for the help."

There wasn't much else he could do at 5:30 on Friday afternoon. He didn't usually write for the weekend editions. He ran up the steps to his desk, pulled the loose papers into what approached a neat pile, and headed back downstairs and out the door. It was already dark. As he stepped onto the sidewalk, the green letters over the doorway glowed into the night, IF IT'S NEWS, YOU'LL KNOW IT. READ THE EVENING   HRONICLE. He glanced up and noticed the first "C" in Chronicle was burned out. He slid behind the wheel of his Tempo and rumbled the block and a half to his apartment. As he pulled up, he could see that the little Wises across the street had pushed their plastic reindeer onto the porch for Christmas. They already had them plugged in. Rudy's nose glowed bright red in the gathering dark.

About an hour later, Berman glowed slightly, too, as he sat in his dark apartment, working on a tall glass of white wine. He couldn't decide what to have for supper, so the alcohol was getting a head start through his empty stomach. He finally decided to walk over to Brady's, the restaurant and bar across the street. Might be someone there he could eat with, but in case he drew a blank, he stuffed the latest *New Yorker* into his back pocket. He'd never expected to work in his hometown, but after nine years, Berrington felt pretty comfortable. *The Evening Chronicle* had given him his first chance, he had some good luck getting started, and the people liked him, so he stayed on. Not that he never considered moving up. He knew he could do it, but the longer he stayed here, the less reason he saw for going anywhere else. He ran through the old debate about being a big frog in a little pond or a little frog in a big pond over and over in his mind. So far, he always ended up preferring to belch out big frog croaks in this little pond. But it was tempting to think about other possibilities, like a really big paper, where they actually paid you for what you did.

Brady's attracted a fairly diverse crowd into its homey interior. Square chrome-edged tables for four filled the center of the dining room in two long rows. Along the edges, people jammed into upholstered booths with high backs, that gave you the feeling of a tiny, private salon. The problem was that you couldn't tell who was in the booths without walking right by them. Berman had long ago figured out how to stroll toward the back of the room and catch a peek in each booth as he went by. In the third one on the left he spotted a familiar face, Jane Filips. She was alone, so he walked over to her table.

"Looking for company?"

She had spotted him coming in the door; she wasn't surprised to see him by her booth. They had spent a little time together over the years, after her ex answered the call of the west. She smiled and motioned to the bench opposite hers.

"Have a seat, pardner. What'll ya have?"

Berman slid into the booth and out of his jacket. He

19

smiled back, pleased to find her here. Of all the Berrington regulars, she ranked at the top of his list. She was cute, smart, and fun, and extremely well built. More than once her figure had surfaced in his dreams. But she had never made it into his bed in real life. She sat smiling at him, but she made him start the conversation. He came up short on originality.

"How are you? How was your week?"

Before she could answer, the waitress stopped at the end of the table.

"Can I get you something to drink?"

Berman ordered a glass of wine, Jane asked for a marguerita. People really got excited about margueritas around here, although he couldn't understand why. The idea of that worm in the tequila bottle always convinced him not to have one. The last thing he wanted was to chomp on a chunk of pickled worm. Enduring unusual and unpleasant experiences seemed natural when he was working on a story, but on his own time he just wanted things to move slowly and smoothly.

They picked up the menus the waitress laid in front of them and reread the list of entrees for the umpteenth time. He was debating between the Beef Manhattan and Brady's special spinach salad with hot bacon dressing when Jane finally answered his question. At least a minute had passed since he posed it, but there was no awkwardness in the delay. He had noticed that about their relationship since the first time he met her. It always felt very natural. She answered as though the conversation had already been underway.

"Seemed like this week would never be over. I had to drive to every school in the system, that's more than fifteen buildings and at least fifty kids. I'm wiped out."

Jane Filips worked with kids who couldn't or wouldn't

read. She had a reputation for getting through to even the most resistant subjects. Kids loved her. Her rank among local teachers equalled Berman's standing among reporters. Berman's feelings for her went well beyond respect. He'd never been married, but she seemed like the right kind of person to consider if he ever wanted to tie the knot.

"How do you keep it up? Those kids would drive me absolutely nuts day after day, going through the same basic stuff, forgetting half of what you taught them last week, refusing to learn the new stuff this week."

"It's not that bad. Besides, I'm pretty good at finding the key to each kid's head. And once I figure them out, and manage to unlock their minds so they can read, it's a wonderful feeling, a real natural high. Sometimes they surprise themselves so much they yell out loud. And sometimes they forget about being cool or resistant and they give me a big, sweaty hug. That's the stuff that keeps me going. But enough about me. What kind of trouble are you in these days?"

"I'm feeling pretty much defeated tonight. I heard a rumor that Child Welfare was going to grab Charlotte Spanner's kids, and I planned on exposing the caseworker as an overzealous, religious freak. But she got the drop on me and took the kids this afternoon. I'm bummed."

The waitress slid a very large marguerita in front of Jane and a drinking-glass size goblet of wine in front of Berman, then pulled the order pad from her apron pocket and a pencil from behind her ear. Jane ordered the Brady Special lasagna and Berman settled for the spinach salad. This time Jane picked up the conversation.

"I know you won't give up on that story until you win, but it sounds a little messy. Isn't there always room to debate whether Child Welfare was right or not? Do you

21

know for sure Charlotte Spanner is a good mom?"

"I'm fairly sure, but I have a little more leg work to do before I put it all together." He sighed and slouched on the bench. "What the hell, it's a challenge, you know?"

She nodded and smiled. He knew she respected what he did, and he considered her the best teacher around. It mattered to him that she excelled in her field. He had little tolerance for mediocrity. He valued people who drove themselves as hard as he did. Plus, she turned him on.

"Enough shop talk," he concluded. "Wanna catch a movie after we eat? I'll treat."

"Deal. What's playing?"

"I think there's a Stephen King horror thing, some family movie, and the new James Bond, with Pierce Brosnan. Any of those sound good? I have to warn you, I'm not usually up for horror stuff."

"Bond it is," she concluded, pounding her hand on the table, and nearly upsetting both glasses. They laughed and then sat quietly for a moment. Before long the waitress returned, arms full of plates and bowls. They dined on lasagna and spinach and a potpourri of their favorite movie scenes.

*   *   *

Three screens served Berrington's population of just under twenty thousand very well. The Bond film, dedicated to the memory of the recently expired Albert "Cubby" Broccoli (producer of the long and illustrious run of secret agent flicks), featured lots of new gadgets for Brosnan to use in foiling the bad guys, but, as usual, the story line sagged. The good part was the length, two hours plus, during which Jane leaned her tired head on Berman's shoulder and casually rubbed her hand along his leg, thigh

high, enough to get a response. Her touch seemed as natural as the pace of their conversations. He decided to invite her to his apartment after the show. Something told him she would come and that maybe they were ready to move to a new level. He was right on both counts. They walked into Brady's for breakfast a little after nine the next morning.

Around 9:15 Sunday morning, Dee Morgan pulled into the lot at Pruitville's biggest church, the Full Gospel Resurrection Bound Fellowship. She smiled to realize the actual name wasn't that far from Berman's cynical rendition Friday afternoon. A steady stream of cars rolled off the highway and nosed into neatly lined parking spaces on newly refinished asphalt. Before she even got out of the car, she saw Hildy Mazer glide into a spot in a new-looking Lincoln Town Car. Morgan considered the likelihood of an underpaid social service worker tooling around in something that nice. Mazer was alone, but Morgan figured there must be a Mr. Mazer in the picture with a fairly good job, or else Mazer lived on the edge of financial ruin. But that didn't seem likely for someone as fussy and fastidious looking as Hildy Mazer.

Mazer slammed the door of the Lincoln and marched toward the church without looking right or left, which gave Dee a chance to fall in behind her and appear to be making her own way into the building. Inside, a young couple surrounded by at least six kids greeted the new arrivals. They looked like something out of the mid-'50s, very straightlaced and dull. The handshake they offered had a too-soft quality Morgan hated. She called it a "fish."

A short staircase led up to the sanctuary. Dee could feel lots of eyes following her as she tracked Mazer into the room. Here and there someone smiled or offered a quiet "Good morning," but mostly everyone seemed intent on getting seated in time for the service. Morgan did not make a habit of attending church on Sunday. It now dawned on her that if Mazer was going to give her testimony on the Spanner situation, it probably wouldn't happen until the Sunday school hour, which meant sitting through this first hour for nothing. Morgan made a mental note to make sure Berman knew the extent of her sacrifice on his behalf. She slid into a pew on the outside aisle, about three rows behind Mazer.

As it turned out, Morgan didn't have to wait for the second hour. Right after the sermon, which chastised people for not giving enough money and condemned the homosexual element infiltrating the God-fearing troops of the United States armed forces, the minister stepped down from behind the pulpit with a cordless microphone and asked if there were any prayers, petitions or blessings. He started down the aisle, and before he reached the second row Hildy Mazer jumped to her feet reaching for the mike. In a clear loud voice, tinged with a slight southern accent, she held forth on the sinful situation she had moved to correct in the week gone by.

"My brothers and sisters, I am so grateful to the Lord this morning. For some months now I have shared with you the burden on my heart for six little children in Berrington, caught through no fault of their own in a den of iniquity, a cesspool of sinfulness, with an unmarried mother living in unrighteousness with a man, outside the bonds of holy matrimony. My soul ached for these children as I watched them being smeared with the slime of their mother's degradation. And I have implored our heavenly Father to show me a way to rescue these little ones from the clutches of evil. For many of these past weeks I have worked, as on a mission, to find a way, and this week, through the grace of God, I did. I am happy to share with you this morning that those little angels are safe in the arms of loving foster parents across this county, each in a different home, and each in the care of a mother and father committed to the Lord. I believe this is what the Lord wanted, and I know in my heart that they are far better off than ever before in their young lives. Please share with me the joy and celebration of seeing God's will done once again, not through my power but through His loving tenderness, made evident through his gracious son, Jesus. Amen." Mazer never mentioned Charlotte Spanner by name.

The congregation erupted in applause. They obviously knew what she was talking about and clearly endorsed Mazer's accomplishment. As the sound of clapping and shouted amens washed over her, Mazer's face shone triumphantly. Three rows back, Dee Morgan had taken careful notes, figuring it wouldn't be a good idea to flash the palm-sized tape recorder hidden in her bag. What she had just heard didn't give Berman everything he needed, but it supported his theory that Mazer went after Charlotte Spanner out of religious zeal. And it sounded like she had crossed the line between church and state in doing it. There was no law against single mothers, or against a single mom living with a man. Yet Mazer had pulled off a court order to take the kids! *Berman better take a close look at the paperwork on Monday*, Morgan thought. These people liked what they'd heard, but Morgan realized Mazer had not really outlined the path God revealed to her for getting her hands on those kids. Maybe those details would surface in Sunday school. For the first time in a long time, Morgan looked forward to sitting in a Sunday school class to find out.

She wasn't dispappointed. Mazer stood around and drank some coffee during the break after the service, then headed downstairs to a classroom. The chairs ringed the room, and they quickly filled up with women who fixed their hair a lot like Mazer's and men whose heads glistened with some sort of old-fashioned dressing like Brylcreem or laid stylishly in place, thanks to gel and hairspray. Double knit appeared to be the most popular fabric. From Morgan's point of view, these people were not slaves to current fashion.

Several people stood up and shook Mazer's hand as she walked in. She was still glowing from her victorious testimony upstairs. And she was obviously eager to expand on what she'd already said. A bell rang and the class leader called everyone to order, then asked Mazer for more details on her encounter with Satan.

As Morgan took a seat near the door, the woman next to her turned and extended her hand.

"Good morning, I'm Flora Wilson. Are you new here? I don't seem to recognize you."

Morgan played along.

"Yes, I'm just visiting. It's wonderful to be here. Everyone is so nice and friendly." Mazer was about to launch into her explanation. When Flora Wilson turned away from Morgan to listen, Morgan reached into her bag and clicked on the recorder.

"You all know how long I've been a caseworker," Mazer began, obviously comfortable in these surroundings. "And you know my only concern has ever been for the children, the babes who find themselves in heathenish places where they are unable to bask in the light and love of the Lord. That's exactly what was going on with these little ones, six of them living with a mother who was only ever married to the father of her first three offspring.

"I first spotted them in a grocery store in Berrington, dressed in worn-out clothes, the littlest ones looking dirty. I asked some people about the children and their mother and learned that she lived in sin with a man. A couple of months ago, I visited the home and went through everything. It is amazing how little there was to check. The mother looked weary and I thought I saw marks on some of the smaller ones' faces, where she might have struck them. The man was not around, but I asked about him. She admitted he was not her husband, but he did father the youngest child. As I was leaving, I asked her if she was right with the Lord. You can imagine my shock when she refused to answer me. The answer was right there as plain as can be—a single mother with too many children, no husband, a frustratingly poor life, and children bearing the signs of abuse.

"I left her there that day, and drove back to my office to begin drawing up papers to get those children away. The report of my inspection noted the decrepit conditions of the house and my suspicions about mistreatment of the children. When my supervisor read it she urged me to send the mother a warning that things must change. I sent it, but, as I expected, the woman didn't respond. Our rules require a six-week waiting period after a warning, so I waited. It was the longest wait of my life, knowing that each day those sweet little things lived and breathed a world of sin. And finally, this past Friday afternoon, the waiting ended. With a sheriff's deputy along in case the mother resisted, I served a court order granting custody of the children to the county, and hustled the little ones off to foster homes."

As Mazer finished the story, she threw her hands into the air with a flourish. Most of the people in the circle nodded and smiled, relishing her achievement with her. But Morgan saw a chance to nail down the details. Assuming no one in this group would recognize her, she posed a question.

"Did the judge want proof that the children were being abused? Was it hard getting him to give you the order?"

Mazer turned on her with a gloating smile.

"It was old Judge Frank. He accepts whatever I tell him. He didn't even read the papers, just signed them."

Morgan pushed the issue.

"Did you really have proof those poor little things were being abused?"

"No, not at all. But that doesn't matter. It was the Lord's work and they are the Lord's creatures and that mother doesn't deserve to have them if she's not going to raise them properly. I suspect she'll try to fight me somehow, but I know I'm going to win, the Lord is going to win. I've done this sort of thing before. These people can't fight the power of the state and the Lord put together. Praise God, those children are safe this morning."

Morgan couldn't believe how easy this had been. She had what she needed. She waited until the conversation moved on and then faked a coughing fit. With her hand over her mouth, she stepped out of the room and kept on going to the parking lot. When she got to her car, she reached into her bag and snapped off the recorder. Berman would be pleased. She drove back to *The Chronicle*, put a label on the tape and laid it on his desk along with her notes from Mazer's testimony during the morning service. The rest was up to him.

*　　*　　*

It didn't take Berman long to get it all together. First thing Monday, he listened to the tape, deciphered Morgan's notes, and then drove to Pruitville. He parked outside the Child Welfare Office and waited for Mazer to arrive. It was early, about a quarter to eight; all of the white county cars

28

were still in their reserved spaces. Promptly at eight o'clock, Mazer pulled up in the Lincoln Town Car Dee Morgan had described to him. He jumped out and ran to head her off as she reached the front door.

"Ms. Mazer, I'm Jed Berman with *The Chronicle*. Could I talk to you for a moment?"

Mazer never lifted her hand from the door handle. She wrenched it open, nearly whacking Berman in the head in the process, and steamed past him into the building. He followed her down the hallway.

"Ms. Mazer, I'm writing an article that involves your work here at Child Welfare and I need to get your response to what I'm going to say."

At least this time he knew she was listening. Without breaking stride she tossed a threat over her shoulder.

"Don't try to frighten me, sir. If you print something that harms me I will sue you and that rag you work for for every penny you've got. Who do you think you are, anyway, the *National Enquirer*?"

He gave it one more try as she pulled out a key to unlock the door to her office.

"Ms. Mazer, I have reason to believe you have abused your authority and misled the courts to gain custody of Charlotte Spanner's children. Did you intentionally lie about Charlotte abusing her children? Did you misstate the facts with regard to the conditions in the Spanner home? Did you ask Charlotte Spanner questions about her marital status and her religious life that violate her right to privacy? And were you improperly motivated by your religious zeal rather than the guidelines set down by the state for dealing with child custody cases?"

Berman spewed out all of his questions in one breath, hoping something he said would stop Mazer in her tracks, but it didn't. She unlocked her door, pushed it open and

29

stepped inside without comment. The door slammed shut in his face. By now several other workers had stepped into the hallway to see what was going on. Berman turned around and walked out without looking at them.

He had one more stop to make, at the courthouse; but he couldn't do much for another hour until Judge Frank came in. Frank's court was notorious for starting late. The annual survey of local lawyers always ranked Frank at the bottom, but he appeared to shrug it off without changing anything. Berman walked across the grass quadrangle from the Child Welfare Office to the courthouse and climbed the inside staircase to the judge's second floor office. The outer door was open, so Berman walked in.

The judge's secretary was already hard at work cranking out documents from yesterday's rulings and assembling the pile for today's proceedings. She ignored Berman until he coughed loudly into his hand.

"May I help you?"

"Yes, I'm Jed Berman with the Berrington *Evening Chronicle*. I must speak with the judge if he has a moment before court starts."

"Well, I can't tell you if you can or can't speak with the judge."

"What does that mean?"

"It means, I don't decide who the judge will see and who he won't see. Why don't you ask him yourself because he's standing right behind you."

Sometimes Berman grew tired of the endless smartass comments reporters endured at the hands of these minor functionaries, but if you burned them, you could kiss your chances of ever getting any help from them good-bye. He swung around and greeted the judge.

"Good morning, Your Honor." He observed the proper title even though he agreed with the lawyers that of all the judges in the county, this one deserved respect less than anyone else. "Do you have a couple of minutes before you pull on the old robe and start meting out justice to the masses?" Berman had dealt with this guy many times before; he wasn't worried about offending him. As cooperative as Hildy Mazer found old Judge Frank, reporters knew him to be the kind of man who enjoyed joking around and never seemed to take himself or anyone else too seriously. The judge answered through his double chins, in a deep gravelly voice.

"Sure, c'mon in. Wipe your feet so you don't get mud on the rug."

There was no rug, just an old, creaky hardwood floor, scuffed by many a poor soul coming to plead one case or another with the judge in this worn-out space euphemistically referred to as his chambers. The judge shrugged off his jacket and hung it behind the door. Berman kept his on, and stuffed the leather gloves he'd been holding into his coat pocket. The judge pointed to a stiff-looking chair in front of his desk and then sank into an old leather office chair on the other side.

"So, what is it this time? Did I forget to answer the questionnaire on who's the greatest reporter in the county? That must be you, Jed, 'cause you're the only one who seems to stay here. All the talented ones get snapped up by the folks in big cities."

Berman usually enjoyed the banter, but he felt impatient today. The same nonchalance the judge used to entertain him had cost Charlotte Spanner her kids. He hoped Frank would be as quick to correct his mistake as he had been to make it, especially when he realized he'd been had by Hildy Mazer.

"Your Honor, I think a big mistake has been made, and it involves your court."

31

Frank's good humor evaporated in an instant. The judge leaned over his desk and glared at Berman.

"Are you suggesting I made some sort of mistake?"

"Not exactly, sir. I think you were ill-used and poorly informed by a Child Welfare caseworker who wanted to do something for the wrong reasons."

"Tell me more."

Berman launched into his tale. He didn't refer to his notes, he didn't need them. He'd been so close to this story for so long he recited it from memory. The judge sat back and listened quietly, the scowl fading from his face. Berman brought the old man all the way to the present, including his encounter with Mazer just moments ago across the quad. He couldn't read the judge's expression, but retelling the story made him hope he was about to get results. He got results, but not what he expected.

"How dare you?" the judge roared in an unbelievably loud voice. "How dare you walk in here and accuse, on the strength of hearsay and rumor, not just one officer of the court but two, Mrs. Mazer and myself? Do you think we're playing court here in this building? Do you imagine Mrs. Mazer has nothing better to do than fabricate court documents and reports to support her personal religious convictions? What on earth did you think I was going to do after I heard this story, from a newspaper reporter, no less? I suggest you get out of my office and find something worth writing about. The Spanner case is none of your business— A, and B—whatever action this court may have taken will not be reversed on the strength of your amateur grade spying and intimidation."

Berman stood up and turned to walk out of the office. The judge wasn't finished.

"And one more thing. I don't want to hear that you are continuing to harass Mrs. Mazer. If I do, I promise you will have to deal with me in front of my bench. Do you understand me?"

"Yes, I do understand you, Your Honor. And I want you to understand me. I've got this one nailed down, and I'm going with it. I came here to give you a chance to respond to it. I don't suppose I expected a judge of your reputation to actually admit anything or take steps to correct it until you're forced to. I'm confident that hour is not far off. Thank you for your time."

He spun on his heel and walked out of the office, stomping down hard on the wooden floor. The judge's secretary had obviously heard the entire conversation through the open door. She bent her head toward the file on her desk and refused to look at him as he walked out. Just for effect, he slammed the outer door as he stepped into the hallway. The glass rattled. For an instant he thought he might have overdone it and actually broken the pane, but it remained intact. He looked at his watch: twenty after eight. Not a bad morning's work so far. On his way out of town he drove through McDonald's for a cup of coffee and headed back to the office to start writing.

As he crested the steps into the newsroom, he saw Dee Morgan reading a magazine at her desk. He walked over and sat down beside her.

"So, what happened?" she asked.

"You want the long or short version?"

"Make it short, I gotta get to a meeting."

"Mazer stonewalled me, and the judge threw me out of his office without comment, other than to praise Mazer as a dedicated public servant."

"Can you go with what you have?"

"Don't see why not, I've covered every base I can think of. And every day I delay is another day Charlotte Spanner and her kids have to be apart."

"Well, then, stop bothering me and get busy."

"Right, chief." He tossed her a half-hearted salute. "But seriously, Dee, thanks for the help. Your tape really is the smoking gun on this one. I have half a mind to share the by-line with you."

"But you won't, will you, you egotistical slob?"

"Probably not." She pretended to take a swing at him, but smiled. They both knew it was his story. She really was glad to see what he was doing, and didn't mind not being in the limelight when it came time to take the bows. Berman strolled over to his desk, logged onto his computer terminal, spread out his notes and began to write. Two hours later, the editor shipped his story to layout for page one.

Mother Loses Children to Zealous Caseworker
by Jed Berman

Charlotte Spanner lives a hard life; six kids, no husband, welfare income supplemented by food stamps, trapped in a worn-out house most of us wouldn't want to spend the night in. Yet, with all of these obstacles, Charlotte Spanner loves her children and spent most of her time caring for them—until a Child Welfare Department caseworker named Hildy Mazer paid her a visit late last Friday afternoon. Hildy Mazer took Charlotte Spanner's children away.

Judge Allen Frank signed a court order last Friday authorizing Mazer to take the children into custody to protect them from alleged abuse and neglect. But an *Evening Chronicle* investigation has uncovered a different explanation, one that smacks of a different kind of abuse—abuse of the system charged with protecting children in the first place.

In documents signed by Judge Frank, Hildy Mazer asserts that the children were living in squalid conditions in a decrepit house on the edge of Berrington. Mazer alleges that her personal inspection of the children found them to be dirty and poorly fed. She also documents the discovery of marks on several of the children which she judged to be signs of physical abuse. The report does not include any eyewitness accounts of abuse from the other children or any adults. Mazer appealed to the court to grant her custody of the children so they can be removed to county approved foster homes.

Apparently Judge Frank took little time to review the documents. They are dated as having been assembled last Friday, the same day the judge signed them. The order was carried out immediately. This reporter was present when Mazer handed the papers to Mrs. Spanner Friday afternoon, conducted a cursory inspection of the children, and then herded them into two separate cars, her county issue sedan and the backseat of a sheriff's department cruiser, sent along with her to maintain order if she met with any resistance.

There was no resistance. As this reporter watched, the mother made only a silent plea, reaching out her arms to touch each child as he or she was hustled by. The entire exercise took less than ten minutes. When it was over, Charlotte Spanner collapsed into a chair in her shabbily furnished living room and sobbed.

If Charlotte Spanner were a child abuser or a negligent mother, her histrionics would count for little in the face of vigilant enforcement of the law by Hildy Mazer. But there is no evidence of that to be found. What *The Evening Chronicle*'s investigation has uncovered, however, are clear indications that the caseworker acted out of her personal religious beliefs in seeking and carrying out the court order.

We attempted to confront Mazer with our findings, but she refused to comment. Judge Frank also declined any comment, other than a glowing endorsement of Mazer's performance as a county worker.

Acting on a hunch, *The Evening Chronicle* stationed an undercover reporter at the morning services of Hildy Mazer's church last Sunday. During the first hour, that reporter heard Mazer declare to the congregation that, in her words, she had found a way to "rescue these little ones from the clutches of evil." Mazer defined that evil as a mother (Spanner was not identified by name) living unmarried in "unrighteousness with a man, outside the bonds of holy matrimony."

During a visit to the Spanner home some weeks ago, according to Mrs. Spanner, Mazer asked numerous questions about Spanner's marital state. In her testimony on Sunday, Mazer made it clear that Spanner's living arrangements were unacceptable to her. When she came to take the children last Friday, Mazer's parting words were, "They're mine now."

But Mazer's testimony did not end with the morning worship service at her church. In the second hour session, Mazer was asked to elaborate on the experience she'd had. She referred to the situation involving the six children and their mother, telling the class that the children were dirty and that she had found signs of what she took to be physical abuse. But she also asked questions about Spanner's religious life, a clear violation of federal and state privacy guidelines for Child Welfare investigations. Mazer told the group she left Spanner's house, with no more evidence than a few dirty faces and a bruised arm, and "drove back to my office to begin drawing up papers to get those children away."

According to Mazer, she drew up a report which she submitted to her supervisor, who advised her to begin proceedings for a court order to take custody of the children. The supervisor's decision, based on the report, might lend credibility to Mazer's actions, until you hear Mazer's response to a question from our undercover reporter.

Our reporter asked Mazer, in the Sunday school classroom, in the presence of at least two dozen adults, if the judge asked for proof of abuse before signing the order. Mazer's answer, "It was old Judge Frank. He accepts whatever I tell him. He didn't even read the papers, just signed them."

To a follow-up question, "Did you really have proof those poor little things were being abused?" Mazer responded, "No, not at all. But that doesn't matter. It was the Lord's work and they are the Lord's creatures and that mother doesn't deserve to have them if she's not going to raise them properly."

It is clear from our investigation that whatever Hildy Mazer thought she was accomplishing with her campaign against Charlotte Spanner, what she actually managed to do was to tear a family apart, present unsubstantiated charges in court to support her request for custody of the children, and run rough-shod over Charlotte Spanner's constitutional rights. The next step should involve Child Welfare officials and possibly the prosecutor's office bringing about a speedy correction of these apparent injustices and reuniting Charlotte Spanner and her family.

The story hit the street Monday afternoon. Child Welfare officials and the prosecutor checked it out on Tuesday. Hildy Mazer was suspended on Friday, the same day Charlotte Spanner's children were sent back home. A sheriff's deputy was dispatched to collect the children from the foster homes and elementary schools and bring them to Charlotte's house. Berman knew when it was going to happen and he again pulled into the driveway behind the police car, but this time he witnessed a much happier scene. Charlotte ran onto the porch with tears streaming down her face. She snatched up the smallest children as they climbed the steps and hugged them until they could hardly breathe. The bigger kids crowded around her, arms around her knees, laughing. The deputy made a U-turn through the yard and accelerated back to the highway. Berman stood in the yard watching, tears filling his eyes, too. As she began shepherding the children into the house, Charlotte looked up and noticed Berman. She dashed off the porch and threw her arms around his neck.

"You said you'd get 'em back for me, and you did. You are a wonderful man, Jed Berman. I can never thank you for this. You've given me back my life."

Berman smiled and pulled her arms away from his shoulders. He pointed toward the house.

"You'd better get in there before they tear the house apart. I'm happy I could help."

She took his advice and ran inside, where he could hear children racing around and shouting in joyous, high-pitched voices. *Thank God it worked out right*, he thought. He climbed into his car and drove slowly away, trying to figure out what to work on next and wondering if Jane Filips would show up at Brady's for another Friday night dinner.

Three

Transitions

Berman's story about Charlotte Spanner's brush with injustice provoked a stack of mail and a pile of phone messages. Most of the responses praised Berman for his crusading good deeds and condemned the state for crashing into people's lives and harming their families. A couple of callers, who refused to identify themselves, suggested Spanner was guilty of abuse, but when Berman pressed them for details they hung up. He assumed they had some sort of grudge against Spanner, maybe a grudge against anyone caught on the lower rungs of life's ladder, dependent on the goodwill and generosity of society to keep going. Sometimes, especially in the past few years, Berman had the feeling generosity was an endangered species. People still seemed committed to the essential elements of American life they'd learned in school—life, liberty, and the pursuit of happiness. But the understanding that those qualities are best sought by a community working together appeared to be fading. Maybe his youthful idealism was in decline, but he just didn't have as much confidence in the goodness of people as he used to.

One of the phone messages was from someone named Fred Demarco. The name sounded familiar, but he wasn't sure why. He dialed the number and got a receptionist.

"TV 10, your best friend, morning, noon, and night. This is Donna. How may I help you?"

Berman had little contact with the broadcasters in the area. He knew a couple of jocks from the Berrington radio station, but TV 10 was in Pruitville. He'd never been there or bothered to talk to anyone who worked there.

"May I speak with Fred Demarco, please?"

"I'll connect you with the news department right away. Have a nice day."

The line into the news department rang at least six times before a gruff voice picked it up.

"News, what is it?"

Nice touch, Berman thought. What if he had some hot tip for these hair spray specialists? That sort of greeting could convince him to take his goods elsewhere in a hurry.

"This is Jed Berman. Is Fred Demarco available?"

The voice on the other end didn't answer him, but he heard whoever it was hollering across the room for Demarco.

"Fred, line three is for you." Berman heard a snatch of rock music as the voice put him on hold. Demarco picked up an instant later.

"Fred Demarco, who's this?"

"Hi, this is Jed Berman at *The Evening Chronicle* in Berrington. I have a message here that you tried to reach me. What can I do for you?"

"Oh, Jed." Demarco sounded genuinely pleased to hear from him. "Thanks for calling back so soon. I'm the news director here at TV 10. I'd like to talk with you about something, a possiblity I think you might find very interesting. Are you free for lunch today?"

Tomorrow looked better. They set it up for noon in Pruitville. But Demarco hadn't given much away, so Berman probed a little.

"The suspense is likely to kill me, Mr. Demarco. Can you give me some idea what we have to talk about?"

"Let's put it this way, Jed. First of all, call me Fred. Second, they say each of us is likely to pursue several career paths in our working lifetime these days. I think I may know where your path leads next."

"Are we talking about a job?" Berman could hardly believe this guy.

"I'd rather not say too much until we sit down face-to-face. But you might want to think about where things stand for you right now and where they're going from here. I don't mean to be coy, but I think we have a lot to talk about. I'll see you tomorrow."

"O.K., Fred. See you then."

Berman put down the phone and sat motionless. The idea of moving to TV had crossed his mind now and then, when he had to stand behind the cameras at a press conference and the newsmakers seemed much more intent on getting on the tube rather than in the paper. But he also shared much of the common print attitude toward TV reporters: weak journalists with pretty faces and expensive clothes, who skimmed the surface of a story like a hockey puck flying across the ice. If they hit the goal, it often seemed like luck to him. They didn't show much depth or much awareness of how shallow their work usually was. Why on earth would this Demarco guy want to talk to him about a job? He stared at the pink phone message. He couldn't imagine what this guy could say to convince him to leave a job he loved, where he felt like he was doing something worthwhile. But a free lunch was a free lunch. He'd let Demarco do the talking, enjoy a good meal, and get back to real reporting.

*　　*　　*

Berman headed for Pruitville around 11:30 the next

41

morning. Before he reached the restaurant, he drove by the TV 10 building. A school bus had just pulled up in front, and eager little kids tumbled down the steps, apparently on a field trip. It was tough to fight—people really like TV, they get all excited when the local anchors show up at a concert or in a parade. Berman had some trouble with that. All some of these people did was sit there in very bright lights and read news someone else wrote.

But there was something about most TV stations that made a certain statement. They always had impressive lobbies with shiny floors and big portraits of the stars on the walls. Often, a modern-looking stairway curved up to the second floor. It reminded him of an airport, somehow. At those moments, whether he agreed with it or not, he could see that television was the air travel of the communications industry, classy, obviously well-heeled, and popular. Newspapers, even a fairly successful one like *The Chronicle*, seemed more worn down, the Greyhound buses of the communications trade, dependable, able to go the distance, but with no shiny parts.

From what he heard around the circulation department these days, fewer and fewer people wanted to ride the bus. Yet, they shelled out more and more money for TV, cable, satellite, big screens, digital stuff, video cameras and recorders. People sat around his newsroom and condemned broadcasters, blamed them for ruining the journalism business, made fun of the anchors. But he knew most of his colleagues harbored a certain envy of TV types, their popularity, their larger incomes, even their celebrity status. You couldn't attend a public function without seeing at least one of them in the audience, surrounded by admirers, or worse, serving as master of ceremonies, telling stupid jokes all night.

Berman's jaundiced attitude had warmed into quite a

head of steam by the time he reached the restaurant. If this TV guy wanted to recruit him, it wouldn't be easy. Ink flowed in his veins; his whole professional life, his self-respect, revolved around print. Convincing him to abandon newspaper journalism would not be easy.

When he stepped into the restaurant, he realized he had no idea what Fred Demarco looked like. He saw a stocky guy with obviously dyed hair sitting alone at a table across the room. He stepped close to the hostess at the front desk and asked, "Excuse me, but is that Fred Demarco over there?"

She turned in the direction of his nod.

"It sure is. He's our regular lunchtime celebrity. Comes in here almost every day. "

"Thank you."

As Berman crossed the room, Demarco stood up and looked straight at him. He was short, and as Berman got closer he could see that the black hair was a piece, and not an especially good one at that. Demarco smiled warmly.

"Jed Berman?"

"Yes, and you're Fred Demarco."

"That's right. I got the impression on the phone that you didn't know who I was. Don't you watch TV?"

"I have to admit, not much. My work keeps me out a lot at night. Plus, to be honest with you, there's not much on that I like."

Demarco laughed easily. Berman's criticism didn't seem to bother him at all.

"Frankly, Jed, I agree with you. My wife and I watch some of the sitcoms, and a little PBS, but that's about it." He remembered a category he'd left out. "Oh, and the news, of course. I'd just as soon my kids don't see much of anything, except maybe sports." He laughed again, and Berman laughed with him. This guy seemed more reasonable than most TV types. Not so impressed with himself. And willing to admit his medium lacked quality. Berman was inclined, on the basis of first impressions, to like this guy. After the waiter took their orders, Demarco got down to business.

"Jed, I didn't invite you here to waste your time. Let me tell you something about myself and then I want to hear more about you. I've been in the news business for about twenty years. I started out in radio, worked my way up from a little station in my hometown to reporting and anchoring for a fifty-thousand-watt giant in Buffalo, New York. I switched to TV about ten years ago. Why? Two simple reasons: it pays better, and, more importantly, that's the news medium people really pay attention to. That's not to say they don't read newspapers. Obviously, you're having an impact with the things you do. But by and large, TV has become the primary source of information for the American public. I still like radio, but if you want to reach people today, I honestly believe you must do it with TV. What do you think?"

Berman took his time answering. He'd read Demarco's argument in magazines, but he wasn't quite ready to agree with it. No doubt TV was popular, but the thought of people abandoning newspapers for what they got from the box still galled him.

"I understand what you're saying, Fred. I see the reaction people have to TV. My problem is that I'm not sure we should encourage it. I mean, I have the impression much, if not most, of TV is smoke and mirrors, cardboard and klieg lights, a promise of more information, more value, than the medium has so far delivered. It's hard to argue against the research that shows people rank TV as their most important source of news. But what are they actually getting? From what I've seen, not a hell of a lot. Plenty of hype, sensational coverage of the tragic side of life, but where's the substance? Where's the reasoned approach to important issues?"

Demarco took it all in and continued to smile, not quite as broadly as before, but still a smile. He jumped back in while Berman took a bite of his sandwich.

"I don't disagree with anything you've said, Jed. Hell, I've watched it happen. Maybe I've helped it happen, although God knows I tell myself that's not true. When I started in radio I committed myself to maintaining the same kind of professionalism in broadcast as I know you do in print. It's probably easier to do in radio, because you aren't fighting the 'star factor.' Most people don't know who you are, so you can move around the community and keep an eye on things without somebody asking for an autograph. As long as you've got a telephone, you can track things down and get the story on the air at least as quickly as TV, and if you're a good writer, you can make the story as vivid in people's minds as anything we put on the tube."

This time Berman cut in.

"So what are you doing in television?"

Demarco swallowed some soup before he answered.

"Good question, Jed. It goes back to what I said a moment ago about the popularity of TV. The bottom line for me as a journalist has always been to keep people informed, raise issues, challenge their thinking. When I first got in the business you could do that with radio, even newspapers. But that's all changed. Today, if you really want to have an impact, you've got to be in TV. Look what happens if there's some sort of crisis, the Gulf War for instance. Did you see people crowding around their radios or standing in line to buy a newspaper after Bush ordered the Air Force to bomb Baghdad? No, you didn't. And you and I didn't do that either, admit it. We all switched on the

45

tube and watched those weird infrared pictures of the night bombing of Baghdad while Bernie Shaw crouched by his hotel window and told us what was going on. It was riveting stuff, people lost sleep watching it. I know I did. And what about the families who had kids or fathers and mothers stationed somewhere in the Middle East? They may have read the Reuters dispatches in your paper, but I know they were glued to their TVs 'til it was over. You just can't match the power of TV. It has people's attention and I want to be there to let them know what's going on."

Demarco argued his case with passion. That impressed Berman. But the idea of praising television still stuck in his throat.

"Sure, I watched the war. In special situations, I grant you, TV has the edge. But what about day-in-day-out type of coverage, the crime stuff that we all have to cover. How impressive is TV when it comes to that sort of thing? What I see is mostly sensationalized bullshit—blood-and-guts shots, mothers screaming over their sons after they're shot down in a gang fight. Do you feel good about being part of that?"

Demarco never flinched, but the tone of his voice changed; it was lower and quieter as he answered. His smile faded.

"You think I'm going to sit here and defend that crap? I don't like it any better than you do. But think about this: is the coverage really sensational or does it have more to do with the way people respond to the medium?"

This was a new point of view. Berman listened carefully.

"The research into TV tells us that the pictures automatically give it a power no other medium besides movies has ever had. It makes things concrete in an amazing way. There's no need to imagine what it looks like, we'll show it to you. All you have to do is react. If the pictures are strong, or ugly, or dramatic, that reaction is likely to be strong or ugly or dramatic. We're the medium of emotion. People don't stop to remind themselves it's just a picture on a cathode-ray tube. They react to it as though it were real."

Berman tried to interrupt, but Demarco waved him off.

"You think I'm just rationalizing, don't you? Well, I'm not. There is research today that tells us people react to TV and even computer screens the same way they would to a real person or event. For instance, they had people take some sort of orientation course on a computer. Then they wanted the group to evaluate the course. Half the group did the evaluation on the same computer they'd used during the course, the other half moved to a different computer. You know what happened?" Berman shook his head. "The people who did the evaluation on the same computer as the course gave the computer a more positive evaluation than the people who moved to a different computer. What's that mean? The scientists say it means the first group didn't have the heart to be as critical when they were face-to-screen with the computer that taught them the course. It's the same reaction they'd have if they took the course face-to-face from a real, live person. They treated the computer as though it were a real person, as though it had feelings. Can you imagine that happening with a newsaper or a radio?"

Demarco's pace quickened as he spoke. His eagerness to explain the research to Berman left him almost breathless. Berman waited for him to explain how all of this connected to the shabby way local TV news treated tragedies. Demarco was ready with the answer.

"So, you're sitting there wondering how does all of this justify the way TV news treats those terrible stories, aren't you? I'll tell you how." He wolfed down a large bite of his sandwich and continued.

"Stop me if you've heard all of this before. I respect your intelligence too much to talk down to you. But here goes. Are you familiar with the term 'salience'? If an event or a person or a TV picture has salience, it tends to stand out for people, sometimes beyond normal proportions. That's what TV pictures do, especially the violent, ugly stuff. Television news frequently takes a beating from people who say we focus most of our attention on negative stories. But when you actually sit down and count them, you find out we do at least as many neutral or positive stories as negative. It's just that the negative ones stand out more, they are more salient for the viewers, they remember them more vividly. So, do we sensationalize or do people simply have stronger memories of dramatic or violent stories? Do you know what I mean?"

Berman took a moment to consider Demarco's argument. He'd never heard TV defended quite this way. Demarco seemed to have done his homework on this, or else he spent a lot of time formulating rationalizations for his line of work. Maybe he'd been a bit hasty in his condemnation of TV news. But something still nagged at him.

"Okay," he agreed. "Maybe people have a special attraction to the violence and ugliness, but don't you fan that interest with those provocative little commercials you run between newscasts? You know the ones, 'A mother loses her only child in a fiery crash, details at eleven.' What's that all about?"

Demarco conceded the point.

"Hey, man, I don't like those things any better than you do. They're called topical promos, a kind of ultra-mini-newscast designed to make you stay up and watch the news rather than going to bed around 9:30. Is it really so different from some of the headlines I see in your paper?"

Demarco was trying to turn the tables on the newspaper guy. It hit home more than Berman wanted to admit. The paper's response to shrinking circulation also included more pictures and goofy features, but there was no denying the attempt to punch up the headlines to grab more readers.

"Touché," he said, reluctantly recognizing Demarco had scored. He half expected Demarco to circle in for the kill, but he didn't. Instead, he sat back from the table and looked at Berman with a twinkle in his eye.

"Jed, you are convincing me I did the right thing by inviting you to lunch. I respect your commitment to reporting and I admire the obvious principles that guide you. Your work speaks for itself, but your reactions just now prove you mean it. Now let me ask you something point blank: How would you like a chance to get the word out to ten times as many people as you reach now, maybe a hundred times? What if the power of your words suddenly multiplied a thousand times? What if you could pick up the phone and make a call and people knew they had to pay attention to you, had to give you the explanation you were asking for? You see where I'm going with this, don't you?"

Based on Demarco's comments the previous day on the phone, Berman thought he knew very well. This was a sales pitch, no doubt about it. But what exactly was Demarco selling? He decided it was time Demarco laid it all out.

"Fred, I appreciate your enthusiasm for TV and I am grateful for the kind words about my work with *The Chronicle*. Lunch has been good, the conversation stimulating. But what exactly do you have in mind?"

Demarco's smile returned.

"All right, Jed. I won't beat around the bush anymore.

We have a staff of competent reporters who can cover their beats and handle the ordinary happenings pretty well. What we don't have is a big gun, someone who finds the stories before everyone else does, who can dig out the big ones, put together investigative and enterprise reports that really make a difference. You do all of those things better than anyone in this market. How would you feel about doing it for us?"

Even though he'd expected it, the offer, lying right there on the table in plain sight, gave Berman a funny feeling. He'd been in print for so long, helped cut up so many TV newscasts as he watched with his friends in *The Chronicle* newsroom. He knew his place at *The Chronicle*. Editors basically thanked him for his stories and seldom made many changes. What reason did he have to consider leaving all of that? Demarco waited for his response.

"You know, Fred, I expected something like this. But now that it's happened, I'm not sure what I think. Are you sure it would make sense to hire someone who's never done TV? I don't know much about hair spray and makeup."

Demarco laughed. "My friend, that only makes you more valuable in my opinion. We have plenty of prima donnas in TV already. If some of them spent more time developing reporting skills instead of assembling their knock-out wardrobes, I might not be sitting here talking to you right now. We can teach you everything you need to know about the cosmetic stuff. You've got the important ingredients; you know how to dig. I want that on my staff."

Berman thought of another objection.

"I'm really settled in at *The Chronicle*. I have my place and I feel respected. No one gives me a hard time. If I can come up with a good story and nail it down, into the paper it goes. I have a nice sense of freedom and security.

Could it be like that in TV?"

"Absolutely. I might even be able to give you a field producer to help you dig, or whatever you needed."

The offer made little impression on Berman.

"That won't work, Fred. I travel mostly solo, with only an occasional cooperative venture."

Demarco rubbed his chin and pondered Berman's comment.

"Might be some trouble there. TV is a very close environment, lots of elbow rubbing. It's not uncommon for several people to help pull a piece together, couple of reporters, couple of photogs, a producer or two and I often throw in my two cents worth. Is that really something you couldn't learn to live with?"

Berman couldn't believe he was actually having this conversation. He really didn't know whether he could live with any of it. He tried to answer Demarco honestly.

"That's a tough question, Fred. This whole idea comes as a surprise. I feel as attached to print as you do to broadcast. I'm used to wrestling with words, not big cameras."

Demarco sensed Berman's attraction to the proposition. He tried to nudge him closer to a "yes."

"Listen, Jed, you don't have to give me an answer this minute. Think it over a day or two. Come over to the station and take a look around, talk to some of our people. Get the feel of twenty-first-century journalism. I would love to have you on our team. You're the best at what you do, and you can make a difference for us."

Berman rubbed his forehead and grinned at Demarco. This guy sure knew how to make you feel good.

"I don't know, Fred. You make a good pitch. It's just hard to picture myself on TV."

"Jed, you're a natural. You're a good-looking guy, you're smart and you have a nice, solid voice. The visual part is a given. I might even be able to swing you a wardrobe allowance to help with the transition. No offense, but I've never been particularly impressed by the way any of you print guys dress."

Just listen to him, Berman thought, *every sixty seconds he adds something to sweeten the pot.* To Demarco he said, "That reminds me of another reason why this is not such a good idea. We have a great retirement program at *The Chronicle.* I'm nearly a decade into it. If I walk away now, I fall way back to the beginning, assuming you even have something like that."

Demarco beamed. He had held back the financial incentives until he got a good feel for Berman's reaction. It was time to put the money on the table.

"Jed, money is not a problem here. You're a long way from retirement, but I'll bet you that our program is at least as good as the one you're in now. You can transfer whatever you've accumulated at the paper and never miss a beat in earnings. The station contributes seven percent of your gross salary, whether you kick in or not. Does that compare with what you've got now?"

Not only did it compare, it was better. Berman's wall of resistance started to shake.

"That sounds very good. But there's also the matter of keeping body and soul together until I'm ancient enough to hobble into retirement. I'm at the top of the scale with the paper. I'm not anxious to drop back to entry-level wages just for a new thrill."

"And you won't have to. We'll more than match whatever you're making now, no sweat."

"Wait a minute. I'm making $35,000 a year right now. Can you top that?" As he issued the challenge, Berman thought about how tough it was to make ends meet, even at that rate. His cracked and peeling Tempo with the perforated muffler drifted into his mind. Thirty-five grand wasn't a lot, but no one in his trade, at this level, made more than that. He expected Demarco to fold his tent and walk away, but he was wrong.

"Jed, look at me."

Berman looked squarely into Demarco's eyes. A smile spread across Demarco's face and there was an excited twinkle in his eye. It was not the face of a man ready to admit he had just been defeated in a bout of verbal jousting.

"I want you to know that I value honesty and straightforwardness above almost anything else. There's enough of the old days in me to think a man's word should stand for something. I came here today intent on luring you over to TV. I believe your work would benefit my station in its competition for ratings. I also believe your work, disseminated through TV, would benefit thousands of people in this community. I have argued my case in the way I thought you would most appreciate: philosophy first, then practice and now, finances.

"What I sense is that I made some progress on the first two counts, but the scales haven't tipped. Now, on this third issue, the important issue of money, I think I'm in a position to bear down real hard. Jed, as we sit here this minute, I am prepared to offer you a three-year contract starting at $45,000, climbing to $48,000 the second year and settling at an even $50,000 in the final year. What happens after that depends on how well things go. That's a significant jump over what you're making now. Is it enough to ease your concerns about finances and maybe salve your conscience a little about forsaking print for broadcast?"

With his last card played, Demarco sat back and waited. Berman let the numbers soak in for a moment. Demarco didn't have to spell it out any clearer for him. He knew, in a time when most workers felt lucky to see a three-to five-percent raise, that he would be exceedingly lucky to shoot from 35 to 45 thousand in one year. There really was more money in TV, or at least they were willing to shell out what they had. He stared back at Demarco as the idea spun around in his head. He felt a strange sensation around his mouth. A smile, much like Demarco's, spread across his face as his wall of resistance crumbled before him. He stood up and reached across the table. Demarco jumped up, grabbed his hand and shook it firmly.

"Jed, welcome to the wonderful world of broadcasting."

"Thanks, Fred. I hope I'm not going to hate myself in the morning."

"Forgive me for using this trite expression, but 'trust me.' We're going to do some great things together."

"I hope you're right. At the moment, I feel like I've just sold my birthright for a bowl of soup and a sandwich."

They sat down. Demarco asked another question.

"How much notice do you need to give *The Chronicle*?" A question Berman never imagined he'd have to answer.

"At least two weeks, maybe more, considering I'm their big gun."

"No problem. This is the middle of December. How about starting the second week of the new year? In the meantime, we can get together and get you up to speed on the mechanics of TV news. What do you think?"

Berman welcomed the gradual transition. It would not be easy saying goodbye to everyone at the paper. Some would consider him a traitor for going over to broadcast. Some wouldn't care either way. One thing he had learned a long time ago was that you can't wait for everyone else to make life's big decisions for you. You've got to do what you think is best. This step, as dizzy as it made him feel right now, was right. He could feel it. He suddenly realized Demarco was waiting for an answer.

"Sorry, Fred. I'm a little caught up in this right now, but yes, I think three weeks' notice is enough for the paper. Let me take care of that right away and I'll call you about the indoctrination sessions."

They stood up and shook hands again.

"You won't regret this, Jed," Demarco assured him with that crazy grin.

Berman grinned back.

"I hope you're right, Fred. I'll call you later this afternoon."

They walked out to the parking lot where Demarco climbed into a bright red Porsche and Berman slid into his faded red Tempo. As he started his car, Berman noticed the time on his digital clock: 12:58. In less than an hour, he had decided to foresake the world he knew so well for unfamiliar terrain. Without the warmth of Demarco's confident smile before him, the thought chilled him a little. But as he watched Demarco tool out of the lot in his German-made status symbol, he decided the shock wouldn't kill him. In fact, he began to look forward to this new challenge.

*   *   *

As he drove up to the *Chronicle* building, Berman thought it looked different than before, older, more drab. He knew that wasn't true. The change was in him, even in these brief moments since he left the restaurant with Demarco. This would not be his second home anymore. He wouldn't come up over the rise of the stairway into the newsroom to see his old coworkers cranking away on stories or twisting someone's arm over the phone. He wasn't socially involved with most of them, other than Dee Morgan, and their friendship was more professional than personal. But he felt close to them. Their combined efforts each day added up to *The Chronicle*, a paper people depended on to keep them informed, at least the people who still read the paper. He mounted the old wooden steps slowly, listening to the creaky ones as though he'd never heard them before. He ran his hand along the railing he never used. There were dents in the wall, maybe from a careless photographer's tripod or an angry reporter who just got beat on a story. He was looking down at the worn stair treads when a pair of shoes came into view. He looked up to see Dee standing over him, a curious expression on her face.

"My God, Jed, you look like you just met stairs for the first time in your life. Are you okay?"

"Yeah, I'm fine," Berman answered, flashing her the smile he'd caught from Demarco.

"Hold it, buddy. Something's up. You never smile like that."

"Something is up, Dee, something big, at least for me. Wanna hear about it?"

"Yes, I do. But I gotta check on something over at the mayor's office first. Wanna walk along with me?"

"No, I'd better get to work. I'll talk to you when you get back, or maybe we can grab dinner tonight."

"From the look on your face, you'll explode if you have to wait that long to tell me what's up. I'll catch you back here in about half an hour."

"Okay, I'll be here."

Morgan sidestepped him and was out the front door. With his reverie interrupted, he walked into the managing editor's office and announced that he was leaving to take a job in TV news. He had expected some sort of outcry, a lament over losing him. What he got was a look of surprise that metamorphosed into dismay and ended in resignation. They agreed his last day would be January seventh. He could take care of the exit paperwork in the meantime. That was it. No pleas to stay or reconsider. No counter-offers. The deed done, he stood up and walked out into the newsroom, where life went on as usual. The soft click of computer keys mingled with voices droning on about important and trivial events. The sports guys argued over which team looked most promising in the NBA.

He sat down at his desk and stared across the room. Everything had changed and yet nothing had changed. In three weeks, someone else would be assigned to his space. They probably wouldn't keep a picture of Ralph Nader beside their dictionary. It was unlikely they'd drink coffee in a plastic Star Wars mug. Few, if any, other reporters would tape a poster of Janice Joplin to the side of their desk.

The disjointedness of the move settled over him as he gazed into the not-so-distant future. You invest yourself in a place for years, sacrifice important hours and days of your life, and when it comes time to go, you leave hardly a trace. No one could distinguish your footsteps from the thousands of others in the grooves on the old wooden steps. The paperclip tray in your desk drawer harbored no memory that you had used it. When the computer keys you pounded all those months wore out, they'd throw away the keyboard, not bronze it to commemorate your great journalistic accomplishments. Shit, this was some business. A throwaway business, where you existed only as long as your stories showed up in print. Remove yourself and you vanished. When you tore apart this newspaper thing and examined it closely, it revealed little more substance than any other medium. Why was he reluctant to give it up for TV? Because someone had convinced him real journalists didn't do broadcast? Sure they did, and he was about to become one of them. A tap on the shoulder halted the downward spiral of his thoughts.

"Hey, Berman, what are you doing? You look like you just lost your best friend."

Dee Morgan had returned and was standing by his desk. He looked up at her.

"You know, Dee, in a way I think I just did. Let's get out of here and I'll tell you why." They walked down the stairs together and out the front door.

"Wanna come over to my place for a while?" he asked, as they stepped onto the sidewalk.

"Sure. I'll get my car around back and be right over."

Ten minutes later they were lounging in his living room, a chilled bottle of white zinfandel beginning to sweat on the coffee table between them. Morgan spoke before Berman had a chance.

"You're leaving, aren't you?"

He nodded. This didn't feel like the right time to grin.

"Yes, I am, Dee. I had lunch today with Fred Demarco. Have you ever heard of him?"

"Sure. The TV guy. He used to be a reporter for TV 10, then he moved up the ladder. He's news director now, isn't he?"

"Yeah, he is. How come you know these things and I never heard of him?"

"Because, unlike some snobs I work with, I watch TV. He hasn't been on the air for a number of years, but he used to be a pretty good reporter. At least he did okay on the tube. What kind of deal did he offer you that convinced you to abandon us?"

"Oh, he had a plan. He claimed to be as bothered by the crap TV gets into as I am. That lulled me into dropping my defenses. Then he flattered the hell out of me, told me how much I can do for his paper and the viewing public. Then he offered me ten thousand dollars more a year than

I'm making now, to do exactly what I'm doing now, investigative type stuff. Could you have said no to that?"

Morgan took a while to respond. She emptied her wine glass and refilled it. Berman grew a little uneasy about what she might be getting ready to say.

"C'mon, Dee, you'd go for it, wouldn't you?"

"To be honest with you, Jed, I'm not sure. We've had a lot of talks about why print is better than broadcast. We've had some great laughs making fun of the local TV news teams. I never stopped to think about whether I could go over to the other side. But now that I reflect on it, and considering the deal he offered you, I don't see how you had much choice. Let's face it, we may be in this gig because we've somehow managed to hang onto more of our youthful idealism than the average working stiff, but we're not martyrs. Why should you struggle to make ends meet in a medium that's facing a harder and harder struggle to survive when this guy's throwing money at you and promising to let you do the kind of reporting you believe in? All things considered, Jed, I think I'd do the same thing you're doing."

She smiled at him as she leaned across the coffee table to shake his hand. He felt relieved to know she didn't consider him a deserter.

"Dee, I hope you know how much your opinion matters to me. Of all the people in *The Chronicle* newsroom, you're the one I respect most. Hearing what you just said helps ease some of the anxiety I've been feeling since the moment I sealed the deal. Do you think anyone in the shop will give me shit about it?"

"Buddy, the minute you allow yourself to think other people really care that much about what you do, you're cruising for a let-down. I don't mean to be critical of our staff. We have lots of good people there. But their bottom line isn't much different from yours and mine, figuring out what's best for you or me, and working for it. Did you tell the chief yet?"

"Yes, I did, while you were at the mayor's office."

"Was he upset to hear it?"

"Not especially. He told me he was sorry to lose me. He said some nice things about my work."

"But did he beg you to stay? Did he make you a better offer?"

"No."

Morgan finished her second glass of wine and plunked the glass down firmly on the table.

"I didn't figure he would. You know, it's kind of interesting. These companies push us to commit ourselves and our talents to them, to feel like we're on some sort of team doing what we do. And we do it. We work long hours for not enough money, thinking we really are part of something important. But if we show a little bit of commitment to ourselves and it doesn't jive with what they've got in mind, tough luck for you."

She poured herself another glass of wine and drank most of it in one gulp. Berman was only partway through his second glass, but he could already feel the heat rising in his face as the alcohol crept through his system. Obviously Morgan felt it, too. The cynicism in her voice surprised him.

"Dee, I hope I haven't upset you with this. You've never sounded so pessimistic before. I hope we can keep in touch, maybe work on some stories together like we always have. "

Morgan drained her glass and set it down. She sat staring straight ahead as the sun's rays streamed into the darkening room. She spoke without looking at Berman.

"Those are nice thoughts, Jed, but you know and I know how often we've cooperated with TV 10 on any stories in the past ten years." She formed a circle with the thumb and first finger of her right hand. "Am I right? Zero, nada, rien, zippo, *none*. So I doubt if we can pull that off. I can tell you right now I'll miss working with you. Maybe we'll see each other here and there. That's cool. You know I respect what you do and how you do it. I'll miss having you there. But I'll get over it, and you'll get into your new stuff and that'll be that. I really do hope it goes well for you. And I'd better head for home before the wine catches up with me."

She stood up and shook Berman's hand again. He walked her to the door of his apartment and put his arm around her shoulders. She slipped her arm around his waist and gave him a hug. Theirs was an affectionate relationship, but not a romantic one. They both knew that journalism is a journey marked by many "hellos" and "good-byes," but that didn't make it any easier to do when the time came. They would be working together for another three weeks, so tonight didn't have to be a final moment. But they would never work together again in the same way, and as two professionals who respected each other, they both felt sad about parting company. Morgan opened the door and stepped into the hallway. She patted Berman on the arm and walked toward the stairs. Berman closed the door, returned to the couch and sat down to finish off the wine while it was still cold.

Four

Switched On

Learning the ropes of TV news proved easier than Berman expected. He spent several nights at the station with Demarco during his final three weeks at the paper. By the time his last day came, he already had one foot in the new camp, and leaving didn't feel that bad. He still worried about losing his reputation as a serious journalist, but he was determined to work so hard in TV that no one could accuse him of skimming the surface of the news.

Some of Demarco's staff had seen him hanging around during his training sessions, but Demarco saved the announcement of Berman's arrival for his first day. Starting time was nine o'clock, a considerable change from the seven A.M. punch-in time at *The Chronicle*. The drive from Berrington took about twenty minutes, which meant he really didn't have to get up much before eight to get to work on time. No wonder, he thought, that print people get the jump on these electronic guys so often. Hell, these were banker's hours.

As Berman walked into the lobby, in the new blue suit Demarco had paid for, he saw a young, blonde-haired woman at the receptionist's desk. She hadn't been there when he came to train after hours with Demarco. Berman caught her eye as he swerved to walk down the hall to the newsroom. She raised her hand and stopped him.

"I'm sorry, sir, I can't let you go back there unescorted. Can you tell me your name and who you're here to see?"

She was simply doing her job, but it annoyed Berman to be treated as some sort of intruder. His eyes flashed irritation as he turned to look at her, but he obeyed her orders.

"My name is Jed Berman. I'm the new guy in the news department. I need to see Fred Demarco."

The receptionist was young and very cute. He didn't want to get off on the wrong foot with her, so he added a weak smile at the end of his explanation.

"If you don't mind waiting over there for a moment, I'll contact Mr. Demarco."

She motioned toward a furnished area on the other side of the lobby. The furniture looked new and stylish. It sat on a floor so highly polished it reflected the furnishings like a mirror. It fit his theory about TV stations and airports. Shiny places, very clean, very classy. The front and side of the lobby were glass with heavy curtains running floor to ceiling. The curtains were pulled back and fastened against the wall. A giant plant stood in the all-glass front corner by the couches and chairs. He walked away from the receptionist's desk and stood by the nearest couch. His heels clicked on the hard-waxed floor. As he turned his back to the young woman, he heard her on the phone to the newsroom.

"This is Cindy at the front desk. Would you tell Mr. Demarco there's a man named Jed Berman out here who says he's here to start work?"

As he turned to look at her, she hung up the phone.

"Mr. Demarco will be out in a moment. Would you care to have a seat?"

It had been a long time since he felt like the new kid on the block. Berman smiled again, but he didn't feel like sitting down. He wanted to get started.

"Thanks, but I think I'll just stand. He won't be long, will he?"

"I'm sure he'll be out soon."

Just as she offered that encouragement, he heard a door swing open and quick steps coming up the hallway. Demarco swept into the lobby and past the receptionist's desk.

"Thanks, Cindy." He extended his hand to Berman as he rushed across the floor. "Good morning, Jed. We're just about to start the morning meeting. Come on in and meet the rest of the gang." They shook hands and Berman followed Demarco toward the hallway. At the desk, Demarco stopped and motioned toward Jed.

"Cindy, I'd like you to meet Jed Berman, our new ace reporter. Jed, this is Cindy Owens, our trusted receptionist, who makes sure undesirables don't get past the lobby and into our top secret newsroom. No need to screen Jed from now on, Cindy, he's one of us."

Cindy reached out to shake Berman's hand. This close he could smell her perfume, one of those newer scents that he liked. He took her hand and shook it firmly.

"Nice to meet you, Mr. Berman," she said. She smelled so good he held her hand a little longer than he needed to.

"It's nice to meet you, Cindy. And please don't call me Mr. Berman. It's just Jed, although you may be tempted to call me a few other things after you work with me a while."

She liked the joke. She flashed him a big smile that showed off her beautiful teeth. Looking down at her from this angle, he could see that she hadn't always been a blonde. That didn't matter. She was very cute and he knew he wouldn't mind working with her. Demarco grabbed his arm and started to pull him back to the hall.

"I can see you two are going to be the best of friends. Let's go, Jed. I'm paying you now. I want to see some work."

The newsroom occupied most of the front half of the building opposite the lobby on the ground floor. Double doors opened into it from the hallway. Along the hallway hung portraits of the on-air people, reporters, anchors, weather guy (holding a goofy umbrella and making a wacky face), and the sports guys holding baseball gloves or basketballs. No matter what they were doing, they were all well dressed and fairly good looking.

Berman was a little worried about how well he compared with these beautiful people. He had spent some time staring at himself in the mirror since Demarco told him he had the looks for TV. He felt a little stupid even thinking about it. He decided his brown hair and dark blue eyes filled the bill, but his nose seemed a little too long and straight and his jaw maybe a little too square. He'd never really thought about it at the paper. Obviously, this was going to be different. The bottom line was that he didn't expect his looks to trigger an ego trip just because he showed up on TV.

Demarco banged open the door into the newsroom and started to shout.

"Hey, everybody, gather round. I want you to meet someone."

A scattering of old desks filled the newsroom, some standing alone, others pushed together to form islands of three or four here and there. The staff gathered in front of Demarco. Berman counted about ten well-dressed people he took to be reporters, and another ten wearing jeans and more casual looking shirts; he assumed they were photographers. They all crowded together, jostling and joking around. Demarco raised his hand to quiet them down.

"I'd like to introduce Jed Berman. Some of you may recognize his name from bylines in the *Berrington Evening Chronicle*. Jed's the guy who's been breaking all those great stories around the county, most recently the story about the welfare mom who lost her kids because of the whacked-out caseworker. Today, he starts breaking those stories for TV 10. He's still a little tender, after giving up his place in the vaunted halls of print journalism, so be gentle with him."

Demarco delivered the last sentence with a slightly sarcastic twist. The TV people laughed and Berman squirmed a little. Demarco went on.

"I've given Jed a basic orientation to this madness we call TV news, but just like some of you when you arrived here fresh out of J-school, he may need a few tips and reminders till he gets his feet planted firmly on electronic ground."

"And he may get shocked before he has a chance to really plug in," a voice interjected from the back of the group.

Everyone groaned. Demarco turned to Berman to explain.

"That's just Donnie. He's a frustrated stand-up comic masquerading here as a newsman. Pay no attention to him."

Berman scanned the back of the crowd looking for a face to connect to the voice. Donnie Kurtz waved and grinned. Berman detected no malice. He wasn't looking for any trouble today. Demarco wrapped up the formalities.

"So, my friends, give Jed a hand while he's feeling his way, and don't hesitate to confer with him on stories. Like all of you he's a helluva reporter and he hits the ground running for us because this is his home territory and he's been reporting here for nearly ten years. He may have some good contacts for you, so don't be afraid to pump him for info.

"All right, enough break time. While I've got most of

you in one place, let's get started with the morning meeting."

The crowd backed off and sat down in chairs or on desk tops as Demarco collected their ideas for the day's stories. Berman found a spot off to the side and listened to get a feel for how they did things. He already knew his assignment for this day: to get acquainted with the computer system and work on learning the basic newsroom terminology. Demarco had shown him how to operate a video camera and how to edit, but he didn't expect to do any work as what Demarco called a "one man band," shooting, writing and editing his own stories. Demarco had told him he had all the good shooters he needed. From Berman he wanted great reporting, reporting that would help TV 10 blow away the crosstown competition, Channel 3 News. Once he got the basics under his belt, Berman felt confident he could deliver what Demarco wanted.

*   *   *

By his third day, Berman felt ready to venture out in his new guise as broadcast journalist. At the morning meeting he told Demarco he wanted an assignment. The only thing left was a news conference called by the Salvation Army. It had been a long time since he covered anything that routine, but he agreed with Demarco that it might be a good idea to go through the motions on a few not-so-serious assignments before digging into the kind of stories he normally handled.

He walked into the Salvation Army building behind Lenny, the photographer assigned to him this morning. Berman carried the camera tripod. It felt funny to lug something so big to a story; he was used to traveling fairly light—a notepad and sometimes a small tape recorder.

Lenny marched on into the chapel where the "presser," as he called it on the way over from the station, was going to be held. Two other camera crews were already there, one with its tripod and camera planted squarely in front of the pulpit, the other just to the right of it. Lenny staked his claim to the left, bantering with the other two photogs, whom he obviously knew from other assignments. A couple of radio news people parked their microphones on the pulpit with their microphone cubes strategically placed so the cameras could pick up their call letters and provide some free advertising. Berman recognized the print reporters from the Pruitville paper. They stood apart from the electronic crews. That's where he would have been, too, in his other life. You didn't want to give these space-consuming, arrogant broadcast types any more status than necessary. Berman walked over to his former colleagues-in-print.

"Hey, Georgiana, Judy. How goes it?" He didn't know the guy standing with them.

They turned to look at him with expressions of genuine curiosity. "Berman," Judy said, "how are you? We ran the blurb the other day that said you've jumped ship to the great mindlessness of electronic news gathering. Is that really true?"

He'd expected some of this. He hoped they'd get over it soon.

"Yeah, I'm working for TV 10, but no, it's not a mindless job. These guys work pretty hard. And," he paused for dramatic effect, "they actually think about things besides hair spray and makeup."

"Whatever, Jed, I guess I'm still not so sure that's true. You're a pretty good reporter. We'll see how long it takes you to get sick of being superficial. By the way, do they really pay as well as we always assume?"

Berman smiled and put a finger to his lips.

"Company secrets, can't talk about it." He lapsed into his best George Bush impression. "Can't do it. Wouldn't be prudent."

They laughed, and Judy dropped her interrogation. Berman waved and walked back across the room to Lenny.

"You want anything special here, Jed?" Lenny asked. "Doesn't look like they have many props for us to shoot. What's the issue this morning?" It was a two-part question, with one part easier to anwer than the other.

"They called us over to urge the public to give more money, especially for their homeless shelter. Seems the big Christmas bell-ringing thing hasn't worked so well this year. Their press release says they're about thirty thousand dollars behind on their budget. "

He pulled a sheet of paper from inside his jacket.

"Says here they're kicking off a new campaign today called 'Extend the Spirit'—I guess that's the Christmas spirit—so they can raise enough money to keep things going."

Lenny nodded without enthusiasm. He had shot many news conferences before, talking heads sitting at a table, often in front of a blank wall. With that kind of set-up, he had trouble being creative with his shots. That's when Demarco chewed on his ass back at the station. His question to Berman about special video requests was sincere since he saw another dull and boring story shaping up.

"Not a helluva lot to shoot here, Jed. What're we gonna do to make this interesting? Right now it's a great newspaper story."

Berman flinched. That was the part of the question he couldn't answer. He felt a little helpless. His reflexes were still oriented toward what he could do with words, in this case, to drive home the Salvation Army's appeal to contributors. But now he had to make it visual. Before he could come up with any good ideas, the Army's chief exec, known as "the major," stepped up to the microphones. He squinted as the photogs snapped on their stand lights. Before he launched into reading the press release word for word, he adlibbed a greeting to the line of reporters.

"Good morning to you all and God bless you for coming." Then his eyes dropped to the sheet in front of him. "We want to wish all of you another Merry Christmas and invite you to help make it a happier New Year for dozens of our brothers and sisters here in the tri-county area. Apparently our traditional kettle drive during the holidays failed to ring a bell with as many people as usual. Our coffers are thirty thousand dollars short of the budget we proposed for our homeless shelter."

Lenny leaned over to Berman, who was reading along with the major.

"Let me know when I can break loose for some cutaways. At least that'll give us a little variety in shots, if we have to make something out of this. It's probably just a vo or a vo-sot, don't you think?"

Two days ago, Berman would have accused Lenny of speaking another language, but now he understood the reference to a vo, or voice over story read by the anchors while viewers looked at pictures of the event, or a vo-sot, which started with voice over copy and included one of those infamous sound bytes, a chunk of the spoken words related to the story, in this case the major's comments. He had to agree with Lenny that this story had little potential visually. The major droned on through the press release.

"Homelessness needs everyone's help. If you see one of our bell ringers at your grocery story or on a street corner, please show your support with a generous donation. It's not for us, it's for those who are part of us who are far less fortunate than we are."

That sounded useable to Berman. He got Lenny's attention with a tap on the shoulder and drew his finger across his throat, to signal that he had all he needed from the official announcement. Lenny unsnapped the camera from the tripod and started moving around the room, shooting from a number of angles. Demarco had explained to Berman the standard editing progression: wide shot (to establish the setting), medium shot, close-up, sound byte, medium shot and back out to a wider shot. Armed with Demarco's explanation, Berman had begun paying closer attention to the shots edited into stories. Some followed tradition, others looked more like a hodge-podge of pictures, not assembled in any particular order. Some went for extreme close-ups, from down below looking up, or from the side. He wondered if the major would appreciate one of those up-the-nostrils shots.

Lenny had just moved behind the major to get a shot back toward the gathered media when the officer finished reading. Lenny made a circular motion with his hand to urge Berman to keep the major talking until he got the shot. Berman had a question ready.

"Major, can you explain why your holiday fund drive fell so short this year?"

The major looked perplexed.

"No, we really haven't figured that one out. We didn't change anything on our end, and the employment picture is pretty good right now. Seemed to us people have enough money to donate to a cause like this. We're taking a closer look at the whole bell-ringing idea to see if there's anything we can do differently to have more success."

Lenny shut off his camera and lowered it from his shoulder. He flashed Berman the OK sign and walked back around the room. He set the camera on the floor and began

71

collapsing the tripod. No one else asked any questions. The major thanked them again for coming and the other crews switched off their lights and began breaking down to leave. The room had seemed reasonably bright when they walked in, but now, without the TV lights, it looked dim, almost dark. Berman had noticed the effect while he was still at the newspaper. It really showed up if the TV crews turned off their lights before the rest of the reporters finished asking questions. The brilliance of the illumination somehow gave whatever they were there to talk about an extra sheen of importance. When the lights went out, so did some of the significance. It was another way TV tended to take over whatever it touched. Before, Berman had felt some resentment about that. Now he was part of it. He hoped he could use that power to do something worthwhile.

Berman and Lenny picked up their gear and paraded outside with the other media people. They stowed the tripod and light in the trunk and slid the camera onto the backseat. Then they drove back to the station. They used the back newsroom entrance, off the parking lot. Before Berman could say anything, Lenny gave Demarco his evaluation of the assignment.

"Pretty much bullshit from the Salvation Army, Fred."

"I didn't expect it to be earthshattering, Lenny," Demarco responded.

"Well, then, you were right. All we got was the major standing up there talking at us. How do you propose we put this together, or do you want it at all?"

"Oh, I want it." To Berman he added, "What if you write it so we can use some file of bell-ringers. That at least makes it visual and it was the failure of the bell-ringers that created this shortfall, right?"

"Right."

"Okay, how about if you take a crack at writing up a

forty-five-second vo-sot, and I'll take a look at it. It probably won't need any help in the writing department, but there may be some adjustments to make on the format, since it's still relatively new to you." Lenny tossed Berman the tape, and Berman headed back to the editing bays to decide which part of the major's comments to include in the story. Demarco had one more bit of advice as he walked past.

"Remember, Jed, sound bytes have to be really good to be long. I'd look for something around ten or fifteen seconds. Then wrap your copy around it. I still prefer vo-sots that end in video rather than cutting out right after the sound byte or coming back to another mug shot of the anchors. "

To Lenny he added, "Why don't you dig up some bell-ringer stuff while you're waiting for Jed to get this thing written?" Lenny tossed Demarco a sloppy salute and headed to the tape archive room.

At six, Berman and the reporters sat on desk tops or stood around to watch the show go down alongside the other two stations on monitors mounted near the ceiling on the far side of the newsroom. Berman had tried to come up with a snappy first line for the Salvation Army story. Demarco insisted that's what it took to get viewers to pay attention. Jed wanted to hear how well the anchors read it. He knew from the rundown in the computer that it hadn't made it into the first block of news, but it came up early in the second block after the commercial break. The male anchor, Steve Kimmel, started it.

"Looks like the Salvation Army's traditional Christmas fund-raising drive didn't ring true this year."

Kimmel's co-anchor, Sally West, nodded at Kimmel and turned to the camera to continue reading.

"That's right, Steve. The leader of the Pruitville Salva-tion Army Corps told reporters today the Christmas bell-ringing drive fell thirty thousand dollars shy of its goal. He introduced a new campaign called 'Extend the Spirit' to help fill the cash-shy coffers."

Next came the major's sound byte.

"If you see one of our bell-ringers at your grocery store or on a street corner, please show your support with a generous donation. It's not for us, it's for those who are part of us who are far less fortunate than we are."

The shot had changed to bell-ringers when Sally West started reading. After the sound byte, Lenny had edited in some of the cutaways he'd shot, including one of Berman standing by the tripod listening to the major. It caught Berman off guard. It was the first time he'd seen himself on the air. Donnie Kurtz saw it, too.

"Hey, Berman, nice cutaway. Looks like you really give a shit what that guy's saying. You're gonna do just fine in TV."

"Thanks for the encouragement, Donnie. I thought it would take a lot longer to learn how to fake it like you do," Berman grinned.

He wanted to add, but didn't, that he really did care what happened to the Salvation Army's fund drive and the program it was designed to support. He was no stranger to cynicism, or the gallows humor reporters often resort to in order to combat the awfulness of the things they write about. But the level of callousness seemed even higher in TV, based on what he'd heard in this newsroom so far. He figured no one wanted to hear how he really felt. He stopped talking and focused on the screen. Sally and Steve were into the weather tease. A gorgeous winter sunset captured by the weather camera on the roof of the station filled the screen as the anchors promised all the weather details with Bill Boynton "in just a moment." Berman headed toward the drinking fountain in the hallway. As he passed

Demarco's office, he got a thumbs up from the news director. The story had gone well, but he didn't feel at home, just yet. Maybe it was too soon to expect that. When he got back to his desk he logged off his computer, pulled his jacket off the back of his chair, and walked out the back door to his car. He called Jane Filips when he got home and they spent the evening watching videos at her apartment.

*   *   *

At the next day's morning meeting, Demarco threw Berman into the mix. The assignment editor reeled off six or seven routine events of the day: council meetings, a news conference about a new literacy program at the library, police kicking off a new fingerprint-your-kid project—all stuff everyone had done before. They groaned as the list was read, but when Demarco asked them for better ideas, they avoided making eye contact with him, like a junior high school class that hadn't done their homework. Finally, Demarco turned to Berman.

"Got any ideas, Jed? Anything you had left over from the print side that you could crank out in a day?"

Berman felt a little uneasy trotting out his ideas in front of people he didn't know very well; he hated making himself vulnerable, tossing a story idea on the table for everyone else to bat around and maybe tear up or dismiss as unworthy. But he also had considerable confidence in his own news judgment. He saw himself as an ordinary person who had the good fortune to be granted access to the four corners of the community. He wanted to be the eyes and ears of working folks who couldn't be where he could, who didn't have time to track down details they nonetheless wanted to know. He spoke softly as he made his first contribution to the TV 10 news meeting.

"Well, something that came up back in November during the election was an idea by one of our state legislators to create a legislators' hall of fame. His opponent tried to use it to convince people the guy was an egotist, but he got reelected anyway. I never heard whether the lawmaker really wanted to do it or not. If he's in the area this week, it might be interesting to find out. Personally, I can't think of anything we need less than an expensive monument to the politicians we tend to despise most of the time anyhow."

"What visual possibilities do you see, Jed?" Demarco wanted to know.

"Hell, not many, Fred. I mean, as far as I know there are no drawings of this proposed political palace. I just thought if this guy really does want to build this thing, and he's been reelected, people ought to know what he's up to."

Donnie Kurtz tossed in an obvious criticism.

"Wouldn't that have been a better story during the election? Seems a little dated now, unless this guy actually intends to push for it. Do you know what he's going to do about it?"

Berman shook his head and sat back, assuming the idea was dead. Demarco cleared his throat and moved on.

"Interesting idea, Jed, but I don't think it's gonna fly today. I agree with Kurtz, the timing is off. Got any other ideas in the hopper? We need something with some zip."

Kurtz tendered his own suggestion.

"I have an idea, but I need to ask a question first. Did we get shots of that bad accident last night, where the two teenagers from Danforth High School got killed?"

One of the photographers answered him.

"Yeah, I shot it, I was on call. It happened about one this morning. Nasty crash. Just one car. They slammed into a tree when they missed a curve. Must've been doin' about ninety. The car closed up like an accordion. I got some great shots before they got the bodies out. The one kid's arm was chopped off and lying on the ground outside.

Most of the group found the graphic description more than a little distasteful, with the exception of one of the other photographers who seemed excited by it.

"Where's the tape? I wanna save the arm part on my 'blood and guts reel'. Nice shooting."

Demarco drew them back to the main discussion.

"C'mon, you ghouls. Get with the meeting, we don't want to be here all day." To Kurtz he said, " So, Donnie, what do you see in this crash for today?"

"Nothing earthshattering. I just thought maybe we should go over to the high school and see how people are coping with it. It's always traumatic when kids lose one, let alone two of their own."

"OK, Donnie, why don't you and Smitty head over there and see what you can get. But do me a favor, don't try to find the parents today. They may want to say something later, but we need to give them a chance to grieve a little before we put a camera in their face."

Kurtz raised his index finger to make one more point.

"I agree with your approach, Fred, but you should know that Channel 3 is likely to have the parents, grand-parents, brothers, sisters, and the dog if it can talk. You wanna get scooped on this?" Kurtz had enough years on the street to know what he was saying. Demarco gave him the response he always gave reporters who showed signs of tilting toward sensationalism.

"Donnie, you know where I stand on these things. If I err in covering tragic events like this, I want it to be on the conservative side. I can't help it if the other guys decide to pander to the morbid side. We're not going to do it here until management walks into this newsroom and insists on it. And the day they do that is the day I walk out the door for good."

Demarco delivered his policy statement with enough heat that Kurtz backed away with his palms raised in front of him.

"I got ya, chief. I just didn't want to be standing here tonight at six, when they run that stuff, and have someone say, 'How come we got caught with our pants down?' "

"Don't worry about that, Donnie," Demarco assured him. "We will continue to take the high road as long as I'm in charge. We're not the networks or those phony tabloid shows. I believe in showing people some respect and here's a chance to do it. So get going,."

Kurtz and Smitty grabbed their gear and shuffled toward the back door. Berman felt refreshed by the conversation he'd just heard. It was a little bit like the theory he'd heard about car commercials. Some researcher had said car commercials were on TV to convince people who'd already bought a car that they'd made the right choice. Listening to Demarco spell out his news philosophy, in the face of cheesy practices by the competition, gave Berman even more reason to believe he'd made the right choice in coming over to TV 10.

After Kurtz left, Berman walked over to his desk and shuffled through his idea file. Most of the other reporters were scanning last night's paper to find a story they could copy for the six o'clock show. Berman detested the thought of stealing good stories from the paper. He'd always had enough contacts to generate his own assignments. He wasn't about to start taking the easy way out now. He came across a crudely scribbled note he'd received just before he left the paper but hadn't had time to check out. The writer charged that county highway workers were stealing supplies from the county garage and selling them. Berman picked up the note and walked over to Demarco.

"Hey, Fred, here's something I'd like to work on. Somebody sent me this note accusing county highway workers of ripping off supplies to make money. Can you give me some time to check it out?"

It sounded good to Demarco, but it also sounded like a story that might take more than a day. He felt the usual newsroom pressure to get a good package out of every reporter each day. He was reluctant to tie up a news team on a chance, but if Berman got lucky it would almost certainly be today's lead. Plus, he knew viewers would love to see someone nail those fat, lazy bastards who got their jobs through patronage and acted as if no one could make them do any real work.

"Get on it, Jed. Stay in good touch with me. If it's not working out by noon, let me know. We may have to switch you to something else you can pull together today."

Berman protested without thinking.

"Hey, Fred, this isn't the kind of story that just jumps into the boat. I'm gonna have to do some fishing around to see if this is really true, probably even a little stakeout stuff, to get pix of these guys in the act. It's likely to take time."

"Welcome to TV, Jed. I understand good investigative work takes time, but we need a serious contribution from each reporter every day. So be prepared to do some of the work on this today and then shift gears into a quick hitter you can crank out for six, okay? Why don't you and Carol get going and see what you can find?"

Carol loaded up her gear while Berman grabbed his notepad and jotted down a few phone numbers he thought he might need. As they drove toward the county garage, he did a little prying with some of his best contacts.

"Good morning, Fletch. This is Jed Berman, how are

you doing? I'm fine, but I've changed addresses. I'm working with TV 10 now. No, they didn't hire me for my looks. What? Oh, yeah, I knew you were kidding.

"Hey, listen, I gotta ask you about something. Can you talk? Good."

Listening to Berman, Carol could tell he was no rookie. It sounded like this guy had some connections.

"Fletch, I got a note from someone accusing county highway workers of ripping off supplies. Have you ever heard anything about that? I know just about everybody lifts something from time to time, like a screwdriver or a box of paperclips. But this note said these guys were stealing enough stuff, like ice-melt for instance, to make money selling it."

Berman stopped talking and started jotting down notes. Carol assumed "Fletch" had the scoop. When Berman hung up, he clapped his hands together and looked at Carol.

"This is going well. He knows about it, but he says it's not at the main garage, it's out on the east side of the county at the equipment shed. Do you know where that is?"

Carol shook her head. "No, I don't."

"It's over on Beasley Road. My source thinks it goes on during the day in broad daylight. Let's just cruise on over there and watch from a distance, see if anything looks funny. If they're taking this stuff out in bulk, it ought to be obvious. He says they're supposed to be hauling it in their own pickups. If we see anyone loading supplies into a P.O.V., we're on the right track."

"What's a P.O.V.?" Carol asked.

Berman thought to himself, *These kids are really young. How could she not know that?* To Carol he explained, "It's police shorthand for personally owned vehicle, as opposed to a police cruiser or company car. Haven't you ever heard that before?"

Carol shook her head again.

"No, but that's no big deal. I've only been doing this for a couple of years. I figure there's a lot I have to learn. I'm glad to be working with you. It's nice to be teamed up with someone who really wants to cover the news. No offense, but some of our people seem a lot more concerned about being TV stars than getting the really good stories. Do you know what I mean?"

Berman laughed. He had expected to be the one pointing out TV's shortcomings.

"Yeah, I know exactly what you mean 'cause that's the impression I had looking at TV from the newspaper side. We didn't think anyone over here was worth much as a reporter and we thought even less of most of the coverage you guys put on. I'm glad to know you're serious about this, and I actually think a fair number of the others are, too. And Demarco seems pretty committed to doing good stuff, which ought to help any of us who are willing to do it right. So let's kick a little ass on this one, whaddya say?"

Carol smiled and offered him a high five. He returned the gesture and smiled back. Other than making him feel like the old man on the mountain, this conversation encouraged him, as Demarco's speech had earlier.

They came up on the equipment garage from behind, down a short hill onto a level space, where fields stubbly with mashed-down cornstalks surrounded the building. The garage was really just an oversized pole barn, like the ones farmers put up cheap, with a basic set of poles and rafters inside supporting panels of corrugated thin-gauge steel. The main doors were apparently around front. From this vantage point all Berman and Carol could see was a single door, in the middle of the back wall. The sides had no windows at all. The same corrugated panels covered the roof, except for four opaque fiberglass panels on each side to let in light. Berman had Carol pull up behind a stand of big trees that bordered the field right behind the garage. There was no sign of activity in the parking lot around the building, but several cars and pickup trucks were parked along the side of the building.

Berman slumped down into the stakeout position he had used so many times before. Carol sat upright behind the wheel, staring hard at the steel shed.

"Berman, how long till we see something?"

"We may not see anything at all. We're sitting here because some guy I tend to trust told me a couple of the guys working here are ripping off stuff. Chances are they don't do it everyday. They may not do it every month. So the odds that they're gonna do it the first time we come to watch are heavily against us."

Carol looked at him in amazement.

"And Demarco approved this? There's no way this is a story tonight, is there?"

"No, Fred warned me we'll probably get pulled off of this to do something else. But if we don't start watching, we'll never see anything."

They'd been sitting motionless for about three hours when Berman noticed a man dressed in overalls, wearing a heavy sheepskin vest, walking up behind the car. He waited as the figure passed out of the mirror and came up to his door. He motioned for Carol to switch on the ignition so he could lower the window. He hoped it wasn't some guy trying to shoo them off his property. As the window slid down, Berman sat up.

"Hello, sir. Can I help you?"

The man held a small paper bag in his hand. He raised it for Berman to see as he answered. "On the contrary, newshound, I may be able to help you." He showed Berman the paper bag he held in his hand and winked, as though Berman should know what was in it. Berman thought to himself, *All we need now is one of those militia guys with a bomb in a bag. I don't feel much like being a hostage today.* Either way he had to find out.

"I'm not sure what you mean, sir."

The man pushed his face close to Berman's.

"I assume you're not out here enjoying the fine winter day, are you?"

"No, we're working on a story. "

"Shit, I coulda guessed that. And I think I can guess which one you're workin' on 'cause I'm the guy that wrote the note."

Now the man had Berman's full attention.

"You see, newshounds, I know what's been goin' on at this place for a couple of years now. Others know, too, but they all work for the county and they're not about to take a chance losin' their cushy jobs by blowing the whistle on one of their own."

Those comments pretty much convinced Berman this was the correspondent who scribbled the anonymous note.

"How come you're willing to rat on these guys, then?"

"Let's just say I owe 'em one. Besides, I'm a county tax-payer and it pisses me off to see these guys taking tax dollars out that back door for their own benefit. My question for you is, what took you so long to check it out?"

Berman smiled as he answered.

"Oh, hell, that's an easy one. I switched jobs since I got that note. I'm with TV 10 now." He pointed to the TV 10 News logo on the door. "But I have a question for you: Why'd you send that note to me?"

"'Cause I read *The Chronicle* and I saw the kind of stuff you report on. You seem to be a straight guy who can be trusted to check out this kind of crap if someone tells you it's going on. I guessed right, didn't I?"

Berman felt flattered.

"Yeah, I guess I do care about this sort of thing. I'm a taxpayer, too. It bothers me to see anyone abusing the system when we all have to pay for it." He motioned toward the garage. "But it doesn't look like we're gonna catch anybody in the act today. How often does this go on?"

"About once a month, but you don't have to wait for it. I got it right here on my own handy-dandy videotape." He hoisted the bag again in front of Berman's face.

Berman looked over at Carol, who remained impassive, and then back at the man by the window. He forced himself to stay calm as he took in this very welcome news.

"Can I have that tape, or at least borrow it for a while?"

"Sure, if the price is right."

Berman's heart sank. Even in this age of checkbook journalism and tabloid news, he had never paid a source for information, and he didn't intend to start now. But he might as well find out the asking price for the tape.

The man's face creased into an evil grin and a raspy laugh rose from his throat. His eyes widened and he raised his voice.

"It'a simple price." He pointed to the bag. "The two guys on this tape are Franky Smith and Tom Pickett. I want you to screw them to the wall." His grin faded and he almost ground his teeth together as he continued talking. "They fucked me over worse than anybody ever could, and I swore I'd get 'em one way or the other. I want them sent up for this and I want everybody to know about it. I figure you're just the right guy to do it. Am I right?"

Berman was repulsed by the evil intent in this man. He was reluctant to become his avenging angel. But he wanted the tape and the story. He tried to answer in a way that would secure the tape without letting the man think he was calling the shots.

"Hey, look. I can imagine how you feel. These guys must be slime. And if they screwed you over, I don't blame you for wanting them hammered. I assure you I have every intention of letting everybody know what's been going on out here, and I have no doubt that's all it will take to do these two in."

That was enough. The man pushed the bag into the car, but he held on as Berman's hand closed around the top.

"Just one warning, newshound. You better do this story. If you don't, I have copies of this tape and I'll give 'em to the rest of the stations and the paper and you won't have your neat little scoop. So you gotta get to work, understand me?"

"I understand," Berman said. "Can I get your name and a phone number in case I need to contact you while I'm putting the story together?"

"You won't need to call me. The tape tells the whole story. I've already done most of the work for you. Just get busy." He slapped the top of the car with his right hand as he let go of the bag with his left and walked rapidly back the way he had come. Berman looked at Carol, who showed no emotion at first. Then, slowly, she began to smile.

"Jed, is this as big a break as I think it is?"

"Only if this tape confirms his allegations. We've got names and maybe pictures. Let's shoot back to the shop and see what's on here." He reached in the bag and pulled out a VHS tape in a white cardboard sleeve. The label on it read "SCUM" in rudely scrawled capital letters. Berman showed it to Carol.

"This is one classy guy we're dealing with here."

"Yeah," she answered and started the car. They turned around and retraced their original route, to avoid passing by the main doorway of the garage. Newscars seldom traveled through this remote section of the county. He didn't want to tip off the thieves until he was ready to confront them. If this tape was good, that wouldn't be too long from now.

Back at the station, Carol switched on the newsroom's only VHS machine and Berman slipped in the tape. The first thing they saw was the closing minutes of *Wheel of Fortune*. Berman wondered why anyone would ever bother to tape such an inane game show. Then the picture broke up. When it settled down again, they were looking at the back of the equipment garage on a clear day. The camera date on the corner of the picture read 10-15-98, months ago. Berman pulled out his wallet and checked his pocket calendar. October fifteenth had been a Saturday. The camera zoomed in slowly on two pickup trucks, backed up on either side of the back door. The door swung open and two men, one behind the other, walked out with small round cardboard barrels, which looked to be about five-gallon size. One man slid his barrel into the pickup on the left, the other put his in the truck on the right. Then they walked back inside the garage. They were obviously loading something, but from this distance Berman couldn't read the labels on the barrels or make out the features of the men's faces. He mentally pushed the zoom button to take the shot in closer. The shot changed as though the photographer sensed his request. As the two men re-emerged from the building with two more barrels, the camera zoomed in fast on the white labels. Berman could just make out the trade name "Quickmelt." No question what they were loading. It was the latest generation of ice-melting product. It was quick, left no ugly residue and preserved concrete surfaces rather than breaking them up like the old rock salt used to. Berman had used the stuff himself, in civilian size containers of two or three quarts. Even that was pricey. He could only imagine what barrels and barrels of the stuff were worth. If these guys started with a five-finger discount, they could undercut the commercial price by a lot and still make some good change.

After holding on the label for a few seconds the camera tilted up so Berman could see the men's faces—good, clear, close-up shots. He didn't recognize these guys, but anyone who worked with the county highway department would. Berman pulled his notebook from his back pocket and flipped to the page where he had written down the names given to him by the man with the tape—Franky Smith and Tom Pickett. Then he looked at his watch. Noon, already. The tape ran on for another five minutes as the two men brought out barrel after barrel, ten for each truck. They slammed the back door and drove off. As they pulled away from the camera, the photographer tried to zoom in on their license plates, but the trucks moved too fast. Then the picture broke up again. When it stabilized, Vanna White was waving goodbye. Carol fast-forwarded through the tape for about a minute. From *Wheel of Fortune* it ran into a commercial break and then into a sitcom. She pressed the eject button, pulled the tape out and handed it to Berman, then switched off the VCR.

"Now what?" she asked.

"A bunch of things," Berman replied. "But I don't think we're gonna have time to do all of them today. Let's go talk to Demarco."

The news director applauded their progress, but as he had warned Berman earlier, he sent them out to cover a special meeting at an elementary school where kids and their parents were protesting the quality of food in their cafeteria. Demarco reminded Berman to be sure he shot a standup to go with the story. Berman was a little disappointed to appear on camera in his first standup talking about people who hated Oscar Mayer. But he did it, and when it ran that night Demarco made a point to compliment him on how relaxed he looked doing it. Two minutes after the hot dog story ended, the news hotline rang. It was Jane Filips for Berman. She laid it on thick.

"Say, is this the famous Jed Berman, TV star and ace reporter? The guy I just saw on TV?" Berman was glad to hear her voice and he enjoyed the ribbing.

"That's right, ma'am. How can I help you?"

"Well, I'm your biggest fan. I'm a little embarrassed to do this, but I'd like to seduce you tonight."

If the other reporters had looked at Berman they would have seen his face flush crimson momentarily. But they were busy watching themselves show up on the monitor. He and Filips were playing this game alone.

"Well, Miss. Management discourages us from engaging in that sort of thing, but I think I'm gonna make an exception in your case."

"That's great. Will you meet me at the movie theater? I'll pay."

"Okay. Is seven o'clock all right?"

"I wish it could be sooner. I'm really hot for you, Jed Berman." She breathed heavily into the phone.

"Well, I sure don't want to disappoint you. How about if I head down to the theater right after the news?"

"Oh, would you, could you? I'll be the one in the real short skirt and tight sweater."

"Great. I shouldn't have any trouble spotting you, then."

"Oh, don't worry about spotting me. I'll find you, you big TV stud."

Berman laughed. Whatever else he saw himself as, it had little to do with powerful sexual attraction.

"Whatever you say, Miss, uh, I didn't get your name."

"You won't need it tonight, Jed Berman, 'cause you're gonna get somethin' much better instead."

"Jane, you've never talked like this before."

"I never went out with a TV star before. I'm pretty excited. So hurry up and get over here to the theater."

"OK, I'll see you a little before seven."

As he hung up, he felt good, about the day, the story he'd done, and the one in the making. When the news ended, the newsroom emptied quickly, except for the late show producer and two nightside reporters. Berman pointed his car toward Berrington. He was eager to see Jane. She taught remedial reading by day. At night, their once casual relationship had begun to intensify.

When he met her in front of the theater, she threw her arms around his neck and kissed him in front of a rowdy crowd of teenagers. But, like the newsroom staff, they had other things to think about. No one noticed or seemed to care what these two grown-ups were doing. That was fine with Berman. He didn't need anyone else when Jane was there. She completed his world nicely. As they stood there looking into each other's eyes, they realized they didn't want to sit through a movie tonight. They drove to Jane's apartment, switched on the local classical music station and descended into the joy of each other's presence. They made love slowly, more deliberately than ever before, savoring each step of the way. They both noticed Ravel's rhythmic masterpiece "Bolero" come on the radio. For an instant they smiled, envisioning themselves as Bo Derek and Dudley Moore in the movie 10. But Ravel soon outpaced them. They slid languorously against each other, touching gently and kissing deeply. As so often happened, any sense of time departed, leaving only an overwhelming feeling of uncalibrated pleasure. Much later they lay beside each other, spent but refreshed. Then they talked. She was curious about his new pursuits in Pruitville.

"You really did look good on TV tonight. How do you like it?"

"It's okay. I feel like I'm getting a slow start working on the kind of stories I'm used to doing. But I'll get there."

"Is it hard adjusting to TV after so many years with the paper?"

"Not as hard as I expected. People are pretty decent about helping me get settled in. Demarco is the right kind of guy. He wants to compete with the other stations, but he's not going to lower his standards to do it. I have to respect that." He stroked her hair as he spoke. "But enough about me, how have you been?"

She rolled onto her side and looked at him.

"Is that all I get to hear? No inside scoop? No secrets about the anchors or the star reporters?" She was smiling, but when he turned toward her he could see her questions were in earnest.

"Gee, I don't know. I haven't gotten to know the anchors very well. They come in late in the afternoon, do a little bit of writing, maybe, read the early shows, go out for a long dinner break and come back to do the late show. If they have deep dark secrets, I haven't heard about them yet. Most of the reporters are younger than I am, some are a lot younger. The photogs are young, too. But everyone seems pretty nice. The on-air types seem to worry more about their appearance than I do. Maybe that's what you turn into after you work in TV for a while."

"Do you miss the paper?"

"Not really. What I do miss is that nice comfortable feeling, that niche you get into after you hang around a place for a long time. I suppose that will come."

"Where'd you get that suit you're wearing today?"

"That's one of the perks of the job. Demarco kicked in with a clothing allowance, after making a few rude remarks about the way newspaper reporters dress. It's a nice suit. I guess I'm gonna have to buy a few more, just to make him happy. It's part of the TV code, sort of like a uniform. Demarco says people expect us to show up looking sharp. I'm not going to argue with him. I have no point to prove by dressing shabby. But if you catch me getting too impressed with myself, kick me in the ass, will you?"

"With pleasure." She reached over and slapped him on the butt and then jumped out of bed. "I'm starved," she told him. "Let's go eat."

They got dressed and drove her car to Brady's.

*　　*　　*

Berman was already standing by the newsroom's VCR, watching the tape when Demarco reached the newsroom the next morning. He was with another man in a vest and blue work clothes. The name Mitch was stitched over the man's shirt pocket. He had a heavy build and long hair, tied back in a ponytail. He looked about thirty. Demarco walked past the editing room without interrupting their quiet conversation.

"Let's just double check this," Berman said, as he froze the picture on the first close-up shot of one of the men. "Are you sure this is Franky Smith?"

Mitch answered in a deep, thick voice.

"Hell, yes, I'm sure. I been workin' with that son of a bitch for ten years. That's Franky stealing ice-melter from the east side garage. I never seen him doin' it, though."

Berman jotted down some notes in his notepad. He advanced the tape to the close-up shot of the second man and froze it again.

"And who's this?"

A note of irritation crept into Mitch's low rumble.

"You fuckin' around with me, or what? I already told you, that's Tom Pickett. He's only been with the county for about five years. I don't know him very well. He moved here from out of state, I think. I wonder whose idea it was to rip off all that stuff?"

Berman didn't have the answer to that, and he wasn't certain how he was going to get it. But Mitch's identification put him on track to make something happen, quickly. He held out his hand to thank Mitch for his help.

"Mitch, I owe ya. Do you think anyone saw you drive in here this morning?"

"Nah, starting time's pretty loose at the garage. They won't even think about me if I get there by 8:30. Is that all you need ?"

"It is unless you know a way to get Franky and Tom to spill the beans on how they got started stealing all that stuff and what they do with it."

"I'll keep my ears open, but don't expect too much. If these guys really have been stealin' stuff for a couple of years, they sure know how to keep it quiet. See ya around, Berman."

He turned and walked out the back door, his girth and heavy gait giving him the appearance of a bear shuffling across the floor. Berman had helped Mitch's mother after a furnace repair guy ripped her off a couple of years ago, so it hadn't been hard to talk her son into taking a look at the tape on his way to work. Berman felt the adrenalin start to flow as he plotted the next steps toward a kill. If he could confront Smith and Pickett today on camera, no matter what they said, he'd have a story to run tonight. And most likely the county would have a couple of openings on the highway crew tomorrow. Berman bounded up the three short steps into the newsroom looking for Demarco. He found him in his office.

"Fred, I'm closing in on the county garage story. One of the guys who works out there just ID'd the two thieves. I want to drive out there and confront them this morning. If all goes well, I should have a great story ready for you by six tonight."

Demarco could feel Berman's excitement. He stood up and looked out into the newsroom. Carol, Berman's partner from the day before, was standing by the coffee maker.

"Carol, are you ready to head out?"

She nodded and raised her styrofoam cup in salute to Berman. "I'm always ready, Fred. What's up?"

"I want you to stick with Berman today, since you know this garage story he's working on. He wants to corner these two guys today, so why don't you two take off. No need to hang around for the morning meeting."

Fifteen minutes later they pulled up in front of the garage. The giant doors had been folded back to expose three dump trucks sitting side by side. In the dimmer recesses of the building, they could see stacks of little barrels like the ones on the tape. Off to the right, stuck like a wooden blister against the wall, was a small office. Berman led the way into the office. Carol followed with the camera on her shoulder, but she wasn't rolling. An older looking man sat at a battered wooden desk shuffling through a stack of papers. He looked up as they walked in, but Berman spoke first.

"Good morning, I'm Jed Berman with TV 10. I'm looking for Tom Pickett and Franky Smith. Are they in yet?" The man at the desk stood up and brushed past the news crew to poke his head out the door. He hollered into the dimly lit recesses at the back of the building.

"Tommy—Franky! You got company."

As he headed back to his desk, he spat a giant gob of juice from the snuff in his mouth into the trash can. Berman and Carol both swallowed involuntarily, imagining how bad that slimy specimen must have tasted. The spitter slumped back behind the desk and returned to his paper shuffling. Berman kept watch out the door for the two workers. When they emerged from the twilight he motioned for Carol to turn on the camera. The bare light-bulb on the ceiling of the office would have to suffice. He didn't want to snap on Carol's camera light and scare these two off. Smith came in first, followed by Pickett. They both noticed the camera, but Berman started talking right away to get their minds off it.

"Hi, I'm Jed Berman. You must be Franky Smith and you must be Tom Pickett."

They looked at each other and back at Berman and Carol.

"Yeah, that's who we are," Smith said. " Should we know you? And what's with that camera? What are you guys up to?"

Berman got right to the point.

"Gentlemen, we're with TV 10 News and we're running a story tonight that accuses both of you of stealing supplies from here at the garage. We thought the only fair thing to do was to give you a chance to respond to the allegations. Who wants to go first?"

Pickett's face turned crimson.

"What are you, some kind of smart ass or something? Where'd you get the idea we've been stealing stuff? That's the stupidest thing I've ever heard."

Smith joined in Pickett's indignation.

"You two must be crazy. We been workin' for the county for a long time and we ain't never had any trouble, right Lenny?" He tried to draw the man at the desk into the conversation, but the man only raised his head to reveal a noncommittal expression on his face. Smith tried again. "C'mon, Lenny. Tell these guys we're just a couple of workin' joes doin' a job for the county."

Lenny responded by standing up, coughing another big lump of brown spit into the trash can and walking out into the garage. Watching him go, Berman wondered if Lenny was one of the people who knew what Smith and Pickett were up to and hadn't done anything about it. This promised to be some interesting video. He repeated his offer to the two men.

"As I said, we're here to give you a chance to respond to some pretty serious allegations. This story will run tonight, so now's your chance. Do you have any comment?"

Smith spoke for both of them.

"Here's your comment, asshole. We never stole nothin' from nobody. We come here every day and do whatever we're told to do. If you think you can prove otherwise, go ahead. In the meantime, why don't you get the fuck out of here?"

Carol was catching it all. These two buffoons hadn't even tried to stop the camera. Berman figured they had all they needed for now.

"OK, gentlemen. We tried. Next stop is TV 10 and the six o'clock news." He started toward the door. Carol still had the camera trained on Smith and Pickett. "Oh, I forgot to mention that we have both of you on tape lugging ice-melter out the back door and loading it into your trucks. Any interest in responding to that?"

Without saying anything else, Smith and Pickett pushed Berman and Carol away from the doorway and stalked out. Carol stepped into the garage and kept shooting as the two figures moved away and became silhouettes in the limited light. When they drifted behind a stack of supplies, she stopped rolling, turned toward Berman and offered him a high five with her free hand. He grinned and slapped her hand.

"We're almost there," he told her. "Let's shoot a standup here and some cover and then drive over to the highway commissioner's office to see if he has anything to say."

Lenny walked up to them as they shot the stacks of ice-melt and other supplies. He suddenly turned talkative. First he spat on the floor by Berman's shoes, then he growled at both of them.

"I just want you to know I had nothin' to do with what those guys were up to. I never done nothin' like that in twenty years with the county. A bunch of us knew about it, but what were we gonna do? If we said anything they was likely to can us all." He hawked another big gob against one of the dump trucks. "You know what I'm sayin'?"

Berman saw no reason to debate with this guy, now that he had the two culprits on tape. He motioned to Carol that he wanted to leave. He turned and walked out of the garage without giving Lenny another look.

The highway commissioner worked in the building where Berman had confronted Hildy Mazer about the Spanner kids. Berman had called ahead from the car on the way over to make sure the commissioner would be in. He was. The news crew needed no introduction. When the commissioner's secretary saw Berman walk in with tripod in hand and Carol lugging the Betacam, she jumped up and sprinted into the commissioner's office. Less than a minute later, Berman was sitting across the desk from the commissioner and Carol was peering at him through the viewfinder on her camera. The face she saw looked tense. Berman had not gone into detail on the phone. He simply told the commissioner he had an urgent question to ask him about the east side garage. Berman wasted no time getting to the point.

"I appreciate your willingness to see us on such short notice."

The commissioner flashed an uneasy smile; light beads of sweat broke out on his forehead.

"Jed, we've talked before. You know my door is always open to the media. Now, what's your concern today?"

"I'm working on a story that deals with two of your men at the east side garage—Franky Smith and Tom Pickett. I have videotape of those two men carrying barrels of ice-melt out the back door and hauling it away in their personal vehicles. Do they have permission to do that?"

The commissioner looked shocked.

"Are you sure that's what you saw them do? They may have been transferring supplies to some other buildings around the county. We store our whole supply out there 'cause we don't have anywhere else to put it."

"Do you ask county workers to haul it in their own trucks?"

"Well, no, that would be unusual. Are you suggesting these men are stealing supplies?"

"That's pretty much the gist of it, yes. Can you think of any other explanation for what we see them doing on the tape?"

The commissioner picked up the phone and dialed a number.

"Hey, Lenny. Let me talk to Franky Smith and Tom Pickett."

Berman and Carol waited to see if the two men would come to the phone. Several minutes went by. The commissioner offered the news crew some candy, then a cigarette. They declined both. When the commissioner suddenly straightened in his chair, they knew someone had come back on the line.

"What the hell are you talking about—they're not there? Were they there this morning?" As he listened to the answer his eyes locked onto Berman. "Okay, thanks, Lenny. Hey, listen, if they come back, call me right away."

He slapped the phone into the cradle and sat back in his chair.

"Jed, you may be onto something. Those two men have left the garage, without telling their supervisor where they're going. I'm going to check into this thing and if what you suggest is true, those two guys are history. I promise you that."

He lit a cigarette and blew a long stream of smoke up toward the ceiling.

"Do you have any more questions? If not, I have some other business to attend to."

"No, that's all for now." To Carol, Berman said, "That's enough, you can shut down." As he stood up he spoke to the commissioner. "We're gonna run this story tonight, with pictures of the two guys hauling out the stuff. Can you let me know what happens when you talk to them?"

The commissioner stood behind his desk.

"Yeah, sure, Jed, I'll let you know. Is this story gonna touch anyone besides the two guys?"

"Don't see why it has to, if they're the only ones involved. I appreciate your time. Thanks again. C'mon, Carol." As he walked out the office door, Berman could hear the commissioner sinking back into his chair and picking up the phone.

Back at the station, Berman and Carol sat down in Demarco's office and outlined their story. Demarco pushed them on how sure they were that the videotape really showed what they thought it showed. Berman recounted

Mitch's testimony plus the reactions from Smith, Pickett and the commissioner. Demarco wasn't completely satisfied.

"You two are doing a great job on this. We're almost there. But I'd feel better if we had definite proof they were stealing this stuff, like someone who bought it from them. Can we find someone?"

Berman had an idea. He grabbed Demarco's phone and dialed. A moment later he said,

"Hey, Lenny, this is your friend Jed Berman, from TV 10. You know, I was thinking about how I'm gonna play this story and it occurred to me there's something you can do to convince me you really don't have anything to do with this."

The voice on the other end erupted so loudly that Berman had to pull the phone away from his ear. He waited for the noise to subside.

"Lenny, I'm not trying to fuck you over on this. The truth is, I need your help. Just one little bit of help. Can you do that for me? If you do, I won't even mention your name in the story. You will? That's great. Can you tell me the name of anyone Franky and Tom sold that ice-melt to? "

Berman flipped the page on his notebook and wrote down two names.

"Is that all you know?"

Lenny's voice rose again on the other end. Berman tried to calm him down.

"Lenny, Lenny, you're doin' great. No problem. Two names is plenty. Where do I find these guys?" Berman scribbled more notes as he listened. "Lenny, you are a true citizen. Thanks. Talk to you later."

He hung up and looked at Demarco.

"I think I've got what I need. We better get rollin' if we want to corner one or both of these guys so we can run the story tonight. See ya later, Fred."

In less than an hour they had located both of the people Lenny mentioned. One ran a small lawn and garden store, the other managed a convenience store. Both admitted buying ice-melt from the county workers and repacking it in smaller bags for their customers. Off camera they admitted that they thought the price they paid seemed low, but they didn't think they could pass it up. On camera they named Smith and Pickett as the men who sold them the barrels. They said the men claimed to be sales reps for the company, unloading surplus inventory at really good prices. They denied knowing the ice-melt was stolen from the county garage.

Berman called Demarco on the way back to the station to let him know they had what he wanted. Demarco immediately called the Promotions department to make sure they plugged Berman's exposé in the afternoon promos. Before Berman got back to the shop, Promotions had finished writing the fifteen-second spot for one of the anchors to record when they came in. It hit the air before Berman even finished writing his story:

"Tonight, on TV 10's award-winning six o'clock news ... an exclusive report on theft in county government. Investigative reporter Jed Berman uncovers a scheme to steal from the county and sell cheap to the public. He'll name names and point fingers on TV 10 News tonight at six."

By 5:30, Berman and Carol were back at the east side garage setting up to do a live wrap around their package. Berman practiced what he wanted to say before they rolled the tape back at the station. Carol had the mast on the microwave truck locked into position to feed their signal to the tower and into the station. As he paced around in the glare of the lights they had set up on the asphalt by the now

100

closed garage doors, Berman could hear the two-way radio crackling with the voices of the other crews setting up live shots. The system allowed him to hear the two-way communication through his earpiece, so the producer could give him instructions and time cues while he was on the air. At six, he heard the taped opening of the show rolling, and then Steve and Sally introduced his piece.

"TV 10's own Jed Berman uncovered the alleged scheme and he joins us now from the county's east side equipment garage with details. Jed?"

Demarco had encouraged Berman to learn to do live shots without looking at notes, but he didn't feel ready for that. He held his clipboard, with the printed script on it, down low, hoping it wouldn't show in the camera shot, and launched into his opening comments. He could barely see the camera behind the stand lights; his mouth felt strangely dry.

"Steve and Sally, there appears to be big trouble here at the county's equipment garage."

In the newsroom, Demarco watched closely to see how his hand-picked star would perform. At the moment, he looked a little stiff, his voice was tight. But the story came through with force.

"And before it's all over, what we've uncovered here is likely to cost at least two people their jobs."

That was the cue for the guys back at the station to play Berman's tape. In roughly a minute and a half he showed the supplies in the garage, identified Smith and Pickett as the alleged thieves and let viewers hear reaction from the two workers, the commissioner and the store managers who bought the stolen goods. Demarco had urged him to use a lot of footage from the VHS tape he'd gotten from the man in the vest. No one could doubt that the men in the closeups on the home video were the same men who pushed Berman out of the way inside the garage earlier that day. The tape ended with the store managers accusing Smith and Pickett of pretending to work for the ice-melt company. Then the picture cut back to Berman at the garage.

"Franky Smith and Tom Pickett left this garage well before quitting time today. No one has seen them since. But as you just heard, the commissioner has promised to deal severely with them, if he's convinced they've been caught in something illegal. We should know before long where this whole incident will end. Steve and Sally?"

Berman thought he was finished, but Sally asked, "Jed, can you tell us how you uncovered this alleged scheme?"

Berman froze for an instant. He never revealed his sources on investigative stories. He wished Sally hadn't put him on the spot. For what seemed like an eternity, but was little more than two or three seconds, he racked his brain for something to say. When he opened his mouth he wasn't sure what would come out.

"Sally, we had good cooperation from sources in and out of county government in tracking this down. They did taxpayers a favor by speaking up. Back to you."

Steve Kimmel had done some investigative reporting before moving on to the anchor desk. He could tell from Berman's expression that Sally had crossed the line. But he chalked it up to inexperience. She had spent little time on the street before management put her on the desk. Kimmel tried to wrap up the live shot before she could do any more damage.

"Nice work, Jed. We'll stand by to hear how it all works out." As the director dropped the "boxes," the video windows with Berman on one side and the anchors on the other, Kimmel turned to a different camera and began reading the next story.

Berman let the hand holding the microphone drop to his side and breathed a sigh of relief. Carol stepped from behind the camera as they both heard the producer say, "You're clear, Unit Twenty, nice job, you guys."

"Way to go, Jed. I don't know why you were so nervous. You're a natural. We've got people who've been doing this for a couple of years who aren't that good yet. Great story. Let's get packed up and head home."

Carol left the stand lights till last so they could see to gather up the cables and other gear set up for the live shot. When she finally flipped off the lights, Berman found himself standing in the dark beside the truck, still recovering from the encounter. Sally's question basically pissed him off, but as the new guy he figured he couldn't say much about it to anyone. He appreciated Kimmel's efforts to get it over with before she asked anything else. His annoyance and anxiety subsided as the live van bounced along country roads back to Pruitville. Beneath the minor annoyance, he felt a warm excitement. Demarco had said he was a natural for TV. He would have to see a tape of the show to know how he really looked, but he felt pretty comfortable. He had expected to stumble around, but he hadn't. This made the transition complete. He was back in business kicking ass. It felt good.

When he got back to the station, there was a message to call the county commissioner. He made the call. By eleven, he was at home watching Steve and Sally as they read the lead he wrote for the late show version of his story:

"The axe fell at the county equipment garage tonight. The county commissioner fired two workers minutes after an exclusive TV 10 News report accused them of carrying out a two-year-long scheme to steal county supplies and resell them."

Berman switched off the set and went to bed, satisfied.

103

Five

Tied Up

The kudos for Berman's performance the night before started the moment he stepped into the station the next morning. Cindy at the front desk flashed a wide smile and said, "That was a great story last night, Jed. You sure got those guys."

Berman thanked her politely and kept moving toward the newsroom. Donnie Kurtz hollered at him from the coffee maker.

"Hey, Berman. What're you trying to do, show us all up? That was a helluva good piece last night."

Berman was a little surprised by the reaction. His former colleagues at the paper seldom made much of a fuss over a particularly successful story. He liked this response much better.

"Thanks, Donnie. I couldn't have done it without you. You taught me everything I know."

"Damn straight, Berman, and don't you forget it," he said with his usual grin.

By this time Demarco had walked out of his office.

"It was a good story, Jed. The kind only TV 10 can give this community. I told you broadcast news was right for you."

Berman felt a true sense of gratitude, but he also felt a little uncomfortable seeing his achievements played up in front of the other reporters and photogs.

"I'm just glad it worked out, Fred. You know how that stuff can be. You put a lot of time into something and then it sort of runs away like water through your fingers. This one stayed solid."

"You bet it did," Demarco agreed. "Now get to work and do another story like it. You know the deal here, you're only as good as your last story, and when that's done, my only question is, what are you going to do for me today?"

As they formed the circle for the morning meeting, Berman's phone rang. He stepped over to his desk and picked it up.

"News 10, this is Jed Berman."

"Hey, newshound. Guess who this is."

There was no mistaking the low, raspy sound of the man in the sheepskin vest who handed over the videotape of the county workers. Berman hadn't expected to hear from him so soon, if at all. Usually, tipsters got their kicks watching the story go down and seeing the people they blew the whistle on take the heat. If this guy had more stuff, Berman was prepared to listen, but he didn't want to sound too eager. He remembered the sinister quality that radiated from the guy while he was standing by the news car.

"I know who this is. The best source I've talked to in a while. Did you see the story last night?"

"Yeah, I saw it. You fucked up."

That caught Berman off guard.

"What do you mean, I fucked up?"

"Didn't I tell ya a whole bunch of those guys knew what was goin' on and didn't do a damn thing about it?"

"Yeah, I guess you did say that, why?"

"'Cause I wanted you to screw all the bastards. Not just those stupid shits, Smith and Pickett. Why didn't ya put it to Lenny?"

"I guess I didn't think he was really involved in it. He

told me he kept his mouth shut so he wouldn't lose his job. Is that a lie?"

The voice on the other end descended into an angry growl then rose to a howl. "Now you listen to me, newshound. If you aren't afraid to do the job right, meet me back where I gave you the tape and I'll give you the rest of the story. You interested or are you just chicken shit?"

This is an evil man, Berman thought. But he'd worked with people like that before. Sometimes you had to cruise the lower levels to get the story because no one else would talk. If there was more to be told here, he'd better get it. His answer to the challenge sounded more confident than he actually felt.

"Hey, look, I can only report what I know to be true. At the paper, I put my name on it; in TV I stand there and look you right in the eye as I say it. If you know so much, are you willing to go on camera and tell the whole story? I'll be out there in twenty minutes if you're man enough to stand up and name names."

The caller howled again. Berman thought he sounded drunk. The growling went on for nearly a minute. Then the harangue continued.

"You listen to me, newshound. I'm givin' you, that's right, givin' you a story good enough to make you a real big deal. I don't have to go on TV. Don't start tryin' to push me around. I've handled tougher assholes than you. Do you want the rest of the story, newshound? Or do I shop around?"

Berman wanted to see this through, even if it meant putting up with this weirdo.

"All right. I want the rest of it. How do I get it?"

"I already told you, newshound. Meet me back at the tree and we'll talk."

"When?"

"As soon as you can get there. I'll be waiting for you." He slammed down the phone.

Berman walked over to the morning meeting. A couple of people had overheard his end of the conversation. They waited to hear the details.

"That was the guy who gave me the videotape of the county workers. He claims I didn't do the whole story, says other people are involved, including the garage supervisor. He wants to meet me again out by the garage, but he sounds a little strange, maybe drunk or stoned."

Demarco looked concerned.

"Do you want to go back out there, Jed? Could he be dangerous?"

The guy's tone did bother Berman, but he didn't want to admit that in front of everyone else.

"I think he's mostly a big blowhard who apparently got the short end of the stick from the county at some point. He's not likely to do anything physical. I think he gets his kicks out of playing with the media. I think I should go back out there and hear what he has to say."

Demarco trusted Berman's judgment, based on years of experience.

"Do you want a camera there, too?"

"Nah, might scare the guy away. He claims he doesn't want to be on TV, just wants to be Deep Throat for us."

Demarco knew that meeting with unstable sources could be hazardous. He wanted to be sure Berman didn't get into something he couldn't handle.

"Look, even if you don't shoot anything, why don't you take Carol with you just to be safe. Carol, you okay going with Jed, even if this guy is a little strange?"

"Yeah, I don't see how he could do anything to both of us. I'll go."

"All right. Why don't you take off. Keep in touch. I want

to hear from you every half hour, if you're gone any length of time. Keep me posted on everything you do, got it?"

Berman smiled at Demarco.

"Fred, you take such good care of us. Like a mother hen. I appreciate the concern. We'll be fine and we'll report in periodically. See ya later."

Carol and Berman talked about other things as they drove toward the garage, but their thoughts were several miles ahead of them. They both had heard stories of reporters roughed up by people they were trying to work with. Usually it involved criminal types and undercover investigations about drug dealers or gangs. The guy in the vest looked like a loner, a mountain-man type, whose bark was probably worse than his bite. Nonetheless, they both felt uneasy as they came down the hill leading to the garage and stopped by the clump of trees where they'd picked up the tape two days ago. They shut off the engine and flipped on the radio. As the minutes ticked away, Berman wished they'd stopped for coffee before they left Pruitville.

They didn't see or hear anything until the driver's side door suddenly flew open and the man in the vest crouched down and filled the doorway. He held a large revolver.

"So, you want the rest of the story, huh? Well, now you're gonna be part of it, 'cause I don't like people jerkin' me around."

With one startled glance Carol saw the man and the gun. She sat motionless and silent behind the wheel, staring straight ahead. Berman's eyes had snapped toward the door the second it opened and he, too, had taken in the threatening figure in a glance. Now he angled his body around so he could look straight into the man's face. As he did so, he got a whiff of the man's breath. It reeked of strong booze. Berman tried to keep things calm until they knew what the guy was really up to. His stomach was churning.

"Hey, what kind of welcome is that? We're only here because you invited us. It's the first thing in the morning. You sure don't need a gun to protect us out here. All the druggies live in Pruitville."

"Hey, newshound, why don't you shut the fuck up? You, bitch, slide over. I'm the new pilot." He motioned Carol away from the wheel and slid into the car. His bulk forced Carol tightly against Berman, who shoved himself hard against the other side of the car to make room. The situation was deteriorating rapidly, but Berman still hoped this wasn't as bad as it looked.

"You don't have to drive. We'd be glad to take you wherever you want to go so we can talk."

The man in the vest swung the gun under Berman's nose.

"Here's the deal, shithead. From now on, nobody talks unless I tell 'em to. You got that? You fuckin' TV guys think you're such hot shit. Well, I'm in charge here and the sooner you get that straight, the longer you're gonna be around."

Berman felt Carol shaking against him. The man in the vest felt it, too.

"What's wrong with you, babe? You're not scared of me, are you?"

Carol shook her head, but didn't turn to look at him. She said nothing.

"There, she understands, newshound. You got the message yet?"

Berman felt as frightened as he knew Carol was. He had no intention of antagonizing this guy, if he could help it.

"Yeah, I got the message. You're in charge. What are we gonna do now?"

The man in the vest cranked the ignition and yanked the car into gear.

"Whaddya say we go for a little ride. I got someplace to show you that I'll just bet you never saw in this county."

He floored the accelerator and yanked the steering wheel hard to the left. The car spun around and headed back up the hill, the front wheels flinging out a stream of gravel as they came off the shoulder of the road. The force of the turn shoved Carol tighter against Berman. Neither of them spoke as they hurtled up the hillside. Less than a mile later the man in the vest slowed down and turned into a lane obscured by heavy brush along the roadside. Roughly a hundred feet off the highway stood an old one room shack, with boards over two of its three windows and a rusty woodstove chimney poking through moss-covered shingles on the roof. The driver slammed on the brakes, nearly throwing Carol and Berman into the windshield.

"How d'ya like it, Berman? This is my home. It's what I get for being an honest county worker. If I'd lied like all those other bastards, maybe I'd be in some nice house in town. What d'ya think, Berman?"

Berman concentrated on answering in a cool tone to avoid setting this guy off again.

"Doesn't look like a very good deal," he admitted honestly, "but I don't understand what's goin' on here? If somebody did something to you, it wasn't us. Why'd you bring us here? Are we gonna talk about the story?"

The man motioned toward the passenger side door with the silver revolver.

"How about if I ask the questions, newshound. Get the fuck out of the car. You, too, bitch. God, I hate women about as much as I hate men. You all suck. Get out and stand by the house."

Berman opened the door and climbed out. His legs felt

weak. When Carol stepped out beside him she was so shaky she nearly fell over. He caught her with his arm and pulled her close to him. The man in the vest got out and walked around the car. He towered over the news crew by at least a foot and a half. The sheer size of him sent another shiver down their spines. He stood about three feet away from them, gun pointed at Berman's stomach, and glowered.

Try as he might, Berman couldn't calm down enough to form an escape plan. He had often wondered how perfectly healthy people accosted by a gunman could simply stand there and let the guy shoot them to death. It always seemed as if they hadn't thought it through, hadn't made the dash that might have saved their lives, hadn't lunged for the gunman and put an end to the lunacy before they got hurt. He now understood at least one reason why they let it happen. He was petrified of this man; the idea of doing anything that would set him off seemed extremely foolish. But if he didn't do *something* he believed this not-so-gentle giant might well pump them both full of lead.

He remembered another stupid thing he had often said: that he didn't want to die some normal death like a heart attack. He wanted to go out in a weird way that people could talk about and marvel at. He swore to himself that if he survived this encounter he would never utter such stupid thoughts again. He looked down at his watch; it had been forty-five minutes since they left the station. If he didn't call in, Demarco might send someone out looking for them. That could be the wedge. He had his flip phone in his jacket pocket. He risked speaking to the gunman without an invitation.

"Say, big guy. Our station policy is that news crews check in every hour to let the desk know what we're up to. I don't know how long you expect this session to last, but it

111

might be a good idea if I called in to let them know we're okay."

The man with the gun stared at him, his mouth hanging slightly open. His eyes looked glazed, but he'd heard what Berman said.

"Sure, give 'em a call, but don't make it sound like you're in any trouble here, you understand? 'Cause if you do, you really *will* be in trouble."

Berman pulled the phone out of his pocket and dialed the newsroom. He tried to think of something to say that would tip off Demarco and the others that he and Carol needed help without antagonizing the gunman. The phone rang three times before Demarco answered.

"News 10, Fred Demarco speaking. May I help you?"

"Fred, this is Berman. Just wanted to check in and let you know how things are going out here on the hillside. We've made contact with my source. He's got a lot to tell us, so it might be a while till we get back. Do you need Carol any time soon for any other shoots?"

Demarco didn't notice anything unusual about Berman's voice, but he wanted to be sure Jed and Carol were okay.

"Jed, are things all right, are you getting more information?"

"Oh, no, Fred, we sure don't need any more cameras or crews out here. This is a one-crew deal, just between us and . . . Hey, wait a minute, Fred," he pulled the phone away from his ear and looked at the gunman. "I just realized I don't even know your name. My boss wants to know who I'm dealing with. What should I tell him?"

Demarco heard Berman's question and he heard the response in a thick, deep voice.

"Why don't you get the fuck off the phone before you get hurt, Berman? Gimme that thing." He reached over and knocked the phone out of Berman's hand. The line went dead.

Demarco had heard enough to realize something wasn't right at the east side garage. He called the police. At first they thought he was kidding around about his ace reporter being in some kind of trouble, but when he insisted he needed their help they agreed to send over a cruiser to talk to him. The officer offered to take Demarco to the garage to see if they could find Berman and Carol. Demarco was eager to do that. He left word at the front desk that he was heading east to check up on Berman, and he told two photogs who were standing around the newsroom to follow the squad car he'd be riding in. He felt a little silly; he had never done this before. But then, he had never heard a conversation quite like the one he'd just listened to, either. He had no doubt that Berman's answer had been a plea for help. And then the nasty sound of the man's voice before the phone went dead. He hoped Berman and Carol were not hurt. This was a hell of a way to break in a new reporter.

On the hillside, things had gotten worse. When Berman bent down to pick up his phone, the gunman kicked him in the ribs. He yelled and fell to the ground. Carol stepped forward to help him, but the man with the gun motioned her back.

"Leave him alone. He's a big boy. He can get up all by himself."

Berman stood up slowly, rubbing the right side of his chest. Anger began seeping through his fear.

"What the hell did you kick me for? Chances are you fucked up this time, 'cause I'll bet Demarco is on his way out here right now to find out what's going on."

The gunman laughed loud, deep, and ugly.

"Newshound, you are so stupid. What chance is there

113

this Demarco guy is ever going to find the two of you in here? Almost nobody even knows the lane to this house ever existed, and you can't see it now for all the bushes out there. You're the one who's fucked, newshound. Why don't you two sit down on the porch while I figure out what I want to do with you."

They walked over and sat down on the edge of the porch. The paint had long since chipped away, the wood felt soft and rotten to the touch. The gunman reached inside his vest and pulled out a metal flask. He unscrewed the top and sucked down a long shot of whatever was inside. He swallowed with a loud gulp and upended the flask again, draining it. Berman and Carol had little choice but to watch silently. Between them they had been covering local news for more than ten years, but none of their experiences seemed useful in facing this ordeal. Carol's shuddering seemed to be getting worse. She leaned close to Berman and whispered, "What are we gonna do, Jed? This guy really scares me. Do you think he'll really hurt us?"

Before Berman could answer her, the man in the vest tossed the flask aside and lurched toward them. He leaned close to Berman's face, the stench of his breath blew foul over both of them

"Here's the deal, newshound. I want the story done the right way. I want every one of those bastards with the county exposed on TV, and I want to see them pay for what they've done to me and everyone else. Do you think we can do that?"

Berman saw no choice but to play along, at least for the moment.

"Sure we can. I'm here and Carol's here and we've got a camera and lots of fresh batteries. Why don't we set up and let you tell people what they need to know and then we'll take it back to the station and put it on the air. That's simple. We'll get those bastards, whoever they are."

"Okay, newshound. Why don't you get set up." He waved the gun in Berman's face. "But no bullshit. One of you do something I don't like, you might just get popped. You hear me?"

They nodded, then slipped off the porch and walked to the car. Berman whispered to Carol as they opened the trunk.

"Stay as cool as you can. I think he might do something if we piss him off. Be sure you're rolling on this stuff. We're not likely to put him on the air the way he wants, but getting him on tape will be good evidence for putting him away," he paused, "assuming we get out of this."

Tears welled up in Carol's eyes. He felt like crying himself. In all those years of newspaper work he'd never gotten into anything remotely like this.

"C'mon, what's taking you so long, let's get going with my interview." They both jumped as the gunman roared at them. They grabbed the equipment and walked back toward the porch to set up.

On the highway, Demarco and the officer had reached the top of the hill leading to the garage. They slowed down as they descended. Demarco spotted the clump of trees where Berman had told him they picked up the tape. As they pulled up to the spot, they saw hook shaped tire tracks, like the ones kids laid down burning rubber. The marks seemed to lead back up the hill. They turned around and drove slowly back up the road, straining to see through the tall weeds and bushes that obscured the shoulder on both sides. Berman heard two cars pass by the overgrown entrance to the gunman's shack. He had no way to signal whoever was out there that he and Carol were here. On the highway, Demarco and the rest of the searchers rolled by the driveway and back toward town. Berman considered making a break for it, in hopes of getting through to the road before the man in the vest could stop him. As the thought entered his mind, he glanced toward the gunman. The silver revolver was pointed straight at him. He helped Carol get the camera set up for the interview.

The officer with Demarco suggested they go back to the station and wait for some contact from Berman or the man he had driven out here to meet. Demarco could see that driving aimlessly around country roads held little potential for finding his crew. He agreed to wait for another contact from Berman.

On the other side of the bushes, just a few hundred feet away from Demarco's car when he gave up the brief search, Carol clipped a microphone to the gunman's vest and Berman went through the motions of interviewing him. The gunman didn't need any questions from Berman. He launched into a rambling diatribe against the county, its workers and its administrators. Berman listened long enough to realize all he was hearing was a drunken harangue, then he returned to racking his brain for a way out. After about ten minutes, the gunman held up his hand to stop the taping. He backed up onto the porch and reached inside the front door, all the while keeping the pistol aimed at his hostages. He fished around with one hand, apparently unable to find what he wanted. He stepped to the edge of the porch and waved his gun in the air.

"Don't either of you move a muscle. I gotta go in here and get something. If I see you try to make a run for it, you're dead. You hear me?" He leaned so far toward them he seemed ready to fall face forward off the porch. Instead, he rocked back on his heels till his body pointed toward the house and away from the drive, and then backed into the house, keeping the gun trained on his captives.

The instant he stepped out of sight Berman grabbed

Carol's arm and pushed her toward the car. She ran around and slid behind the wheel as he jumped in the passenger side. Just as she turned the key in the ignition, the gunman stomped back into the doorway, with a half-empty liquor bottle in his hand. In his inebriated state it took him a moment to realize what was happening. He locked in on the details as the engine turned over and Carol slammed the car into reverse. She floored the accelerator. The tires spun on the loose dirt of the old driveway, but the car started backing away from the house and the man with the gun. By this time, he had the gun up and pointed toward the car. True to his threats, he started firing as he cursed the duo for trying to get away. The kick from the gun threw him off balance. Inside the car, Berman and Carol heard the slug hit somewhere around the right fender. They watched as the gunman staggered back against the house, all the while blasting away. Berman turned toward Carol as she rammed the car backward through the bushes.

"Keep goin', Carol! We're gonna make it." Just before the car slid out of the gunman's sight, he lowered the revolver for one more shot. Berman had just started to turn back toward the house when he heard a bang along his door and then felt a pain like a hammer blow in his shoulder. A moment later the news car burst through the brush and onto the highway. Carol slammed on the brakes, shifted into drive and floored the gas pedal again. With tires screaming, the car headed hard and fast away from the madman and his lethal weapon. Berman shrieked with relief.

"Carol, you're beautiful. You did it. We made it. Oh, God, we made it. Gimme five."

Carol raised her hand to meet him, but when Berman tried to raise his arm, a stabbing pain shot through his right shoulder. He reached over to rub it with his left hand.

When he pulled his hand away, his palm was covered with blood. He craned his neck to look down at his arm and saw blood seeping through his jacket.

"Ah, shit," he said, "that stupid bastard put a hole in my new suit. Demarco isn't gonna like this." Then he slumped against the door and passed out.

Carol hadn't seen the blood but she saw Berman collapse against the door.

"Jed! Jed! What's wrong?" They were at least a mile away from the gunman by now. She pulled the car off the road and made a hard stop, wheels locked up and skidding through the gravel on the shoulder. She grabbed Berman's shoulder and shook him gently.

"C'mon, Jed. What's going on?"

Berman roused slightly and turned his face toward her. His voice was weak.

"Carol, I'm hurt. I think we'd better get to the hospital."

"Whatever you say, Jed. Just hang on." She still hadn't seen the crimson stain seeping down the sleeve of his coat. She ripped the transmission into drive and gunned the engine. As she raced toward the hospital, she punched the newsroom number into the cell phone mounted on the transmission hump in front of the seat. It only rang once.

"Hello, Fred Demarco here. Who's this?"

She talked to the no-hands speaker mounted on the windshield visor in front of her.

"Oh, Fred, it's good to hear your voice. This is Carol."

Demarco's voice crackled with anxiety.

"Carol, where are you? Is Berman with you? Are you all right?"

"Easy, Fred, we're on the old East-West highway, heading back into Pruitville. We have not been having a good time. I'm fine, but Jed is hurt. We're heading to the hospital.

Why don't you meet us there and we'll tell you all about it."

Demarco needed to know more now.

"What do you mean, Jed's hurt? What happened to him? How badly is he hurt?"

"Fred, get in the car and meet us at the hospital. You'll get the whole picture pretty quickly. See ya there."

"Okay, I'm on my way." He hung up.

Carol looked over at Berman who was stirring, trying to sit up.

"Hey, Jed, just take it easy. We'll be at the hospital in a couple of minutes."

Berman nodded and slumped back against the door.

They reached the hospital five minutes later. Carol stopped in front of the emergency room door and jumped out to help Berman. When she opened his door she got her first glimpse of his wound. His sleeve was drenched with blood. She sucked in her breath and leaned against the car. A wave of nausea swept over her. She covered her mouth and crouched down, trying to stop the blackness slipping through her brain. Two nurses spotted the action outside the door and came running out to the car. By the time they arrived, Berman was about to roll off the seat onto the ground and Carol had slumped into a heap. They lifted Berman onto a gurney and pulled Carol to her feet. They had spotted the News 10 logo on the side of the car. They were eager to find out what brought a local TV news crew to the E.R. in such drastic shape. Inside, they revived Carol with smelling salts and propped her in a chair in the waiting room. They wheeled Berman into the examination area to find out why he was bleeding. He was conscious, but just barely, and hadn't managed to tell them anything useful on the way into the hospital.

Demarco pulled up behind the news car three minutes later. The car door hung open and he could see the long blood stain where Berman had leaned against it. Fearing the worst, he stepped through the automatic doors looking for his crew. He spotted Carol, pale but apparently in one piece, slumped in her chair. When he didn't see Berman beside her, he rushed to the admitting desk.

"I'm Fred Demarco. This is my news crew you're treating here. Where's Jed Berman? Is he all right?"

The nurse waited patiently while Demarco fired all of his questions, then she offered him an explanation, in that controlled tone only professional medical people can sustain in the face of danger or disaster.

"Mr. Berman is being examined. It appears he may have been shot."

"Shot? What do you mean, shot? With a gun? Where is he? Is he gonna make it? I saw a lot of blood out there in the car."

"Please, sir, we have just begun the examination. I will be glad to answer all of your questions when I have the information you're asking for. In the meantime, why don't you take a seat over there beside the young lady? She looks as if she could use some of your attention while you're waiting."

Demarco gave up his interrogation and walked over to Carol. She looked pale and dazed. He sat down and put his arm around her. She turned her face to his shoulder and began to cry.

"Fred, it was awful. I was scared the whole time. Do you think Jed is going to be okay?"

Demarco hugged her close and looked down at her.

"Sure, he'll be okay. Tell me what happened."

Haltingly, Carol told him the story. Every so often she stopped to draw a deep shuddering breath, as the tension began to seep out of her. When she reached the details of their getaway, Demarco realized he hadn't told the police what was happening. He eased Carol back in her chair and stood up to find a phone. At that moment, two officers walked in. True to the rules, the hospital had reported to police that a shooting victim had just been brought in. One of the officers was the man Demarco had ridden with searching for his crew. When the cops heard the details, they decided one of them would stay and try to talk with Berman, while the other one would head back toward the east side garage in search of the gunman. Carol agreed to go with them to help find the hidden drive. Demarco would ride along in case she needed support. Before they left, Demarco called the station and arranged for another crew to meet them on the edge of town and follow them to cover what happened.

When they reached the rendezvous point, the TV 10 crew was waiting and so were cars from the other two stations. They had picked up enough from the scanners to realize there had been a shooting and that a news crew was involved. The reconnaissance mission numbered four vehicles as they headed out of town. Only Carol knew what they faced if they found the gunman and his shack. She leaned silently against Demarco, her face pale, shivers still rippling through her body.

She was just beginning to relax when they reached the hillside leading to the garage. She tapped the officer on the shoulder from the backseat.

"Slow down here. I'm pretty sure the drive is on the left side of the road, just after you start down the hill."

The officer slowed the cruiser to a crawl and began scanning the brush and weeds for signs of an opening. Carol leaned forward to see out the windshield.

"There!" she shouted, pointing to the road directly in front of the car. "Those are the marks we made when I peeled out of here after we backed away from the house."

Two short black marks showed up across the yellow line down the middle of the highway. The officer braked to a stop and looked left. He could see broken down brush where the news car had come out of the drive. He pulled off onto the opposite shoulder and shifted into park. He turned toward Carol and Demarco.

"Is that where you came out?"

Carol had spotted the same ragged weeds and brush. She nodded.

"Okay," he told both of them, "you stay here and I'll see if he's still in there."

Before he got out, he picked up his radio and squeezed the switch.

"Two-oh-three to base. I'm here, on the old East-West Highway, about a half mile from the east side equipment garage. We've identified the spot we were looking for. I'm about to step in and check it out. Wouldn't hurt to have some back up out here in case this guy's still in the mood to argue."

"Ten-four, 203. Two-oh-six and 208, proceed to old East-West Highway to assist 203."

The officer waited to hear the other two cars acknowledge the dispatch, then stepped onto the roadway. He flipped off the safety on his revolver, but didn't pull it out. The news crews parked a short distance behind the police car. They piled out, grabbing their gear. The cop walked over to the TV 10 team and motioned the other crews to join him.

"Listen, if I had more people here, they would have stopped you about a mile back. There may be an armed man on the other side of those bushes. He's already shot someone today; I don't want to give him a chance to do it again. I'm warning you to wait here. If you try to follow me in there, I can't be responsible for what happens to you. In fact, if you try to follow me, I may just arrest you. You all got it?"

Demarco's crew nodded right away. They knew that Berman was lying in the hospital with a bullet in his arm. The others tried to feign agreement without committing themselves. They hoped to sneak into the brush after the cop had gone in and get some pictures. They didn't want to lie and say they wouldn't try to follow him, but they also didn't want him to keep watching them.

The cop walked slowly across the street and peered into the brush. Behind him, all three cameras clicked on. Branches cracked as the officer stepped into the tall weeds. Carol stood beside the police car, watching the other photogs record this very tense moment. She thought, for the first time since she and Berman fled this place, that her camera still sat on top of a tripod on the other side of the bushes, unless the gunman had done something to it. She had recovered enough to think about the very real fact that Demarco would not be pleased if she lost a thirty-thousand-dollar piece of equipment. The officer took another stealthy step into the brush. Another step and he was out of sight. Carol held her breath, waiting to hear the awful sound of the big silver gun going off again. For several minutes there was no sound at all. Then they could hear footsteps coming back through the thick vegetation. Eight of them standing there suddenly realized that if the man in the vest came stumbling out with his gun drawn, they would provide a convenient shooting gallery. The crew from Channel 3 slipped around to the other side of their car and crouched down with only the camera high enough to be seen from the other side of the road. The other crews stood where they were, as did Demarco. Carol leaned back against the car and began to shake again. The rustling in the brush stopped for a moment, and they heard a grumbling voice. Then the footsteps continued and the cop reappeared. They all breathed a collective sigh of relief.

The officer walked over to them, fingering a tear in his sleeve where he'd snagged it on a branch.

"It's okay. The guy's still in there, passed out on the porch with a bottle of whiskey in his hand. I cuffed him to one of the porch posts. As soon as my backup gets here we'll bring him out." He turned to Carol. "Ma'am, I know you've already had a rough day, but I could use a positive ID in there, to make sure I'm arresting the right man. Can you do that for me?"

"I guess I can, " Carol agreed.

They walked back through the brush and were gone for less than two minutes. Just as they came back out, two squad cars pulled up. The first thing the reinforcements did was to tie yellow crime scene tape across the entrance to keep everyone out. The TV crews booed them, disappointed they wouldn't be able to get inside while the scene was fresh. All three cops went back through the weeds and dragged the gunman out. The photogs rushed them as they stepped through the undergrowth, their cameras zoomed in on the large man in overalls and a sheepskin vest. He sagged between two officers as they guided him to a cruiser and shoved him into the back seat. They put him in sitting up, but he slid sideways onto the seat as soon as they closed the door. One of the TV crews turned away from the car and started across the street toward the house. The first cop yelled at them.

"Hey! You can't go in there yet. We need to process the scene, and right now the scene is everything from the other side of that brush to the front porch of the house. If you set foot in there before I tell you to, I'll bust your ass."

The photog tried to push the issue.

"C'mon, man. The TV 10 guys already have shots from

in there. It's not fair to keep us out here."

The cop had had enough. He walked quickly to the photog and grabbed him by the arm.

"You listen to me, pal. You guys are always pushing your luck. We do everything we can to tolerate your presence in the middle of dangerous situations, but I can tell you honestly we don't enjoy having you around. It's tough enough trying to look out for the people we're paid to protect. Having your ass in the way all the time, and having to worry about whether you're gonna get popped, too, gets to be a little too much. Now get your ass back across the road before I haul you in. You got it?"

He let go of the photog's arm and glared into his face. The crew turned around and moved back in line with the others. The oficer pointed to all them as he spoke to one of the cops who had just arrived.

"Sammy, keep an eye on these assholes and make sure they stay out of our way. Jimmy, let's go over this place so we can get out of here."

They stepped back through the brush, leaving the news crews with little to shoot. The Channel 6 crew approached Carol, asking for an interview. When the other crew heard the request, they rushed up with camera rolling and shoved a microphone in Carol's face. Demarco put an end to it before it started.

"Sorry, kids. This woman has been through enough for one day. I hate to spoil your fun, but she's not giving interviews right now. If she has anything she wants people to know, you can catch it on TV 10 tonight at six."

The crews protested loudly.

"Hey, Fred. We're all in this together. You can't shut us out just because your crew happened to end up in the middle of it. It's news and our viewers have as much right to hear about it as yours do."

Demarco was adamant; Carol stood silently while he fought the battle. Finally, the other crews gave up and powered down their cameras until the cops let them walk in to the house to get some shots. Demarco went in with Carol. Her camera stood exactly where she had left it. Nothing else had changed except that the man who had terrorized her and Berman barely an hour ago was no longer there. She waited until her own crew got shots of the scene, including the camera on its tripod, then broke it down and headed back to the news car. Demarco didn't press her for an interview at the scene. He could see she wanted to be away from the place, as quickly as possible. He didn't need to force her to react on camera here. If they needed an interview with her, she could do it back at the station. In fact, he was already thinking about putting her on set so the anchors could interview her about the ordeal. Having her live, talking about the most traumatic thing she'd ever lived through, would be much stronger than a taped interview. He wished he could have Berman there, too, but after seeing the blood all over the car door at the hospital, he didn't expect it. They loaded the gear in the news car and headed back to the station. Carol put her tripod in the trunk with the other photogs' gear, but she clutched her camera in her arms, on her lap, as they rode back to town. Inside the camera was the tape of the gunman—she knew it would be a haunting reminder of this terrible day. Finding herself on the receiving end of a crime was a lot less interesting than watching it through a viewfinder.

Demarco had the crew drop him and Carol off at the hospital so they could pick up the other car. The police had gone over it while they were away. He'd have to have someone run it by the local detailers in the next day or so to get the blood stains cleaned off the door and the seat. He ran his finger over the neat hole in the metal where the bullet had crashed through and into Berman's shoulder. He'd have to think about whether or not to get that repaired. It made one hell of a souvenir for TV 10 News the way it was.

Before he drove back to the station, Demarco went inside to check on Berman. The nurse at the desk said he was out of surgery and just waking up in recovery. She told Demarco he could go up and see how Berman was doing. An attractive woman stepped into the elevator with Demarco. She looked familiar, but he couldn't place her. When he got out on the third floor, she followed him down the hall toward surgery. When he stopped at the nursing station to check in, she did the same thing, giving Berman's name. Demarco turned to her as they walked together.

"Are you a relative of Jed's?"

"No, I'm a good friend. My name is Jane Filips. Who are you?"

"Fred Demarco, news director at Channel 10. I work with Jed. How did you know he was here?"

"One of the E.R. nurses is a good friend of mine. When she saw Jed come in she gave me a call. I work as a reading tutor for the county schools. Jed and I have been seeing each other for a while now. I can't believe he got shot."

She looked worried. There had been no smile from her when Demarco introduced himself. She moved ahead of him to be first in the recovery room. Berman was the only patient there. He was propped up on some pillows, looking around the curtained area where they'd rolled his gurney after removing the bullet from his arm. Other than being very pale, he seemed fairly normal. He grinned widely when Jane parted the curtains and stepped up to his bedside.

"Jane, am I glad to see you. You're the first nice thing I've seen all day."

Jane bent down and kissed him. He gave her a one-arm

127

hug; the other arm was wrapped against his chest in a sling. Demarco was close behind Jane. He heard Berman welcome her.

"Hey, Jed, you saw me this morning. That should have been a pleasant way to start your day."

Berman laughed carefully, holding his right arm gingerly against his chest. He seemed to be in some pain.

"Does it hurt a lot?" Jane asked him.

"You know how your finger feels if you smash it real hard with a hammer? The way it throbs later? That's what it's doing, only a lot more of it. The doc says it'll probably last a couple of days like that. He gave me some nice pills to help make it go away. I just took the first one, but I don't feel much yet. Jane, how did you know I was here?"

"My friend Betty Frist works down in E.R. When you rolled in here, she gave me a buzz. She told me not to come right away because you were heading into surgery. I finished a couple of lessons and then came right over. I was a little afraid. To be honest with you, I didn't know what I was going to find. I'm glad you're doing okay."

"Me, too," Berman told her, lifting her hand to his lips and kissing it. "I'd hate like hell to check out of here just when you and I are getting along so well."

Filips blushed to have Berman speak so personally in front of Demarco, but Fred was thinking about other things. He cut in on their reunion.

"Jed, I got an idea. Could you do a live interview with us at six, from right here in the hospital? I'm thinking about putting Carol on set with Sally and Steve. We obviously have the exclusives on this one. I'd like to capitalize on that as much as we can."

Berman turned to answer him, but his speech got fuzzy as the pain pill kicked in. He started to say something to Demarco, but instead he smiled into Jane's eyes and fell asleep. Demarco grabbed the arm of a nurse standing nearby.

"Hey, Berman just passed out. Is something wrong with him? How long's that going to last?"

The nurse pulled away from Demarco's grip, walked over to the foot of Berman's bed and picked up his chart.

"I don't think your friend has passed out. He just took a pretty good dose of pain killer. It's designed to knock him out for several hours. Considering what he's been through, he may sleep 'til tomorrow morning. He's okay; he just needs some rest."

Demarco moaned with disappointment. He stood with his hands in his pockets, thinking, then walked out. He looked at the clock on the wall by the nursing station. It was three P.M., time to get back to the station and see how they were going to put the story together. In the recovery room, Jane Filips smiled. She leaned over and kissed Berman on the lips. She would go home and fix something to eat, then come back and wait to see if Jed woke up again and wanted to talk. Until he told her the story, she could only imagine what he had gotten himself into this time. She was thankful he came out of it alive.

*   *   *

At six, all three stations led with the story of the local news crew abducted and shot at by a disgruntled ex-county highway worker, fired after thirty years with the county for being drunk on the job. The only pictures the other stations had were the man in the vest being dragged to a police car and shots of the house where he had taken Berman and Carol. TV 10 had it all—close up shots of the gunman and his gun during the interview, shots of Berman talking to the gunman in front of the house, the blood-stained door of the news car, shots of Carol and Demarco waiting across the highway as police nabbed the gunman, a sidebar piece detailing the theft allegations and the link between the gunman and the other county workers, and they had Carol on set talking with the anchors. They gave her two full minutes to talk about it. The anchors went over the questions with her before the show so she could think about what she wanted to say. Most of the questions focused on her reaction to the experience. They ended with the classic question in local TV news: how do you feel now? She paused before she answered that one. The emotions started flooding back as she tried to speak. She shared her conclusion that it was more satisfying to look through the camera than to stand in front of it. She tried to tell them how frightening it all was, but the feelings were too fresh. She choked up and tears welled in her eyes. Steve and Sally quickly ended the interview. When Carol came off the set, Demarco gave her a big hug and told her to go home.

"Do you want to take tomorrow off, just to pull yourself together?" he asked her.

"No, I don't think I need that. It's probably better if I get right back into it. One drunken asshole isn't enough to get me down for long. I'll see you in the morning."

Jane Filips returned to the hospital around five. Berman showed no signs of waking up, but she didn't want to take a chance on not being there if he did. He'd been moved to a private room on the fourth floor. When the late shift nurses made their first rounds they saw two sleeping people in the room: Berman lying still on the bed and Jane, wrapped in a borrowed blanket, slumped over in a chair close to Berman's bedside. They thought about telling her visiting hours were over, but after seeing who it was, they closed the door and let them both sleep.

When Berman stirred the next morning, Jane was

standing by with a fresh cup of coffee and some muffins she had picked up down in the hospital cafeteria. He smelled the coffee before he realized Jane was still there. Seeing her made waking up easier.

"Hey," he said drowsily. "When did you get back here?"

"Last night, I slept right here in case you needed me."

He felt a little sheepish about having her stationed by his bedside all night.

"Did I need you?"

"Not really. You never woke up after Demarco left. How do you feel this morning?"

He started to pull himself up and stopped short when he tried to move his right arm.

"Ouch! This thing still hurts, at least when I try to move it around. That jerk on the hill out there really messed me up."

Jane held up the coffee and muffins.

"Before you get into all of that, how about a little breakfast? How soon do you think you can get out of here?"

He didn't know. He remembered the nurses telling him they'd take a look at his wound this morning and maybe discharge him early in the day if it looked good enough.

"If I'm lucky, I may get out of here soon. What's your schedule today?"

"You are my schedule, macho man. I've cleared the decks so I can take you home or wherever you want to go as soon as they untie the ropes."

A nurse pushed open the door and rolled in a cart full of juices and charts.

"Good morning, Mr. Berman. That was quite a story they told about you on the news last night. How are you feeling today? " She unfastened Berman's sling and started unwrapping the bandage around his arm.

131

"I feel pretty good," he told her, but he winced as she pulled off the last of the wrapping. "The question is, how does it look?"

Without a mirror, Berman couldn't see the hole in his arm. Jane Filips walked around beside the nurse. A large ugly bruise spread over much of Berman's upper arm and in the middle of the bruise was a small hole, neatly stitched shut with five or six sutures. The whole area was swabbed in brownish colored iodine. It looked sore, but there was no sign of reddening that might signal infection setting in.

"You're doing just fine, Mr. Berman. This doesn't look bad at all, considering you got shot with a .357 magnum. They said the bullet went through a car door before it hit your arm. That may be what saved you from losing it, or worse, from having the bullet zip through your arm and into your chest. Once it got in there, no telling how much damage it might have done. The way I see it, you are lucky to be alive."

The nurse's review of the situation left Berman a little light-headed as he considered the prospects. He could still picture the panicked getaway, he and Carol backing frantically away from the gunman as he tried to kill them. Berman considered himself a fairly tough journalist, but he would admit to anyone that that moment frightened him worse than anything he had ever experienced. He felt lucky to be alive. He wondered if Carol felt the same way. He thanked the nurse for her evaluation, and turned to Jane.

"I can't believe I haven't thought of her until right now, but how's Carol?"

"Oh, she's doing all right. She had recovered enough after she brought you here to lead the police back to your news car and the gunman. She seems like a spunky kid."

Berman agreed. "She is. I just hope this ordeal doesn't convince her she made a bad career choice. This sort of thing certainly doesn't happen very often."

A shadow of concern darkened Jane's face; she reached over and took his hand.

"That's true, Jed. But who ever thought it could happen at all? I'm a little worried about the things you could get yourself into. I know I don't own you, but I'm getting awfully attached to you. Are you sure you're in the right line of work?"

Berman squeezed her hand.

"Thanks for caring so much, Jane. It really does mean a lot to me. I promise not to go looking for any new trouble for at least a couple of months."

The nurse was still examining his arm when a doctor walked in. He obviously knew Berman's recent history.

"So, you're the celebrity patient in Room 403. You guys must be in ratings, huh? Needed an exciting story to pump up the audience? Looks like you bit off more than you could chew this time, eh?"

"Thanks for the analysis, doc," Berman responded with a grin. "Now that you've figured us out, how soon can I get out of here to start working on my next sensational assignment?"

The doctor took a quick look at Berman's arm and asked the nurse to rewrap it.

"My friend," he said to Berman, "you are ready to go right now. I don't recommend doing too much lifting with your right arm until that wound has a chance to heal. But, otherwise, there's no reason for you to stay here. I'll sign you out at the front desk. You're kinda new to the TV news game, aren't you?"

"Yes, I am. I used to be with the *Berrington Evening Chronicle* until the beginning of the year. I never realized how exciting TV could be. I wish I'd come over a long time ago."

The doctor laughed. "Well, too much of this kind of excitement could mean a short career. I'd be a little more careful next time, if I were you. We usually watch TV 10 News. Now that I've taken a personal interest in you, I'll be watching to see how you treat yourself. You can check with your personal physician about getting those stitches out in about a week. Gotta keep moving. See you later."

He waved as he walked out. Out of habit, Berman raised his right arm to wave back, and felt a sharp pain shoot through it. He put it down on the bed so the nurse could finish wrapping it. After she left, Berman slid his feet onto the floor and stood up. He felt much stronger than he had coming in yesterday. Jane helped him pull on the pants, shirt and shoes she had driven to Berrington to pick up for him this morning. The nurses had thrown away his blood-stained suit and shirt with the bullet holes. As they walked to the elevator and out of the building, Berman was glad Jane was there to lean on. She helped him into her car.

"Where to, sir?" she asked, cabbie style.

"Maybe I better stop in at the station to see if Fred has anything for me to do today."

"My God, Jed, he wouldn't make you work the day after you got shot, would he?"

"I don't know for sure. I'm still the new kid on the block. I better check in." Berman had Jane pull around back so he could avoid attention in the lobby. When he walked up the steps into the newsroom, everyone was gathered for the morning meeting. When they saw Berman, they burst into applause and cheers. He smiled and waved with his left arm. The right was in a sling. He walked up beside De-marco and spoke to him quietly as the meeting continued.

"Fred, do you want me back here today?"

Demarco hadn't expected to see him for a couple of days.

"Nah, you need to give yourself a couple of days to heal. Why don't you take the rest of the week off and get back to it on Monday. Helluva good story yesterday, Jed. Nice job with the interview at the house. That guy was one big looney tune."

Berman realized he didn't know what had become of the gunman.

"By the way, Fred, what ever happened to our friend with the gun?"

"Carol showed 'em where he took you, and when the cops went in he was passed out drunk on the porch."

"Who was he? Why'd he have such a hard-on over the county highway garage?"

"Turns out he used to work there, but he got fired a year or so ago for drinking on the job. He's a real alcoholic. Burned out case, from the looks of things."

"What are the cops going to do with him?"

"Assuming you and Carol will testify, he'll face abduction and at least reckless endangerment with a firearm. Do you think he meant to kill you out there?"

"Hard to say. He acted like a real tough guy, but he was obviously smashed the whole time. I remember when he first ripped the car door open his breath was strong enough to give you a hangover."

"If that's the case, the prosecutor isn't likely to try to press for something as serious as attempted murder. The schmuck, dangerous as he was, probably never really knew what he was doing. Not much doubt he did it, though, with the tape you and Carol shot. He'll probably end up going away for a couple of years, assuming you both agree to testify. You will testify, won't you?"

"Of course. Nuts like that shouldn't be running around on the street endangering people, not even journalists. I'm glad they got him without anyone else getting hurt." He rubbed his arm gingerly. "Are you sure you don't need me the next couple of days?"

"I didn't say I don't need you. I said you need to go home and heal up. So get out of here. How'd you get here, anyway?"

"Jane brought me. You met her at the hospital, didn't you?"

"Oh, yeah. She seems very nice and extremely well put together. You two serious?"

"I hope so. She's waiting out in the car. I better get going. I'll see you on Monday, but don't hesitate to call if you need me."

Demarco looked at him with a mixture of irritation and admiration. If only there were more journalists like Jed Berman around....

"No, go on home, Jed. This is some start you're off to in TV news. I can't wait to see what you get into next."

Berman flashed a smile as he turned to walk away.

"Yeah, I can't wait either. You guys in TV really do have all the fun. See ya later."

He managed to drive home one-handed in his own car with Jane following close behind. They spent the rest of the day watching old movies and napping together. He knew he needed the rest, but he was eager to get back on the street. He had some ideas he wanted to work on.

Six

On Air

Berman returned to work on Monday without the sling. Although pain still flickered through his arm, the worst of it seemed to be over. The newsroom greeted him warmly, but the time for dwelling on what he and Carol had gone through had passed. True to the nature of mass media, the public had consumed the story of his shooting, and now it was time to feed them something else.

Word spread quickly among viewers that TV 10's new reporter liked to investigate. His phone started to ring in his new newsroom as it had at *The Chronicle*. He followed up on as many as he could, but Demarco's dictum of a package a day meant it often took a couple of weeks to pull together everything he needed to nail down the story and get it on the air. In the meantime, he covered the same meetings, accidents, fires, and news conferences as everyone else. Demarco never discouraged him from digging into really good stories, but Berman began to realize that he had traded carte blanche at the paper for tracking down tips, for roughly twice as much work at TV 10—investigating the really good stories plus cranking out the routine stuff to fill the shows every night.

Before long, people started to recognize him on the street and in stores. High school journalism teachers invited him to visit their classes to talk about TV news. (Only once had anyone invited him to class to discuss print reporting.) Service clubs wanted to hear the story of the gunman on the hill. Demarco tried to accomodate Berman's increasing schedule of public appearances. He knew the public relations value of circulating Berman and establishing the personal link between audiences and the TV 10 News team. The Promotions department featured Berman in a new spot touting TV 10's hard-hitting team, led, of course, by anchors Steve Kimmel and Sally West.

Berman did his best to stay afloat as his journalistic landscape shifted. He sensed that some of the other reporters didn't appreciate all the attention he was getting. He overheard one conversation between two of the younger reporters who came close to accusing him, in absentia, of getting shot on purpose so he could make a name for himself. In general, the newsroom buzz gave little credit to anyone for long. The TV scene mirrored the print world—most people spent most of their time focused on themselves. The difference was in degree: TV's higher visibility stoked egos until they glowed much hotter. Once, he heard the beautiful young blonde who sat next to him tell someone on the phone that it was taking longer to become a star in this area than she'd ever imagined. She had decided to find an agent who could get her to a major market as soon as possible.

The most encouraging element was Fred Demarco. He proved to be everything he professed to be the day he talked Berman into jumping ship and coming over to TV. Demarco led by example: he could track a story, write it, edit, figure out ways to make news visual, and produce a newscast better than anyone in the room. He showered his staff with praise when they deserved it and he called them into the office for a serious chat when they fell short of expectations. The formula worked. Demarco's staff was amazingly stable for TV news, an industry where the quest for the big time usually created a cast of vagabonds always preparing to hit the road in search of a bigger and better deal.

All of which did not mean that Berman agreed with every decision Demarco handed down. Many times, he thought TV 10's coverage was too shallow, or, in cases where pictures were hard to come by, non-existent. He wanted TV 10 to be the station of record just as *The Chronicle* had been the paper of record, especially for Berrington. That meant covering council meetings and commissioners' meetings, making sure the public knew about big decisions before they were made and what they meant after they were made. He broached the subject with Demarco from time to time, but the approach seemed set in stone. They'd cover the story if a really big hassle flared up between the politicos and the public, but no one seemed interested in bird-dogging these elected officials from day to day to make sure they spent money wisely and made the right calls.

In spite of Berman's frustration, TV 10's ratings started to rise. After years of threatening to break out of third place, they jumped into a resounding second place and started edging toward first. Demarco watched it happen and willingly credited Berman with part of the success. The move from third to second place first showed up in the May book, the ratings period when Berman pulled off his five-part series on corruption in the Pruitville police department. Three uniformed officers and two detectives lost their jobs, and the city broke up the theft ring the bad cops had helped set up to fence the goods they stole from crime scenes. That same month, TV 10 ran series on caring for pets, getting hooked up to the Internet, and how to lose weight. The reporter in the weight loss series actually shed thirty pounds in the process. Cards, letters, and phone calls flooded the station from people who wanted to know more about the system the reporter used.

139

Demarco was waving the preliminary May ratings over his head when Berman walked into the room two weeks after the sweeps period ended.

"Jed, you gotta see this! These are the best numbers this news department has ever had."

Everyone gathered around as Demarco called out the preliminary results: at six, a ten rating and a 22 share, compared to Channel 3's seven rating and 15 share and Channel 6's twelve rating and 24 share. Berman had to remind himself what the numbers meant: rating was the percentage of all possible TV viewers in the market tuned to TV 10, the share number was the percentage of people actually watching TV during news time who tuned in to his station. The numbers at eleven o'clock were roughly the same. For the first time ever, TV 10 came in second during both time slots. By late afternoon, the Promotions Department had cranked out a spot trumpeting the results. After his story was edited, Berman walked into Demarco's office and sat down. Demarco looked up from his desk.

"Hi, Jed. What's up?"

"I'm still trying to get a handle on this ratings business. In newspaper work, we didn't have that kind of competition. I mean, we knew the Pruitville Gazette wanted to sell papers in Berrington and we peddled our stuff over here, but no one ever tried to figure out exactly how many people actually exposed themselves to the stories we published. We had circulation figures, which were going down last time I looked. But we didn't have this little snapshot of our progress. How important are these numbers to what you're trying to do here?"

A somber expression replaced the happy smile Demarco had worn when Berman first sat down.

"To be absolutely honest with you, Jed, these figures are very serious. The competition for advertising dollars is getting severe, with all the TV options out there today. If we want to convince people to spend their money to put a message on our air, we've got to be able to show them we have the viewers they want to reach. Don't think for a minute that we can just concentrate on reporting the news and let the chips fall where they may. If these numbers ever start going back down, yours truly will be in a world of hurt. One of the first things a station does to try to get better numbers is replace the news director. Last time I looked, the life expectancy of someone in this office was about two years. It's true that up until recently this company didn't think that way, but times are changing." He got up and closed the door, then walked back to his desk. "Just between you and me, the G.M. made it clear to me over a year ago that I'd better show some improvement down here or he'd be looking for someone else. The company wants to make money, Jed. And good ratings translate into better money. So we've got to do everything we can to keep those numbers rising and that money rolling in. I know you and I think we're in the news business, but the people who own this station are in 'business' business and that means getting as much out of this operation as they can."

Berman had never heard Demarco explain things this way. The focus on hard cash cast a cold shadow over them as they talked.

"Fred, I feel a little naive. I see you as a news man through and through. I had no idea you were under this kind of pressure. How much does it affect the way we do our job here?"

"That's the good news. So far, Jed, I've been able to keep reporting news the way I think it should be done, for the most part, and it's working. But I'm always thinking about how it's going to play with viewers. Why do you think I came after you? I know you believe in the stories you dig out, but that investigative stuff is real promotable, it draws people to the show. You've become an important part of our operation in a very short time. I appreciate what you're doing, and I hope it's the right ingredient to keep us moving up. But you never know what the other guys are gonna come up with. We have to keep our eyes and ears open and work very hard. You know what I mean?"

Berman felt uneasy hearing their work couched in these terms, but he respected Demarco and his point of view.

"Yeah, I think I know what you mean. We better continue to kick ass if we want our happy little newsroom to hold together. I hope you know you can count on me, Fred."

"I know that, Jed. I think I can say the same thing for everyone out there." He motioned toward the newsroom. "I just hope it's enough."

Seven

Behind the Scenes

Demarco held his course, but the ratings didn't. The November book dropped TV 10 back to third place at six and eleven. By May of the next year, Demarco's news team was slipping fast. Channel 3 had brought in a new anchor team plus a hotshot consumer reporter. Viewers responded by awarding them renewed control over second place. Berman worked long hours turning in solid investigative pieces, and the rest of the news team delivered steady coverage of day-to-day events, but it wasn't enough. Two weeks after the May book came out, Berman noticed a tall, well-dressed stranger in Demarco's office when he reached the newsroom. As everyone gathered for the morning meeting, the stranger walked to the head of the circle and stood beside Demarco, who looked like he'd just swallowed a peach pit.

"My friends," Demarco said, "I want you to meet Autry Domain. He's with Mangold and Foreman, the second largest broadcast consulting firm in the country. I'm not going to kid around about why he's here. The folks upstairs couldn't help noticing our numbers are in free-fall, for some reason. Autry is here to help us figure out why and get us back where we belong. He and his colleagues will be stopping in here from time to time to offer us ideas and advice. I think it's to our best advantage to consider that advice very seriously. Autry, is there anything you want to say?"

Autry Domain stood six feet three, with a slim build and thick black hair. He had the good looks of a model, his suit fit extremely well and appeared to be expensive. He scanned Demarco's staff slowly with pale blue eyes and then spoke in a strong, deep voice.

"I don't have a speech for you today, but I do have one plea—give me a chance. You may already have your own ideas about what consultants can do or have done in this industry. Please don't automatically reject my advice because you think all consultants are worthless. I've been around TV news for nearly twenty years, ten as an anchor/reporter and five as a news director. My orientation is news and I know, from talking to Fred, that's where all of you are coming from, too. But if TV 10 is going to get that news out to the people of this community, we've got to make sure we're doing it in the best possible ways. We've got to be on the cutting edge; we've got to be trend-setters, and make everyone else follow us. If you're willing to give me and my staff a chance, I know we can help you get back where you belong in the ratings. I've seen your work, I know you're a good team, and I know Fred is a great leader. With a little help from us, you're going to be the best damn kick-ass news team this area has ever seen."

Demarco shook Domain's hand when he finished his pep talk.

"Autry, I know every one of us wants to be number one. I also know these are serious news people who have seen some of the excesses consultants have brought down on our heads over the years. But I believe you mean what you say and I think I speak for this staff when I say we want to work with you." To his staff, Demarco said, "As for all of you, Autry wants to get going by meeting with each of you to look at your recent work and get a feel for what we're doing. I'll be posting a schedule on my door. Please try to be ready with tapes at the assigned time. You'll have to work around your other duties the next couple of days, but I know it'll be worth it. Any questions?"

A hand went up in the back of the group. It was Donnie Kurtz.

"Fred, was this your idea?"

Demarco's face reddened slightly.

"Donnie, it doesn't matter whose idea it was. It's a good one. We can only stand to gain from the expertise and experience Autry and his staff bring to us. Is that a problem for you?"

Kurtz looked irritated, but he shook his head and said nothing else.

Demarco clapped his hands together. "Okay, let's get on with the morning meeting. What's up?"

Autry Domain walked back into Demarco's office. When Berman glanced in that direction a few minutes later, Domain was on the phone, leaning back in Demarco's chair with his feet on the desk.

Berman met with Domain the next morning. He showed him his reports on the police corruption case and part of the station's coverage of his encounter with the disgruntled county worker. He went in feeling a little apprehensive; if Domain had all that experience, he might find a lot of things to criticize in Berman's relatively fresh efforts, but it didn't go that way at all. After looking at the tapes, Domain had only upbeat comments and just a few of those.

"Jed, you are obviously the apple of Fred's eye and I can see why. He told me about stealing you away from the newspaper. How are you feeling about being over here?"

Berman had a ready answer for the question.

"I feel good about it. There are times when TV seems a little shallow compared to print, but our good stories reach so many people and get such powerful results, I have no regrets about giving up print."

"That's good to hear because you're doing a hell of a job. You deserve a lot of credit for what was happening around here a year ago. I admire your investigative work. I also have a lot of good contacts around the country. If I can ever help out with any of that, just give me a call. Fred has my number. Do you have any questions for me?"

Berman shook his head. "No, I didn't think about asking any. I figured you'd be working me over when you looked at my stuff."

Domain laughed and punched Berman's shoulder, buddy-style.

"Hell, no, Jed. You're doing great. I wouldn't dream of trying to rip apart the stuff you're cranking out. Keep it up. It's an important part of the equation here." He glanced at his watch. "Hey, we're out of time. Send me a tape once in a while so I can stay current on what you're doing." He extended a hand to Berman. Berman shook it and headed back to the newsroom.

When Berman and the other reporters compared notes on Autry Domain, they discovered everyone had gotten essentially the same treatment: a positive endorsement of the work they were already doing. They wondered aloud what value this man could be to the station if he never offered any sugggestions for improvement. When Domain had left, Berman took the question to Demarco.

"Fred, what's the point of paying these consultants a lot of money if all Domain is going to do is kiss up to all of us? He met with everyone out there in the newsroom and he didn't have one negative thing to say or one constructive criticism or one new idea."

Demarco sat rubbing his hands together for a long moment.

"You're right, Jed, he didn't." He paused again, still rubbing his hands together, as though he was trying to warm them in the cold. "No, he didn't have any suggestions this time, but mark my words, my friend, he will. He will."

*   *   *

The first sign of Domain's influence came over the summer. It wasn't Domain but a young female assistant who showed up with makeup kit in hand. Shortly after she arrived, another schedule sheet went up. Each of the on-air people, reporters and anchors, had fifteen minutes with this woman who identified herself as an appearance consultant. She had studied tapes of the TV 10 news shows before she arrived to formulate her advice. In every case, she found at least a couple of things that she thought would make a difference in how viewers responded to TV 10's product. Those who had experience in other markets took the sessions in stride, but reporters who had grown up in the business under the no-nonsense tutelage of Fred Demarco chafed at her attention. It was especially hard for Donnie Kurtz. The consultant found little to like about the way he looked on the air. She tried to break it to him gently.

"Donnie, you're pretty serious about what you do, aren't you?" she asked in a soft voice.

Kurtz responded brusquely.

"Hell, yes, I'm serious. I've been doing this since you were watching *Mister Rogers' Neighborhood*."

"Oh," she said, hoping to head off the storm she sensed was building in Kurtz. "You must be one of the most experienced TV journalists in this newsroom."

"I am, and that experience tells me I don't need any advice from a kid about how to look on the air. People here know me and accept me. They don't expect me to be a clothes horse, just a solid reporter keeping an eye on their community. I don't have much time for a fashion show."

"Oh, Donnie, I'm not here to talk about fashion shows. I want to capitalize on the image you already have, to make everyone want to watch your reports. These aren't big changes, just some adjustments in makeup and maybe your hair style. It won't hurt you and it might just improve your image."

Kurtz reached the end of his endurance.

"That's it, I don't have time for this. Nothing personal about you, young lady, but this is fucked. I have better things to do." He delivered his salvo in a loud voice as he stood up to leave the dressing room, but Demarco blocked the doorway, his face crimson.

"Kurtz, if you want to work here, you will sit back down and listen to what this woman has to say. This station is spending thousands of dollars for this service and anyone who works here will be willing to profit from it or they can get the hell out. First I think you should apologize and then start paying attention. This isn't the good old days anymore, Donnie. We're in the battle of our lives and little things like this might just be what turns the tide. Do you understand me?"

Kurtz had been at the station for fifteen years. He had known Demarco for ten years. He couldn't believe Demarco had bought into an approach to broadcast news that most veteran journalists despised. He backed up and sat down beside the consultant, keeping his eyes on Demarco. He couldn't come up with one of his usual cynical observations to help him rise above what was happening. The thought of quitting flitted through his mind, but he quickly rejected it. His roots were too deep in this town, and his contract had a two-year, non-compete clause that meant he wouldn't be able to do anything on air for two full years at any other station in the market if he left TV 10. Yet, the humiliation of having some post-teenage kid sit here and tell him he didn't know how to dress or how to comb his hair seemed like too much. As the options raced through his mind, he realized Demarco was waiting for an answer. Swallowing hard, he gave the only response he could think of—the safe one.

"I understand, Fred. It's just that this is all kind of new to me. You've never talked about these things, other than in a very basic way. We've all done the makeup thing and I've tried to make sure I have decent suits to wear. I accept those things as necessary evils that go with the territory. But this sort of thing scares me. Where does it lead? First time consuming makeup tips and new hair styles. Then the wardrobe makeover. I guess if I look down the road what I see is a news department that picks its staff based on what they look like and how well they dress rather than how well they can report."

Demarco cut him off.

"Donnie, you know I respect you as a professional. You have been a solid part of this newsroom since before I showed up. But times have changed, and if you want to continue doing what you do, you've got to change, too. So give her a chance, will ya?"

Kurtz felt sick to his stomach, but he stifled any further comment. Demarco turned around and walked away. The consultant picked up her yellow legal pad and flipped over the pages until she found the one with Kurtz's name at the top. When she spoke, the tone of her voice gave no hint of the confrontation she had just witnessed. She simply began talking through the points she had jotted down while watching Kurtz on tape. It was a long list. Kurtz started taking notes on her comments, but she stopped him.

"Don't bother with that, Donnie. We always send you a

typewritten summary of everything we talk about so you can use it as a reference. It should be here a couple of weeks after I get back to my office."

Kurtz's session lasted a full hour. Three weeks later, Demarco dropped a five page summary of the consultant's comments on Kurtz's desk. On top was a drawing of a face, shaded with makeup and annotated with brand names so Kurtz could duplicate the results the consultant had created during their session. Kurtz skimmed through the pages and slipped the packet under a pile of papers in his bottom desk drawer.

Berman's makeup session went smoothly; his relative lack of experience gave him little reason to object to anything the consultant recommended. He first felt tension when she took him into the studio to work on his standups.

"You're too stiff, Jed. We need to feel your compassion about the stories you report on. I know you are compassionate, I've seen you on tape. You've got to give more of that to the viewer."

Berman felt frustration inching its way up his back. He questioned how much this kid really knew about reporting.

"Where did you get your experience, if you don't mind my asking?"

"Oh, I've never been on the air, " she said quickly.

Incredulity edged out the frustration. It was tinted by a malicious sort of curiosity. He felt the urge to expose this child who had been thrust on the newsroom by management. He poked a little harder.

"Are you saying you've never worked as a broadcast news reporter?"

"Yeah, that's right. I was a cosmetologist in a drugstore when Autry discovered me. He said he could tell right away that I could relate to—" she hooked her fingers in the air to form quotation marks around what came next, " 'sensitive, ego-driven on-air types.' "

Berman was stunned. He heard himself repeating the same question.

"So you've never been on the air?"

She laughed lightly and shook her head.

"Nope," she offered, without a hint of embarrassment.

"And you're being sent all over the country to tell people like me how to do it? I don't mean to be rude, but that doesn't make a lot of sense to me."

"Well, I was in a couple of plays in high school and college, until I dropped out to go to work. I've always had a good feel for the dramatic." She waved this part of the conversation away. "But we're not supposed to talk about me. I'm here to work with you. Let's try a walking standup; they add so much good energy to your story."

More questions bubbled into Berman's mind.

"Do you mind if I ask how you know that—that my walking around while I talk adds something special to the story?"

"Oh, Autry has reams of research stuff on every aspect of this business. He did the performance study himself to see what people liked best and what kept them focused on the story. He says eighty percent of the people in the study thought the story was more interesting if the reporter walked on camera. You can't really argue with scientific research, can you?" Berman scratched his head. This child was spouting the wisdom of Autry Domain without ever questioning it, and worse, without ever doing the job she was telling him how to do.

"But is it possible walking around may actually distract people from what you're saying? I don't see many network correspondents jumping all over the place to make a point."

"Maybe you don't right now, but we're working with a couple of the networks to teach them the same stuff I'm teaching you. Their people have been real receptive to what we're telling them. C'mon. Do a little walking for me."

Berman backed halfway across the studio and delivered the standup they'd been practicing as he walked toward her. He felt awkward and unsure where to move.

"This really doesn't feel very good to me. How do I know where to walk and how much to walk?"

"What you need to keep in mind is that you're adding energy. If you can find a short set of steps, walk down those toward the camera. Walk out a door, cross a street. Anything that makes it more interesting to the viewer's eye. If there's a wall or a railing you can walk along, use it to steady yourself and give the standup some direction."

"You really have research to support all of this?"

"Autry does and he's one of the top broadcast consultants in the world. He even works with a couple of clients overseas and in South America."

Time ran out before Berman could practice any more walking standups or ask any more questions. He was last on the schedule. When they finished, the young woman headed straight for Demarco's office. A few minutes later Demarco walked out with her to give her a lift to the airport. She waved across the newsroom as she left.

"See ya, everybody. Don't forget to practice. And send me tapes. You're gonna do just great."

No one waved. A couple of people tried to smile, but the young consultant had not managed to charm even one member of the staff. Few knew as much about her qualifications, or lack of qualifications, as Berman now did, but they all sensed that someone was putting one over on them or the station, or both. They all agreed that spending however many thousands were being shelled out for this service was a waste. If this was all they got for the money, it would be better spent hiring more staff or inducing people to work harder through hefty raises.

When Demarco returned from the airport, he called Berman into his office.

"Jed, were you hassling that young woman during your coaching session?"

Berman looked surprised.

"Hell, I don't think so. I asked her a few questions, but I didn't think I was giving her a hard time."

"She told me you seemed defensive and hostile, even after she explained where she got the stuff she was trying to teach you."

"Skeptical, maybe, but not defensive and definitely not hostile. Did you know she never worked as a TV news reporter?" That caught Demarco off guard.

"What are you talking about? A big time outfit like Mangold and Foreman isn't likely to hire people with no experience. You heard Autry Domain's background. What makes you think this young woman hasn't worked in the business?"

"'Cause she told me so herself when I asked her," Berman replied with a certain satisfaction, although he still felt an uneasiness about the whole consulting scene and the fact that Demarco was defending it. He saw Demarco as a newsman's newsman. This consulting stuff was bullshit; he was just waiting for Fred to admit it. The revelation forced Demarco into a stance Berman had never seen him take.

"That doesn't matter. These people sell a service. They promise to take us from where we are to where we want to be. They come in here armed to the teeth with original research and a finger on the pulse of America. Wherever they get the stuff they tell us, we're gonna take it and run with it and come out on top. You're one of the older

153

reporters in here, Jed. I expect you, of all people, to respond to this free training in a mature way, without trying to undercut it or raise questions about it. Can I count on you to do that?"

Berman suddenly wished he knew Demarco better. He wanted to give this man room to admit he was fearful of the future and that was why he was willing to agree to something as annoying as consultants to try to save the day. But they were not really friends, just professional colleagues who respected each other. Now, with the consultant's nose under the tent, Berman doubted whether he and Demarco could ever be really close. He felt pity for them both, sadness that the trends in their business were preventing them from doing news the way they knew it should be done, and worse, preventing them from standing united as they followed those trends into the future. This was not the Demarco who had talked him into jumping ship at *The Chronicle*. This man had a haunted look in his eyes. He realized now that Demarco had no choice in the matter. And that had to be hard for a man who had lived most of his life knowing he could do his job well without advice from a bunch of people with very different values. The times ahead had to look bleak. Berman didn't want to make it worse for Demarco than it already promised to be.

"Hey, Fred, I came here to do the news with you and I still want to do that. If we have to put up with these people from time to time, that's not so bad. Most of the time they won't be here and we can do what we think is best, right?"

Demarco tried to smile, but it looked more like a smirk.

"They're here more than you think, Jed. Have you noticed that my office door is closed a lot these days? You know what I'm doing in here? Talking to Autry Domain. He calls me every week, at least once a week, with all sorts of ideas for stories and how to produce our newscasts." He dropped his voice and looked around as though someone might be listening. "If you breathe a word of this to anyone out in that room, I'll fire you." Jed nodded and Demarco continued, "I'd like to tell Domain to blow it out his ass, but I can't. The boys upstairs get a copy of everything he tells me or sends me. They hired him to boost our ratings, and they expect me to do what he says. Let me just say this, I'm not having nearly as much fun as I used to. Now get out of here and get me some good news."

Berman hadn't noticed Demarco's door was frequently closed until Demarco mentioned it. Once he started looking for it, he saw it swing shut a lot. He started wondering which ideas in the morning meeting came from Demarco and which came from the unseen but omnipresent Autry Domain. For the most part, the content of the newscasts seemed to hold steady. Demarco gave Berman as much leeway as before to pursue the stories he considered important. Now and then, especially around holidays or the beginning of a new season, reporters ended up doing what struck Berman as clichéd stories, obvious reports on the cost of a Thanksgiving dinner or what toy kids wanted most for Christmas. But as he watched the three local newscasts go down every night on the newsroom monitors, he noticed they all did those same stories. He also saw the other reporters walking in more of their standups and styling their hair the same way. The male anchor on Channel 3 started wearing glasses on the air once in a while—a fact of life people at TV 10 noted with some amazement. Contact lenses had ruled the airwaves almost since they were invented. About the same time, Berman realized the network anchors had glasses perched on their noses, too. There was no mystery to it; the consultants provided the same advice to the big markets and to the network people at the top of the broadcast pyramid as they did to TV 10 and the other local stations. To Berman, it seemed like the homogenization flattening so many things in America. Someone gets the idea, it turns out to be good for business, and soon it's introduced all across the country. No wonder broadcast news people bounded around so easily from one end of the continent to the other. Thanks to the steady stroking and handling of consultants, they all looked alike. Personality or news skills didn't matter much anymore. When a station needed to fill a position, the news director or station manager put in a call to the consultants, who checked the faces on their tape reels for the right ingredients: gender, ethnic or racial background, hair color, eye color, voice quality. It wasn't exactly cookie-cutter news, but to Berman's not-yet-jaundiced eye, it came close. Months ago, during that fateful lunch, Demarco had disavowed any interest in this side of the broadcast news business. Berman had no doubt that years ago Demarco would have rejected this approach without blinking an eye. Now, he had to at least acquiesce to it, if not actually endorse it—simply to *survive.*

Berman tried to explain what was happening to Jane Filips over dinner at his apartment. She seemed less surprised by it all than he was.

"Jed, don't you read *TV Guide*? They've been talking about all this stuff for years. The media critics in the national newspapers say the same thing. I can't believe I'm telling you this. It all has to do with the bottom line—these companies will do whatever it takes to make money, even if that means remolding you and everyone else into something you're not."

He hadn't expected to, but Berman felt a little defensive.

"Maybe it's been going on at the networks or major markets like New York or Chicago," he admitted. "But this is Pruitville, we're about the one hundredth market out of two hundred in the country. We've got Fred Demarco in charge. I know he's under some pressure, but I expect him to hold his own."

Jane knew Berman well enough to know what really bothered him.

"If it's any consolation, I don't notice any real difference in the news you're reporting. You're still covering the stuff I want to know about."

"I know I sound sort of maudlin, but I really appreciate your saying that," Berman said. "You remember when I decided to make the switch. The thing I worried about was that TV already seemed kind of superficial. I didn't want to get caught in that and not be able to work on stories that matter, that have a little meat to them."

"Oh, Jed, I don't think anyone would accuse you of that. We all know that TV doesn't give as many details sometimes, but we expect that. On the other hand, where do you think we go looking for the latest news when something big or terrible is happening? TV, where else?" She flashed him a reassuring smile and reached across the table to take his hand. "C'mon. You talk shop too much. Let's take a walk through beautiful downtown Berrington and look in people's windows to see what they're up to. If they're watching TV, which most of them probably are, you can't look, because it'll just get you started again. I'd rather have you thinking about me than the boob tube."

He feigned hurt feelings.

"Hey, you're talking about my chosen medium, the most powerful medium in the world."

She stood up, still holding onto his hand, and started dragging him across the apartment.

"I'm talking about the man I'm crazy about who needs to learn how to leave the job at the office." She picked up the jackets they had tossed on the couch and handed Berman his. "So put this on and let's get out of here and clear our minds with some fresh air. And, if you're really good, I just might stay over and help you forget about work all night long."

As they walked down the hallway toward the front door, they heard televisions blaring in several apartments. Jane reached up and put her hands over Berman's ears.

"And you can't listen to TV, either. Tonight, we're gonna have the unplugged version. You, me, the streetlights and the night sky. Okay?"

Berman grabbed her arm and pulled her close to him just inside the front door. He looked deep into her eyes.

"Yes," he told her, with conviction and the warmth of the love he felt for her. "Tonight's show stars Jane Filips. There is only one channel. Thanks for helping me remember that." They kissed for a long moment and then stepped out into the cool summer night, holding hands as they strolled slowly down the street.

Eight

Changing Channels

When the July book showed no signs of improvement, word began seeping around the TV 10 building that something big loomed in the future for the news department. Berman tried to keep a close eye on Demarco, looking for signs that the veteran newsman might crack under the pressure. Demarco was summoned to the general manager's office almost daily, for long periods of time. When he came back down, the color had usually drained from his face, leaving him with an ashen hue. Berman tried to talk to Demarco about what was going on, but he evaded questions, repeating over and over again, "It'll turn around. If we just keep doing a good job, it'll turn around."

On the first Friday in September, Berman overslept and rushed into the newsroom thirty minutes late. He expected to hear the haggling of the morning news meeting and to receive some well-deserved digs about his tardiness. Instead, he pulled up, out of breath, in the middle of a nearly silent room. Here and there reporters and photogs gathered in small groups, murmuring, with the occasional outburst of raw emotion verbalized in the form of familiar expletives. Berman looked around for Demarco, but the office door was shut, the light off. When he walked up to the windows and pressed his nose against the glass, he realized Demarco's desk was clear, no newspapers, no magazines, no sentimental knick-knacks acquired over more than three decades of tracking down leads and digging out the big story. As he backed away from the office still looking into the windows, he saw Donnie Kurtz's face reflected over his shoulder. He turned around hoping Kurtz could offer some sort of reasonable explanation, a story more comforting than the one Berman was imagining.

"Donnie, what the fuck is going on here?"

"It finally happened, Jed. You could tell it was coming for weeks now, even if Fred tried to pretend it wasn't going to. He's gone."

"What do you mean, he's gone? Where? Why?" Part of him knew the answer already, but Berman asked the questions to buy some time while the shock wave slapped across his brain.

"Exactly where, we don't know. He didn't leave a note or anything. Must have come in here last night and cleared things out so he wouldn't have to do it in front of all of us today. This is some company we work for, isn't it?"

Kurtz was way ahead of him, Berman needed to connect all the dots to catch up. "Okay, so we don't know where he is, then tell me why he's gone. This man knew more about doing the news than anyone in this room. He paid his dues and worked hard. Why would any company dump a guy like that?"

Kurtz looked straight into Berman's eyes without blinking. Berman met his gaze as long as he could, then turned away. Kurtz's voice betrayed the anger he felt.

"They gave him the boot because the numbers weren't high enough and they couldn't make as much money as they wanted to. You're not naive, Jed. You've been around this stuff long enough now to know that's how it works. We got a little spoiled here because Demarco refused to play all their silly games. If he had, I probably would've gotten the heave-ho a long time ago."

Berman struggled to control his own anger, forced himself to speak in a normal tone of voice. "Is there a memo or anything? How do you know so much?"

"The big guy came down a couple minutes after eight. Called everyone who was here together and made a very short statement. Basically admitted they dumped Fred because of the numbers. Says he's looking for someone who can come in here and give us a boost. I tried to ask about Fred's situation, but he said he couldn't talk about that with us because it's a personnel matter. That was it. In less than twenty-four hours, a man we all know and respect ceases to exist. It's fucked."

"Has anyone tried to call Demarco?"

"Yeah, a couple of people, but there's no answer. I think they may have encouraged him to get out of town until we're done reacting to all of this, or maybe he just doesn't want to talk to anyone. God, I hate this business sometimes!"

Five minutes later, as Berman sat at his desk trying to absorb the disturbing turn of events, Steve Kimmel, the anchorman, walked in. He came through the front hallway, not the back door used by most of the staff. Berman had long ago concluded that Kimmel considered himself above the rank-and-file and made that clear every day by refusing to do things just the way everyone else did. Using the front entrance and parking his car in the small front lot with the station executives sent the message that Kimmel saw himself as more of an executive, a big shot, than a run-of-the-mill reporter. Berman got along with Kimmel, but it was closer to coexistence than a real relationship.

Kimmel wore a sweatshirt and faded jeans with sandals, in place of his usual tailored suit. His dark blond hair, normally carefully coiffed and sprayed into place, showed signs of hasty brushing. He obviously had not shaved; a gray shadow lined his handsome, square jaw. Kimmel was no more than five-six, but Berman had the impression he saw himself as much more imposing. Berman tried not to react to it; he wrote it off as typical ego-driven behavior of someone who has succumbed to the seductive allure of celebrity status. After surveying the room, Kimmel planted his hands assertively on his hips and called for everyone's attention.

"Good morning, everybody. I suppose you're all a little shell-shocked by what's happened. I have to tell you I knew about it a week or so ago, but the big guy upstairs asked me to keep it under my hat. I want you to know I share your sadness. Fred Demarco is as good a news director as any station has the right to have. He brought us a long way, from a mediocre news team to within striking distance of the top. Now it's time for us to marshal our resources and get where Fred tried to take us."

As Kimmel spoke, Berman wondered what else he knew about the future. There was no mention of the recent slip in the ratings, just that clichéd jargon about going for the top. Berman figured Demarco would have puked to hear Kimmel's description of him. Kimmel went on.

"By this point, you're wondering what the hell I'm doing here at this hour and why the hell I'm making this speech. Well, here's the deal. The station is searching for a new news director, someone who can pump some serious enthusiasm into all of us and lead us out of the wilderness of third place to the top. I think they've already interviewed a couple of people. The big guy told me he hopes to have our new leader in place within three weeks. In the meantime, I've been asked to keep things moving. Since I'll still be anchoring six and eleven, I can't spend the whole day here with all of you. So what I plan on doing is coming in for the morning meetings, getting things rolling and then going back home till my usual arrival time in mid-afternoon. Of course, if there are questions or problems that I need to deal with during the day, you have my home phone number in the staff list. Don't be afraid to call. We have a ways to go to become the number one station in this market, and we don't want to lose any ground until the new news director arrives. What I'd like to hand over is a newsroom already cranking at high speed, ready for someone to show us how to truly shift into high gear. Are there any questions?"

Not surprisingly, Donnie Kurtz raised his hand. He tried to smile as he waited for Kimmel to recognize him, but Berman had the feeling Kurtz was about to attack. Kimmel nodded in Kurtz's direction.

"What is it, Donnie?"

Berman guessed right. Kurtz unloaded a barrage of anger and sarcasm.

"First of all, Steve, is it possible for you to utter an entire sentence without using trite expressions and clichés? You've been in this business a long time, I can't believe what you haven't learned about using language."

Kimmel's face turned red, but he didn't speak. Kurtz rolled on.

"Secondly, you say you knew this was going to happen. Does that mean you had a hand in knifing Fred in the back? And if so, fuck you. And third, what qualifies you to run this place 'til they find the next victim?"

Everyone in the room waited silently to see how far Kimmel would let Kurtz go. They had never seen the anchor man in this role before. When Kimmel responded, he did not return Kurtz's angry, abusive tone. He looked directly at Kurtz and measured out his words carefully.

"Donnie, the folks upstairs and I talked about how people would react to what's happening here. We called it just about right, nobody likes it, everyone has strong feelings about it and only one person is stupid enough to think he can insult me and station management and get away with it. You've survived around here under Demarco because he thought your reporting skills outweighed your negative attitude. Well, I don't share that opinion and neither does the big guy. We expected something like this out of you and what it amounts to is the last straw. I don't think you would or could be an asset to the new news director. You've just proved to me that you would most likely be a continuing pain in the ass. All of which leads to this, which is already approved by the big guy: Donnie, you're fired. We'll give you two weeks severance, but I want you out of here by noon. I'm sorry to handle something like this this way, in front of everybody. But you didn't leave me much choice. Now get the fuck out of here. We've got a meeting to get through and news to gather."

Kurtz had been standing by his desk. As he listened to Kimmel he wilted into his chair and held his head in his hands. He remained in that position as the rest of the staff gathered in a circle only a few feet away and started shaping the day's assignments. Berman had expected Kurtz to flare up after Kimmel's chilling dismissal, but he hadn't. In short order, he had lost two important colleagues, people who shared his commitment to serious journalism. With the news meeting chatter behind him, Berman logged onto his computer and sent Kurtz a message.

"Donnie, this is all too fuckin' strange to believe. Meet me at Jobo's at 6:30. I'll buy the first round."

Kurtz raised his head when his computer beep signalled the arrival of Berman's message. He punched it up on his screen and then looked across the room. He flashed the okay sign and dropped his head back into his hands. A few minutes later he left the newsroom and returned with two large cardboard boxes. He dumped his notebooks, tapes and trinkets into the boxes and carried them out of the newsroom. The meeting had already ended; reporters were on the phone or heading out the door on assignment. A couple of them stopped Kurtz in the parking lot to shake his hand or give him a hug. As they got into the news cars, Kurtz climbed into his Jeep and drove off.

By the time Berman reached Jobo's, Kurtz had six empty beer glasses lined up in front of him and a half-empty glass in his hand. He motioned Jed to a chair beside him. "Welcome to the celebration, Jed. I've been planning this for a long time."

"Donnie, I'm sorry this happened. This can't be good for you or for the station. You're a pro. We need your talent and experience."

Kurtz spoke slowly when he responded. "You don't need me at that shithole and I sure as hell don't need those people. I gave them some of the best years of my life and what do they give me, first chance they get? The shaft. I say fuck 'em all." He finished off the glass of beer in his hand and waved to the waitress to bring him another.

"Are you sure this is the way you want to end it, Donnie?" Kurtz asked.

"Fuck, Jed, it's basically been over for a while now, since Demarco started bringing in the hired guns from the consultants. Those people have no interest in real news. They're promotions experts, trained to boost ratings at the expense of serious journalism. The hell with it. I'm better off without them."

Berman understood Kurtz's frustration, but he couldn't help thinking that Donnie still felt the urge to report, in spite of the crap. "Listen, Donnie, when this all cools down, maybe you can talk them into taking you back. It'd be good for you and for us."

Kurtz spun around and glared at Berman. "No fuckin' way, Jed. I will never lower myself to beg those fucking assholes to take me back. I say fuck 'em all." He lifted the full glass the waitress had brought to the table. "Join me in a toast, Jed. To all the great stories down the drain and to the crap people are going to get from now on."

"Donnie, I didn't mean to get you fired up. It's been a tough day. I just hate to see you throw it all away."

Kurtz seemed to sober up a little when he heard the sincerity in Berman's voice. "Listen, Jed, I appreciate you coming down here to share my misery. But I can handle it. Maybe you should go so I can sit here and feel sorry for myself."

"Are you all right to get home?" Berman asked.

"Hell, yes. And if I'm not, I'll take a cab. What the hell, I won't need my Jeep tomorrow morning, will I?" He patted Berman on the shoulder. "You can take off. I'll just be here a little longer."

Berman shook Kurtz's hand and walked out.

*   *   *

Early the next day, Autry Domain arrived. He set up camp in Demarco's office, but he had little to say to the rest of the newsroom. In the afternoon, when Kimmel came back to anchor the evening shows, he and Autry sat together in the office, looking through some kind of files. When Kimmel left the office to work on the newscasts, Domain assumed the position Berman had noticed during his first visit: leaning back in what had been Demarco's chair, feet on the desk, telephone to his ear, occasionally gesturing in the air as he made some sort of point to whoever was on the other end. Kimmel had given orders to have every newscast taped, and the tapes were delivered after each show to Domain, if he was still in the building.

Domain's seige of the office lasted nearly a week before he came bounding out one afternoon with bags in hand heading for the airport. This time Kimmel would drive him. Domain nodded to a couple of reporters as he walked by. They returned a perfunctory greeting and got back to whatever they were doing. Berman still wasn't sure what language Autry Domain spoke. He knew he didn't understand much of it and he distrusted what he did understand. Domain was clearly in charge as the station looked for Demarco's replacement. Berman could see some value in getting advice from this man, but it made no sense to him that station management would let him tell them who to hire and what to do with their newscasts. From talking to Demarco, Berman knew that the general manager had always practiced a laissez faire brand of supervision, giving his top people a lot of room to manuever in their part of the organization. Demarco had always thought it worked well. The G.M. wasn't a journalist and Demarco wasn't a business executive; as long as they each did their own jobs well, the station came out on top. The point was that they managed to do it without turning to an outsider, someone who really didn't know the company or the community. *The Chronicle* had hired consultants on a few occasions while he was there, but Berman never felt their influence in the day-to-day routines of the newsroom. Now, this consultant, with his expensive suits and self-important air, appeared to hold all the cards. What bothered Berman was that Domain refused to show those cards to the staff. It made Berman feel as if his years of experience, and the combined experience of the news staff, counted for nothing. Autry Domain, advisor to giant network affiliates and the networks themselves, sat in the driver's seat. Where he was leading TV 10 remained to be seen.

The search for a news director lasted four weeks. Domain did not return, but Berman heard Kimmel greet him by name frequently when he answered the phone in Demarco's office. No one mentioned Donnie Kurtz. His empty desk served as a mute reminder of his sudden departure. His going triggered mixed feelings among the staff. On one hand, Kurtz represented the classic broadcast journalist, steady, aggressive, and accurate, someone you could always count on to deliver a decent story. On the other hand, his bristly temperament had rubbed most people the wrong way at one time or another. He had fallen into his darker moods more frequently in recent years, and no one enjoyed being the target of his wrath when he reached critical mass and decided to unload. They laughed at his sarcasm during the morning meetings, but they avoided spending time with him during lunch or after work. Berman mostly felt regret. He hadn't minded Kurtz's abrasiveness. They had respected each other as professionals and had stayed out of each other's way on stories. Neither of them possessed an inordinate desire for "face time," as they referred to time spent in front of the camera. If management had decided to drive out anyone who raised objections, Berman worried, it might be just a matter of time until his turn came.

Disappointed as he was with recent events, he wanted to be here. He intended to avoid doing or saying anything that would give management an excuse to toss him out. For the moment, he wasn't really worried about it. If the station took its cues from Autry Domain, he should be in good shape. Domain had only praise for his work. Of course, in his skeptical reporter's mind he wondered how sincere Domain was in any comments he made. Now and then he pictured himself working in the *Chronicle* newsroom. It was tempting to wax nostalgic about the good old days, but he denied himself the luxury. He tried to stay focused on doing the best job he could where he was.

Autry Domain returned on the last Friday in September. This time he didn't come into the newsroom, but carried his bags straight upstairs to the G.M.'s office. Word flashed around the building that he had an attractive young man with him, about twenty-five, dark brown hair, cut short, and wearing an expensive-looking suit much like Domain's. Kimmel's face darkened when Berman brought him the report. Berman guessed that Kimmel feared Domain might be looking for more than a news director.

"Steve, you don't look so good. Do you feel all right?"

"Yeah, I'm fine. I have to admit I wish I knew Autry a little better. He's been calling me a lot to ask little questions about our newsroom, but I haven't heard anything about the search. I don't even know if this guy he's got with him is a candidate or what. I have to assume he'll bring him down here eventually."

"They say he's pretty smooth looking," Berman needled. " Are you a little worried management could be looking to kill two birds with one stone by hiring an anchor/news director?"

Kimmel shook his head back and forth several times, as though shaking water out of his ears in a swimming pool.

"No, I don't think they'd do that. I've got a year and a half left on my contract. They'd have to buy me out."

"Hey, if they really want this fresh start, what better way than to clear the decks of all the old faces, anchors, reporters, whatever. They obviously had no problem ditching Kurtz."

"C'mon, Jed, cut that out. You and I both know that Kurtz was a pain in the ass, even if he did manage to do some good reporting. He just never knew when to stop pushing it. I guarantee you, if he hadn't gone when he did, he would have been the first man out the door when the new guy arrives."

A knock on the door interrupted their conversation. Berman turned around to see Autry Domain walk in, followed by the mystery man. Most of the eyes in the newsroom had followed the pair into the office, and now everyone stood watching the office doorway. Domain took charge of the space immediately.

"Steve and Jed, I'd like you to meet John Lenhard. John, this is Steve Kimmel, lead anchor here, and Jed Berman, ace investigative reporter." He waited while they all shook hands. "Gentlemen, John is TV 10's new news director. Should we introduce him to the rest of the staff?" Without waiting for an answer, he ushered Lenhard, Berman and Kimmel into the newsroom and clapped his hands.

"Gather round, everyone. I have important news for you."

His audience was eager to hear what he had to say. Photogs and reporters came running from the editing bays to join the crowd.

"I'd like all of you to meet John Lenhard. He's your new news director. John's presence here this afternoon marks the end of an intensive nationwide search for someone who can step into the TV 10 system and help all of you make the difference that will mean a number one rating for your excellent news product. John comes to you from Philadelphia, where he served as executive producer for the award-winning WPAL-TV. I have no doubt about his ability to lead you where you all want to go. John, do you want to say a few words?"

Lenhard smiled easily, taking in everyone in the room with a sweeping glance of his deep blue eyes. Berman thought he seemed awfully relaxed for a young man about to take on the responsiblity of leading his first news department. Behind the smile, Berman sensed plenty of self-confidence. Lenhard's first comments confirmed the suspicion.

"I don't have a lot to say right now, " he began in a warm, deep voice. "I am very pleased to join all of you. Autry's been showing me tapes of what you're doing right now. It's a good start. We obviously have some real talent in this news department. I'm glad for the chance to work with all of you and help get us in first place where we belong. WPAL was in third place when I signed on there, and now they're number one. I don't mean to brag, but I know I had a hand in making that happen, and I'm confident we can do it here, too. I want you to see me as an enabler, someone who can help each of you reach down into the potential you already have and make it explode into some really dynamic TV news reporting. Together, we're gonna take this market by storm." He raised his arm to look at his watch. " I have to take care of some personal matters this afternoon, like getting moved into my new apartment. I'd like to meet with all of you first thing Monday morning to get acquainted and start plotting strategy for our TV 10 takeover. If it's okay with all of you, I'm gonna take off and see you next week."

Domain had the last word.

"There you have it, my friends. This is a marriage made in heaven. Good luck to you, John, and good luck to TV 10 News. You're gonna do great things. I have to head home tonight, so I'll take my leave now and look forward to working with all of you soon. Thanks for your attention and have a nice weekend."

He took Lenhard's arm and escorted him from the newsroom before anyone had a chance to greet him.

*   *   *

Berman made a point of getting to work early the following Monday, hoping to observe John Lenhard's tenure from its opening moments, but Lenhard was already there, in his office, door closed and blinds drawn. Demarco had never closed the blinds in the time Berman worked for him. Of course, that didn't necessarily mean Lenhard couldn't be as good a news director as Demarco. He was a lot younger, but his record was hard to argue with. He'd been in the big time most of his working life. Surely that meant good things for TV 10.

Everyone appeared to have the same idea Berman had; by 8:45, every desk was occupied. At 9:00 straight up, as Demarco had always referred to the time when the minute and second hands pointed directly to the twelve and the hour hand delineated the ninth hour (he had told Berman it was a leftover from his days in radio), the office door swung open and a neatly dressed Lenhard stepped out. He let his gaze travel across the entire newsroom before he spoke.

"Good morning, everyone. In case you're wondering, I managed to get moved into my apartment and I'm ready to focus my attention on all of you and the task ahead of us. We might as well get right to it. I understand you're used to holding a morning news meeting to plot the day's stories. I'm okay with that, but I expect each of you to have ideas to suggest, rather than waiting for me to hand you an assignment. Are there any questions before we get down to it?"

Berman carefully phrased a question to get a better idea of Lenhard's news philosophy.

"John, I'm Jed Berman, one of the newer kids on this block. I hope you won't mind if I ask for some clarification on how you like to do these things. With our last news director, we had some breathing room to pursue stories as we became aware of them and then we could bring a progress report to the morning meeting. Most of the time Fred Demarco simply acknowledged what we were working on, made note of it and sent us on our way, trusting that we would bring back something good. Is that routine acceptable to you?"

Lenhard looked pleased with the question.

"Jed, I've heard a lot about your work here. In fact, at the risk of embarrassing you in front of your colleagues, you were one of the selling points that convinced me to take this job. Sure, if you've got something working, go for it. I don't want to stand in the way of good journalism. Especially in the early going, I can't presume to have the contacts to pull out the really good stories. I'm trusting all of you to do that. Once I get my sea legs, so to speak, I hope to contribute more seriously to the process. And, as I'm sure you've already been doing, it's likely we'll need each of you to turn a package each day, so you might have to dig out that great story piecemeal and then put it all together when it's ready. Beyond that, I say 'let 'er rip!' " His face broadened in a wide smile as he finished responding. "Any other questions?" No one spoke up. "Okay, let's get to work."

As people moved toward the center of the room, Lenhard ducked back in the office and came out with several dry erase markers and a board leaning on a stand. He set the stand at the head of the circle and pulled the cap off a marker.

"Okay, what have we got?"

As reporters suggested story ideas, Lenhard wrote down slugs for them in a list on the board. After one rotation around the circle, the list had eight slugs:

> annexation
> measles shots

highway funding/speeders
teen murder
repeat rapist
council resignation
school funding
strip joint/neighbor

Lenhard stepped in front of the board, with his back to the group, and stared at the list. Then he picked up the eraser on the ledge at the bottom of the board and stepped to the side so everyone could see the board. He raised the eraser above his shoulder in his right hand as he pointed to the list with his left.

"This is a good list. It's what I would expect from an average day's news meeting. Now let me tell you which of these stories we're going to do today and why. Annexation—how many people are likely to be directly affected by this? Fifty, maybe a hundred. This kind of shit is deadly. Unless the property in question is owned by the President or the Queen of England, nobody cares about this, except that handful of people directly involved. We ain't got time to worry about this, plus the fact that the only likely visuals are shots of an undeveloped piece of land and the meeting where they're gonna hassle over it." He lowered the eraser and swiped the word "annexation" off the board.

"Measles shots—this has possibilities. How serious is the situation here? Are there lots of families that aren't complying with the law on getting these immunizations for their kids?"

"Not a tremendous amount," Joan Kidron said. "The school corporation called yesterday and asked if we could help get the word out so they don't have to hassle with so many kids not having shots in the fall."

Lenhard screwed up his face as though he'd bitten into something sour.

"So, all we really have here is a public service announcement for the school? If they don't have a serious problem with this, like maybe an epidemic of measles or something that's threatening to shut down the system, then fuck 'em. They can find some other way to get the word out. We don't have time for that sort of stuff, either." The eraser swooped across the board and "measles" disappeared.

"What else do we have here? Highway fund/speeders—this may have possibilities. I assume this is the deal where they take away your highway funds if people are driving too fast?" People around the circle nodded to confirm his thought. "But," he paused dramatically, "has this area ever lost money because of that threat?" No one in the circle seemed to know for sure. Lenhard raised the eraser menacingly over his head. "I'm losing interest in this one very rapidly, people. Someone say something to convince me this is actually a story today."

Molly Bingham tried.

"John, this issue has been getting stranger and stranger since the feds eliminated the national 55-mile-per-hour limit. States and local areas aren't sure what it all means. I thought this might be a good time to try to sort that out. We've got state legislators home from the capital and there's a district highway office in the area. It seemed like good information if we could sort it out for local officials and motorists who are always complaining that roads aren't well maintained. Yes, I think it's news today."

Lenhard paused to absorb her reply, then wiped "highway fund/speeders" off the board.

"I appreciate your reasoning," he told her. "But we don't have a hook for it. If we start talking about highway funding tonight, out of the middle of nowhere, when there have been no new developments, nobody will pay any attention. Besides, the only time most people give a hoot about this stuff is when they have to drive over the potholes themselves on the way to work. If you want to dig into it a little more and see what else you can come up with, by all means go ahead. I'm willing to reconsider it another day, if you can put some meat on the bones."

"Let's see, our list is getting shorter and we've got to get things going here. Repeat rapist—this has possibilities, everyone hates these guys. What's the deal on this one?"

Dan Ford offered an explanation.

"The deal is this guy who has been busted for rape at least twice and now he's up on a third charge and the courts are allowing him to run around on bail. Some of his neighbors and the families of his victims think that's a dangerous situation. I thought we could track down the prosecutor and the neighbors and maybe even this guy and see what gives."

Lenhard's eyes lit up. He clapped his hands, then stopped abruptly.

"I'm sorry, I obviously don't know all of you yet. What's your name?"

"Dan Ford."

"Dan, I like it. I see this thing having a number of follow-ups to it. We raise the question about letting a repeat offender walk the streets and then we track him until he goes back behind bars. Great idea. You want to get started while we finish up here?"

Ford nodded. "Sure, I'm always glad for any extra time I can get."

Lenhard motioned toward the door. "Then get going, my man. Any special photog you'd like to work with?" Ford shook his head and the assignment editor teamed him up with the photog sitting closest to him. Lenhard returned his attention to the dwindling list.

"Council resignation—this one has me yawning already and I don't even know the details. What's the story here?"

Molly Bingham had suggested this idea, too.

"It's just an idea, John. A guy who's been on the city council in Berrington for fifty years is stepping down because of his health. I thought it might be nice to salute him with a story as he leaves public service. He's seen a lot of things change since he first got elected."

Lenhard pretended to stifle a yawn, but he smiled at Bingham.

"Thanks, but no thanks, Molly. Other than you and maybe a few members of this guy's family, I doubt if anyone cares whether this old fart leaves office or not. Besides, my general rule is: politics is boring, unless there's a good scandal. Bring me something juicy and the resignation story goes back on the board, otherwise—" He raised the eraser shoulder high and shot a stroke across the board that wiped out the "resignation" slug. Then he stepped back and looked at the short list left on the board. "C'mon, people. We don't have much left to work with here. You better start arguing a little harder for your ideas. How about school funding? What's the buzz on this one?"

It turned out to be one of Dan Ford's suggestions. He had already left the room; nobody defended it and Lenhard wiped it away.

"Last one, folks, strip joint—what gives?"

This was Berman's contribution for the morning. He offered the explanation.

"Simple deal in one way, John. Who wants a strip joint next to their home? This place was just a neighborhood bar, but it started moving in this direction a while ago. The zoning in the area allows adult dancing, not stripping. The owner says that's all he wants to put on. The neighbors say that's bad enough but they're betting he wants the women to go all the way. They say they won't stand for it. It's a NIMBY kind of deal, but I think it has broader First Amendment implications, too. Does the dance club owner have the right to offer this kind of expression? Where does the community stand on the essentially moral issue of nude dancing? Today's story just introduces the whole thing. The city council is supposed to hold a hearing on the zoning approval tonight. Could be lots of follow-ups 'til it's all said and done."

Lenhard applauded again. "Sounds good, Jed. Let me know around lunch time how it's shaping up. Can you get some pix of the dancers?" Berman thought he could. "Good, that will jazz it up nicely. And get some of those pix back here as early as you can so we can use them to promote the story for tonight. We start showing a little T and A now and then, I'll bet we'll get those ratings up." He took a deep breath and let it out in a rush. "Okay, what are the rest of you doing today?"

Cindy Ozick raised her hand.

"John, you skipped over the teen murder story. That's a kid they picked up last night in the shooting death of another teenager about two weeks ago. It's got some pretty strange details associated with it. We probably need to be careful if we're going to report on it."

"What's strange about it?"

"Oh, they're saying it may have some sort of cult connection. I don't know if it's devil worship or what, but I have a couple of leads on the family and some kids he hung out with. I might be able to pull some background together to go with the basic nuts-and-bolts."

"Oh, yeah!" Lenhard's eyes shone as he listened to Ozick. "That sounds great to me. Who wants to do the

178

nuts-and-bolts?" Tim Bricker raised his hand. "Okay," Lenhard said, and paused. "What's your name?"

"Tim Bricker."

"Okay, Tim, get on it and stay in touch with—," he paused again and pointed to Ozick.

"Cindy Ozick."

"Right, Tim, stay in touch with Cindy so the stories complement each other rather than overlap. Cindy, I want you live from the murder scene at six." Above "teen murder" he wrote "murder nuts and bolts." "Anyone else without an assignment will make beat calls and run on spot stuff. Let's get going." He clapped his hands again, spun on his heel and walked back into his office. A moment later he shut the door. As Berman walked past the door on the way to his desk, he heard the news director on the phone.

"Autry? John Lenhard. We're off and running. I came on pretty strong, as you suggested. They seemed to take it pretty well, even when I sank a bunch of their ideas for stories." That was all Berman heard, but it was enough to plant a seed of concern. He didn't know Autry Domain very well, and he didn't know John Lenhard at all, and he really didn't know what to think of a news director who had to turn to a consultant all the time to know how to put together a newscast, if that's what the immediate phone call meant. Lenhard had certainly come across forcefully. Demarco had generally allowed reporters to follow their instincts and bring back the stories they believed would interest the most viewers and have the most impact. Based on first impressions, he had the feeling Lenhard brought a much different frame of mind. It would probably take a while until the full picture of his news philosophy appeared. Lenhard had certainly liked his idea this time around. After the recent turmoil in the newsroom, Berman hoped that was a harbinger of good times to come. Everyone needed some reassurance. Unfortunately, as Berman saw it, they didn't all get it in Lenhard's first morning news meeting. Maybe it would come later.

On Friday night, Berman had dinner with Jane Filips and Donnie Kurtz, whom he hadn't seen since the day Kimmel threw him out. Kurtz wanted to know about the new guy.

"I was talking to Bingham yesterday," Kurtz confided in a conspiratorial tone. "She didn't sound too impressed with this Lenhard guy. What do you think, Jed?"

Jane jumped in before Berman could answer.

"He thinks the guy is probably a puppet, simply doing what the consultant wants, right, Jed?" She leaned toward Kurtz. "He probably won't tell you that; so far he's trying to take the high road on what's going on at the station." She finished and sat back in her chair with a contented smile on her face. Berman paused another moment before he spoke.

"Donnie, it's all happening so fast over there I'm really not sure what I think. I don't want to condemn this guy before he has a chance to prove what he's worth, but on the other hand, first impressions are a little iffy. You had a lot more experience in TV news to draw on in evaluating someone like this. Maybe he's just the new generation of hot-shot news directors—young, aggressive, market savvy—and maybe he's much more in tune with what news should be about for today's viewers. Yes," he turned and looked at Jane, "I have the impression Autry Domain is very close to him, I mean, Domain introduced him to the newsroom rather than the G.M., but that doesn't mean Domain is calling the shots. At the morning meetings, he seems to know what he thinks. He's pretty good at shooting down ideas that people bring up. He's pushing people to come up with more ideas, sometimes racier ideas. Maybe that's what it takes to be number one these days. I don't really know. It's still pretty early."

Kurtz wanted to know more.

"Okay, that's a kind of noncommittal general reaction. How's he treating you? Demarco never laid a hand on you. He mostly just asked what you were working on and let you get on with it. What's this guy think of your style?"

"So far, so good. I've been able to come up with some pretty good stuff since he got here, like the topless dance place. His eyes light up when you give him something like that."

"Then what kind of stories does he shoot down?"

"The kind Molly Bingham brings up, stories that touch the personal side of the community, like a veteran politician calling it quits. Lenhard doesn't seem to have much heart for that kind of thing. He also refused to do a story on measles shots to help the schools spread the word about mandatory immunizations. Oh, and one other step he's already taken: the public affairs shows are gone. He says they're nothing but talking heads without any good production values. They make him yawn, and anything that makes him yawn is gone."

"Doesn't the FCC have something to say about public affairs and dealing with community problems and issues? Can he just dump those shows, talking heads or not?" Kurtz wanted to know.

"It certainly seems like it. They're gone. That's the biggest worry I have after a week of his leadership. He's clearly in touch with the consultants and market research. Much of his criticism of stories deals with why they won't attract enough of the right viewers. But he doesn't seem real interested in the life of the community, the quality-of-life questions, that touch the average citizen. You remember how we used to point fingers at the networks and major market stations for not seeming to care about those things, for pushing the more sensational stuff. I get a feeling that may be the way we're headed now, too. I guess we'll just have to wait and see."

"You can wait and see," Kurtz answered, almost belligerently, "but I've had a bellyful. Call me when you know where it's all going to end up. I'm going out and find a real job."

Jane put her hand on Kurtz's arm.

"Donnie, I hate to hear you talk like that. You have so much experience; you've been at it for so long. You can't just walk away now, can you? Wouldn't one of the other stations be glad to pick you up?"

Kurtz was pleased by her compliment, but unswayed by her argument.

"Oh, yeah, both of the other stations have called me. I told 'em to get stuffed. If the business is headed where I think it's headed, I'm glad I'm out." He turned to Berman. "And I'll bet you anything that one day you're going to wish you'd gotten out, too."

Berman didn't feel like arguing. He looked at Kurtz and Jane and shook his head pensively. "We'll see, Donnie, we'll see."

*　　*　　*

Winter hit Pruitville just ahead of the November ratings period. John Lenhard welcomed both with open arms. The first snow flurries drifted past the newsroom windows just after noon. Lenhard came bouncing out of his office, rubbing his hands together. He called together everyone who was in the room.

"This is it, folks," he told them, a little out of breath. "This is when we start to show this market who's boss. It's time to gear up for Weatherwatch 10. We're gonna cover the arrival of winter weather like it's never been covered before—conditions, how to get ready for it, what's happening on the roads, being sure you have enough food stocked up. You name it, we're gonna have it in our six o'clock show."

Berman had been making some phone calls to dig into research a local college prof was doing on an emerging socio-economic group he called the working poor. He was hoping to introduce the topic tonight, using an interview with the scholar and a couple of families caught in the downward spiral of lost jobs replaced by low paying jobs leading to drastically reduced lifestyles. Instead, he found himself in a hardware store, interviewing a clerk about what tools and supplies you needed to deal with snow. At six, the entire first block of the show was dedicated to the arrival of winter. Three reporters were live, one from downtown Pruitville on city street conditions, one outside of town along a narrow country road, and Berman was live from the hardware store, demonstrating how to scatter ice-melting compounds and the best kind of snow shovel to buy. From the anchor desk, Steve and Sally advised people on what foods they should make sure to stockpile, and Chris Sisko, the weather guy, designed extra graphics to show how snow forms in the air.

Lenhard watched the program with glee, clapping his hands and telling anyone standing near him that TV 10 was beating the hell out of the competition.

"We're kicking their asses," he repeated, without making eye contact with those around him. "We are kicking their asses."

Berman felt a little silly playing his part in what Lenhard had Kimmel and West introduce as comprehensive team coverage. The snow had stopped about an hour before news time, after depositing less than half an inch over the area. Nonetheless, the reports triggered a run on local supermarkets, which promptly ran out of bread, milk and soup, the same products TV 10 told them they should be sure to load up on as the harsh reality of winter bore down on them. Jane Filips found the whole effort amusing when she met Berman for dinner at Brady's that night.

"My god, what a storm that was, Jed!" she marveled, with a twinkle in her eye. "I'll tell you, if you hadn't shown me which end of the snow shovel to hold and how to make that smooth arc with the ice-melter bag to get even coverage on my sidewalk I don't know what I would have done. Of course, the fact that I could have swept that little bit of snow off my sidewalk doesn't mean your advice wasn't worthwhile." She laughed and patted Berman on the hand. "Whose idea was it to get so worked up about a few flurries in November?"

Berman gave her a steady look, tinged with a touch of exasperation.

"You know damn well whose idea it was. Lenhard was so excited I thought he was going to piss his pants. He thinks we showed up everyone in town. He also thinks viewers will see it as evidence of our tremendous strength as a news team, how we're able to swarm all over the big story." He shook his head slowly. "I hope he's right, but I have this nagging feeling all we managed to do is make a whole lot out of nothing. People around here have seen real winter weather and they know how to handle it. Today's little squall was peanuts. It's a little embarrassing to be out doing what we did. What will we do when the real stuff comes along?"

Two days later, Lenhard brought some notes from a phone conversation with him when he came out for the morning meeting. After everyone else had an assignment, he turned to Berman and handed him two sheets of paper from a notepad.

"Jed, here's your story for today. I got a call from a woman who lives in Berrington. Seems her neighbor is a three-time convicted child molester who's looking at a fourth set of charges. She's upset because this guy continues to fondle children every time they let him out, yet the judge made no effort to keep him locked up until his next trial." Berman wasn't sure where Lenhard was going with this. What he'd heard so far didn't necessarily qualify as a great story idea.

"That would probably upset me, too," he admitted, "if I lived in that neighborhood and there were innocent kids anywhere near a guy like that. But I'm guessing that's how the law works. Whatever his prior convictions, he's innocent until proven guilty on this one, which means the judge has to set bail and if the creep can make it, he walks. I don't mean to be rude, John, but where's the story here, other than the woman's displeasure?"

Berman thought he detected a little impatience in Lenhard's reply, along with some defensiveness.

"Hey, the woman's displeasure is plenty to hang a story on. You can probably find other people in the neighborhood who feel the same way. Why not talk to the judge and find out why he let this guy out. And talk to the guy, his name's there on the paper, along with his address and the woman's address. I'd say there's lots of story there." His face reddened slightly as he spoke, his words tumbling out in a rush.

Berman thought it over for a moment before he answered. Despite an occasional silly assignment, he still had little problem with Lenhard. For the most part, he was pursuing the stories he considered important, and Lenhard seemed to focus most of his attention on younger reporters who needed more help gathering and writing the news. Berman was reluctant to say anything that might antagonize Lenhard, but this story was heading down a road that made him uncomfortable before he even left the building.

"John, help me understand how to do this, if there's no law saying this man must stay in jail because he has prior criminal convictions, even for child molesting."

Lenhard took a deep breath and let it out slowly before he spoke.

"Look, Jed, all you have to do is get the complaint on tape from a couple of people who live over there. Try to get the judge to defend his action. And then find this guy. I want shots of you following him down the street, asking him why he should be allowed to wander around and endanger children, after being convicted of these awful crimes three times before. Picture it—this pervert walking down the street with you as the good guy, calling him to account for his evil past. Mix in close-up shots of the concerned mother and maybe even some shots of neighborhood kids, and we've got a winner. People will go through the roof knowing this guy's out there on the street. And I promise you the last thing many of them will ask is whether he has a right to be there. Think about the ratings we can generate for tonight's six o'clock show with this."

Berman sensed there was no use trying to argue the case.

"Okay, John, we'll see what we can do. Can someone here give the judge a call and see if he has time to see us? Considering that the case has yet to come to trial, the judge may not be willing to say anything. Sometimes they refuse to talk even when the trial is over. Let me know if you get something set up. In the meantime, we'll be in the neighborhood talking to residents and trying to track down the sleazebag." He slipped Lenhard's notes into his shirt pocket, pulled on his coat, and grabbed his notebook. Lenhard teamed him up with Carol, the photog who had shared the shooting on the hillside with him.

"Do good work out there, you two. It's been a while since you brought us something really exciting, like that wild man on the mountain." Berman and Carol looked at each other and walked out without responding. Lenhard watched them go, then walked in his office and picked up the phone. A moment later he was deep in animated conversation with Autry Domain.

*   *   *

Berman and Carol found the child molester's neighborhood in Berrington on the first try. If the address of the woman who called Lenhard was correct, the convict lived in a fairly nice house next door. Carol pulled into the caller's driveway and waited in the car while Berman knocked on the door. They had phoned the woman from the car on the way over; the door opened quickly and a plain-looking young woman stepped onto the front porch and pulled the door shut behind her.

"I'd ask you in," she told Berman in a hushed voice, "but my youngest just fell asleep. She was up all night with a fever. I suspect she picked up some sort of flu thing from one of the neighbor kids." She jabbed her thumb toward the molester's house. "I hope it wasn't one of his brats."

Berman tried to introduce himself.

"I'm Jed Berman with TV 10 News."

The woman gave him a strange look and punched him in the shoulder.

"Of course, I know who you are. I watch you folks every night. Do you think I'd just step out of my house and start pouring out my soul to a perfect stranger? You people are like family. You're in my living room more often than my husband."

After all these months, the familiarity people felt toward someone they met only through the TV screen still struck Berman as a little odd. He often felt uncomfortable talking to people who seemed to think they knew him quite well, when they had, in fact, no idea at all who he really was or what he was like. The Promotions department sold them a bill of goods and the die-hard viewers fell for it hook, line and sinker. He suspected that this woman would willingly answer any question he asked. He decided he'd better get to it.

"I'm glad you're watching and I'm glad you called us with your concern. If you don't mind waiting a minute, I'll get my photographer and we'll catch a quick interview with you. We can do it outside here with the molester's house in the background."

"That would be fine," the woman said. "I guess this is my five minutes of fame, thanks to Jamie Wyeth or whoever that artist was who said we'd all get a chance to be famous." She giggled, clearly pleased to have a news celebrity like Berman on her porch in her neighborhood. Berman motioned to Carol as he walked toward the car. She jumped out and grabbed her camera from the backseat. He opened the trunk and fished out the tripod.

"Do you need any kind of light or anything?"

Carol shook her head and walked over to the porch with her camera. She extended her hand to the woman she had been watching from the car.

"Hi ! I'm Carol, Jed's sidekick today. I need to attach a microphone to you so we can hear your comments when Jed talks to you. Don't let it bother you, you won't even know it's there." She clipped a wireless mike onto the woman's blouse, near the neckline and showed her how to stuff the battery pack into the pocket of her slacks. Then she turned and took the tripod from Berman. With practiced ease, she kicked the legs open, set the tripod down with the head facing toward the house next door, and snapped the camera into the groove on top. "Okay," she said to the woman, who had grown quieter as the interview drew near, "now count to ten for me so I can make sure the microphone is working."

The woman counted, but in a voice barely half the size of the one she used to greet Berman at her front door. Some of Berman's confidence about this interview faded. It was common for people to freeze up when they realized what the electronic encounter was actually like. Berman had even run into this phenomenon at the paper, when he'd lay a tape recorder on a desk. Some people simply froze up when they confronted the gear. He knew he'd have to use the first minute or so of the interview to get this woman warmed up again.

"Okay, Carol, are we rolling?" Carol gave him a quick thumbs-up. "All right, let's do some basic housekeeping before we get into the heart of this. Could you tell me your name and spell it for me? The worst thing in the world is to do an interview with some guy from a TV station and then see him spell your name wrong on the screen. " He flashed his reassuring smile, the one that hadn't been successful many months back with the child welfare worker, Hildy Mazer. The woman's voice grew stronger as she met this simple request.

"I'm Sandra Hilverson. That's S-A-N-D-R-A, H-I-L-V-E-R-S-O-N." She paused for a moment. "You don't need my age, do you, like those awful newspaper people?"

Berman wasn't sure whether she was trying to conceal her age or trying to confess that TV 10 wasn't her only media contact. It wouldn't change things much if she intended the latter, but he was curious to know which it was.

"Have you had a lot of contact with newspaper reporters?"

"Oh, no, not before this morning. I called the Pruitville paper right before I called your station. They sent out a nice young woman who asked me a lot of questions and said she'd try to get something in the paper tonight. She took my picture and then asked how old I was. You know what?" She looked a bit impish as she told this part of her story. "I wouldn't tell her. She even tried to guess, but she was way off. Fortunately she guessed low or I would have run her out of my house." That was all Berman needed to know. He laughed gently as she finished her story and moved into the substance of the interview. In the back of his mind he felt a little irritated that the woman had given Lenhard the impression this was an exclusive. But he didn't dwell on it for long. He'd still be scooping the paper because their next edition wasn't due out until tomorrow morning. By then TV 10 would have run the story at least two times and the paper would read like a history book.

"So, Sandra, tell me what it is about your neighbor that bothers you?"

"Well, it's pretty simple. He's a pervert, been convicted a bunch of times for it already. And now he's facing another trial for doing it to some poor innocent child and they let him walk the streets while he's waiting for the judge. It scares me and a lot of other people in this neighborhood."

"Has he done anything or attempted to do anything to any of the children around here?"

"No, not yet. He's only been living here for a couple of months. That's really his girlfriend's house. After all the time he's spent in jail for abusing little kids he probably lost his own house, if he ever had one."

"Do you see him much? Does he come out and hang around where he might be able to do something to the kids?"

"No, he mostly stays inside the house, or before it got so cold he'd sit out in the back yard and smoke. I've never actually talked to him."

The uneasiness Berman felt before he left the station started to grow.

"So how do you know about his past?"

"It was in the paper. I got his mail by mistake one day and then the next day the paper talked about how he's been convicted at least three times before and now he's charged again and the address was the same so I knew it was the same guy. They said he could really go away for a long time if they convict him. I sure hope they do."

"What do you and your neighbors think the judge should have done with this guy?"

"Oh, that's an easy one. They oughta throw him in jail and never let him out where he even has a chance of hurting anyone."

"Have you shared your concern with the prosecutor or the judge?"

"Yes, I did call the prosecutor's office. But he told me there's no way they can hold him if he makes bail after he's arraigned. He said it's not like he's charged with murder where they don't set bail. So, they have to let him out."

"And you think they ought to change those rules?

"Absolutely. Why bother having jails and courts if people like him are going to be able to walk around and threaten innocent children all the time."

Berman had heard enough.

"Okay, that's all we need. I'd like to get some pictures

of this guy. Is there a special time of day when he's most likely to come out?"

"Sometimes he goes out and gets fast food and brings it home for lunch. I don't think he's working anywhere right now. Probably got fired when his boss heard what a creep he is."

Berman wanted to get away from this house and this woman. "Well, thanks for talking to us. You raise an interesting question. We'll have to see what we can find out about it. Oh, I almost forgot. Would you mind if we got a few shots of you with your kids, maybe going for a little walk down the street?"

"No way in hell am I parading my kids past that house for his pleasure. You can come in and take some pictures, if you want to."

Berman and Carol hauled the camera and tripod inside and shot a couple minutes of Mrs. Hilverson with her two youngest children tumbling around the family room. A few minutes later they backed out of Hilverson's drive and pulled up in front of the house next door. Knowing the man inside might be a little camera shy, Berman had Carol rolling as he walked up to the front door and pushed the door bell. As he waited, he noticed someone pull aside the curtain over the front window and peek out. A moment later the front door swung open and a young man, about thirty, with a crisp, almost military-style haircut and an ordinary looking face peered out at Berman from the darkened interior of the house. Berman shuffled to the side to make sure Carol was getting a shot of the guy.

"Good morning, sir. I'm Jed Berman with TV 10 News. Are you Sanford Gilliam?"

The man answered through the storm door without opening it.

"Yes, I am. What do you want?"

"We're doing a story on the charges you're facing and the reaction to those charges and to your presence in this neighborhood."

Gilliam showed no emotional response to Berman's explanation. He simply stepped back and shut the door, leaving Berman to stare at the Christmas wreath hanging in the middle of it. He turned around to Carol.

"Did you get a decent shot of him?"

"Yeah, it's usable, but I'd rather have him outside someplace where we can really see him. Wanna stake him out for a while and see if he comes out?"

"He'd probably see us out here and never come out. But we could hide up the block and follow him if he goes out for that food run Mrs. Hilverson told us about."

They made noisy and obvious work of loading their gear back into the car, but Berman thought he caught a quick glimpse of someone peering out at them again from behind the curtain. He pretended not to notice and climbed in his side of the car as Carol got in her side. They drove around the block and parked back far enough to be out of sight from the house but close enough to see a car pull out of Gilliam's driveway. They were about to give up and head back to the station when Carol spotted a blue Chevy backing into the street. As it pulled into their line of sight, they saw Gilliam behind the wheel. Without looking in their direction, he wheeled the car around and headed out of the neighborhood. Carol started the news car and followed a block behind, guessing that Gilliam was heading to the strip of fast food joints on the edge of Berrington.

As Gilliam approached Burger King, Carol accelerated, ready to pull into the lot right behind him. Berman held the camera, ready to hand it to Carol so she could jump out and get some shots of Gilliam if he parked his car and walked into the restaurant. He still hadn't noticed them. He pulled into a parking space not far from the restaurant door and stepped out of his car. Carol slammed on the brakes, grabbed the camera from Berman and jumped out. Berman sprinted around from the other side. With Carol rolling, Berman approached Gilliam.

"Mr. Gilliam, can we talk to you for a moment?"

Gilliam wheeled around to see Carol and Berman coming up fast from behind. This time he looked angry.

"Look, I don't have anything to say to you. What right do you have to hassle me like this? If you don't knock it off you'll be hearing from my lawyer."

Berman asked the question he knew Lenhard would want him to ask.

"Mr. Gilliam, what right do you have to walk around a neighborhood full of innocent children when you're facing another charge of child molestation after already being convicted three times?"

Gilliam kept walking and talking.

"You listen to me, you creep. You don't know anything about me. And the law says I can be out here if I post bail, which I did. That's how the system works."

"But don't your multiple convictions prove you continue to be a threat to any child you're near? Your neighbors think you should be locked up until your trial."

"I'm not a threat to anyone. I did my time before and I posted my bail to get out now. That's all I have to do. I don't owe you or the people in that neighborhood anything, so get the hell out of my way."

Berman couldn't believe Gilliam had this much to say. A more likely response would have been no comment at all. And if Gilliam's attorney had been here, Berman felt certain that's exactly what would have happened. He decided to push for as much as he could get.

"Did you molest that child in Pruitville?"

This time Gilliam was mute. Berman tried again.

"Is there any reason to think you won't continue to molest children every chance you get?"

Gilliam was silent.

"Does your girlfriend know about you? How can she put up with that?"

Gilliam stopped and looked straight at Berman, his eyes dark and cold.

"Now you listen to me, shithead, leave my girlfriend out of this. You don't know nothin'. So stop hassling me or I'll sue the ass off of you, that cameraman and your bullshit TV station." He turned toward the restaurant, took two more quick steps and disappeared inside. Berman looked at Carol.

"Did you get all that?"

"Yep, but how much of it can you use?"

"Maybe we'll let Lenhard decide."

They piled the gear in the car and drove back to Pruitville.

Lenhard told them to use nearly all of it, with the profanities edited out. And he told them to stay on Gilliam's tail, which they did. Their next encounter came a week later when Gilliam's lawyer filed a motion to have the latest molesting charges against his client dismissed. Berman and Carol were staked out at the lone entrance to the courthouse in Pruitville an hour before the hearing. Fifteen minutes before court was scheduled to start, they spotted Gilliam pulling into a parking space a block away from the courthouse. They hustled down the sidewalk toward the car and reached it just as Gilliam and a young woman got out. They assumed the woman was Gilliam's girlfriend. Carol rolled the camera and Berman started firing even before Gilliam reached the sidewalk.

"Mr. Gilliam, Jed Berman from TV 10 News. Do you

195

have an answer to the question yet: What right do you have to be out walking around after what you've done to children?" Carol zoomed in tight on Gilliam's face as he and the woman headed for the courthouse. He didn't look at Berman or say anything, but Carol could see the muscles in his jaw flexing. Berman changed his tack; he posed his next question to Gilliam's companion.

"Ma'am, I'm Jed Berman with TV 10 News. Mind if I ask you a question or two about the man you're with?"

The woman looked frightened as the camera swung over to point at her. She clutched Gilliam's arm and leaned over to whisper something in his ear. Berman kept at it, sidestepping quickly to stay with the couple as they walked rapidly toward the courthouse.

"Seriously, ma'am, this guy's a convicted child molester. How can you hang around with someone like that? He just keeps on messing with children. Do you approve of that?"

Berman was focusing so hard on the woman that he didn't realize, until it was too late, that Gilliam had taken a step away from her and toward him. In one swift motion he shoved his foot between Berman's shins and tripped him. Berman fell forward onto the concrete, his arms stretched over his head. His face hit the pavement hard; pain shot through his nose and mouth. He heard a loud, ugly laugh that Gilliam tossed over his shoulder as he and the woman stepped quickly away. Carol didn't realize Berman had gone down until she heard him groaning. She moved aside as Gilliam and the woman swept by and shut down the camera. When she looked toward Berman, he was raising his head to watch Gilliam starting up the courthouse steps; blood trickled from his nose and mouth. She ran over to him, put the camera down and helped him up.

"Geez, Jed, what happened? Did you trip on the side-walk?"

"No," Berman answered in a voice muffled by the handkerchief he held up to his face, "the bastard stuck his foot out and I fell over it. I never saw it coming. He's not only a pervert, he's a low-down son-of-a-bitch."

"Is there anything I can do for you?"

"No, just hang outside the courtroom and wait for Gilliam to come back out. I'd better get inside and see what happens."

"Are you sure you're okay? I can go in and listen if you want to get cleaned up."

"Nah, I can handle it." He climbed the steps and walked into the courthouse.

The judge took Gilliam's motions under advisement and the whole hearing was over in less than fifteen minutes. Instead of leaving the building, Gilliam and his girl-friend followed his lawyer into a conference room and closed the door. Berman and Carol camped outside, waiting for them. Thirty minutes passed before Gilliam pushed open the courthouse door. By then Berman's nose had stopped bleeding, but his lips were swollen and he had a feeling his eyes were going to turn black. When Gilliam saw him he burst out laughing, and whispered something to his girlfriend, who started laughing, too. But they brushed by Carol and the camera without comment. Berman took a deep breath and started jogging after them with Carol by his side. He called out to the couple as they sprinted toward their car.

"Are you really going to fight this charge, Mr. Gilliam? The police say they have rock solid evidence you molested a six-year-old girl in the alley behind her house. Her name's Alison, by the way. Don't you feel any remorse for all the harm you've caused these kids? Don't you think they should put you away where you can't ever hurt anyone again?"

Without turning around or responding, Gilliam reached in his pocket and pulled out a remote button to unlock his car. He and the woman parted neatly as they reached the car. In less than ten seconds the car's engine fired up and Gilliam gunned his way into traffic, tires squealing. Berman and Carol stood together on the sidewalk trying to catch their breath.

When they got back to the station Lenhard had Berman write an update on the case for the six o'clock show. Berman stretched the minimal facts of the uneventful hearing into a thirty-second vo that briefly summarized the case against Gilliam and the concern his neighbors had about his freedom. Carol didn't bother to edit the video. She simply laid down thirty seconds' worth showing Gilliam hurrying toward the courthouse, with his girlfriend clinging to his arm.

Two weeks later, Gilliam and his girlfriend made another appearance in court. Again, Berman and Carol awaited their arrival and pursued them down the sidewalk to the courthouse and back to their car when the hearing ended. Berman kept a close eye on Gilliam this time to avoid another fall. The black eyes from his last encounter had finally begun to fade. Gilliam and the woman didn't laugh this time, but they whispered to each other as the news crew dogged their footsteps. Berman asked essentially the same questions and Gilliam refused to comment and avoided looking at the camera. Back at the station, Berman reported to Lenhard. Despite the lack of developments, Lenhard told Berman to write a vo-sot using one or two of his questions to show Gilliam's refusal to cooperate.

"Put it to him, Jed. What right does he have to stiff us like that? He owes this community a lot, including an

198

explanation and an apology for his actions. If he won't talk, then he can just pay the price. We'll make him look like the monster he is."

Berman wrote the story but he wasn't pleased with it. He still felt uncomfortable hounding Gilliam before his trial. He felt nothing but revulsion for what the man had been convicted of doing, and he thought it highly likely that Gilliam was guilty of the latest charges as well, but he didn't like being ordered to prosecute the man on the street. The wheels of justice seemed likely to roll over this guy again. What right did TV 10 have to make a public spectacle out of him over and over? He doubted if Fred Demarco or Donnie Kurtz, or Dee Morgan for that matter, would approve of what he was doing. He didn't really approve himself. But what was the alternative? Lenhard had made it clear to everyone in the newsroom that his word was law and anyone who objected could invite themselves out the door. Berman wasn't ready to leave, but he admitted to himself that he wasn't having nearly as much fun as he had in his early days of TV news.

When Gilliam's trial finally started, Lenhard ordered Berman and Carol to stay on him from the time he parked his car until he drove off at the end of the day. Lenhard had special graphics made up, showing Gilliam's picture and listing his prior convictions. Every story Berman wrote about the trial had to include all of those earlier charges and sentences. Lenhard sent another team back to the neighborhood to interview more neighbors about having a child molester on their block. A third team conducted on-the-street interviews with people in downtown Berrington, who all thought Gilliam should have been put away for good. People in Gilliam's neighborhood refused to allow TV 10 to take pictures of their children, but they admitted on camera that they were reluctant to let the children play outside knowing Gilliam was around.

The trial lasted four days. The little girl Gilliam was accused of molesting testified on videotape. She described what Gilliam had done to her: he had stopped her in the yard behind his house several times, making more aggressive advances toward her each time, until she finally grew frightened enough to ignore his warnings not to tell her parents. After watching the tape, Berman felt angry all the way through the lunch hour. He had paid close attention to the jury as they watched and listened to the little girl's story. They, too, seemed very disturbed by the child's testimony. Berman's concern over Lenhard's attempts to sensationalize the story ebbed a bit as he realized how depraved and sick Gilliam really was. When the testimony ended, including Gilliam's contention that the little girl had mistakenly chosen his picture from police mugshots, the jurors deliberated less than two hours. They found Gilliam guilty on all counts. When his earlier convictions were taken into account, Berman expected to see him put away for a long, long time.

The day after the verdict, Lenhard called Berman into his office and motioned to the chair in front of his desk.

"Jed, I just had a call from the parents of the little girl Sanford Gilliam molested."

Berman nodded but withheld comment, wondering what the child's parents thought about the case and his handling of it. They had declined repeated requests for interviews or even brief comments before, during and after the trial. Lenhard's expression made Berman think his conversation with the parents had not been unpleasant.

"You know what they said? They said they went home every night during the trial and watched all of the stations to see how they handled the case. Know what they decided?"

Berman shook his head, wishing Lenhard would get to the point.

"They thanked us and you in particular for the way you handled the story. They really liked the way you kept after Gilliam to let people see what kind of a real degenerate he is. They wanted me to tell you it was the best coverage of that kind of story they've ever seen." With that, Lenhard sat back in his chair with his arms folded across his chest, smiling like a Buddha. Berman hadn't expected anyone so close to the case to be so positive about TV 10's coverage, coverage dictated virtually line-by-line by John Lenhard, probably with strong encouragement from Autry Domain. Berman chose the wording of his response carefully.

"Well, that's always nice to hear, especially in a sensitive situation like this one. I'm a little surprised they were quite so positive, considering that I was after them every day during the trial and for weeks beforehand trying to get an interview or just some simple comments, as you suggested."

Lenhard waved his hand as if to dismiss Berman's concern entirely.

"That never bothered them at all. In fact, they told me to tell you they were sorry not to give you a reaction, since you were doing such a great job on the story, but the prosecutor urged them to dummy up so they wouldn't trigger a mistrial or something by pissing off the judge."

Berman shook his head again. This wasn't the first time in recent months that he had guessed wrong about how someone closely linked to a serious story would react. He had always prided himself in having the sensibilities of the common man, feeling the way ordinary men and women would feel in the face of life's rough spots. He always tried to ask the questions he thought they would ask if they had the chance, and he tried to fill his stories with the answers he thought they wanted. In this case, he assumed most people would think he had gone overboard in hassling Gilliam before and during the trial. Obviously, he had guessed wrong. Maybe it was the issue—no one has much sympathy for an adult who harms a child. But couldn't they see that Gilliam still had rights, even in the face of such awful charges? He stared at Lenhard's smiling face without speaking.

"Jed, why so quiet? I called you in to tell you about the call right away; I assumed you'd be really pleased to hear the news. Talk about an endorsement!"

Berman tried to make Lenhard see what had troubled him about the assignment.

"Oh, I'm always glad, or almost always, if someone like those parents approves of my work. What bothered me about the whole deal, and still bothers me, is the way we went after this one guy. I see child molesting cases in the paper just about every week. Guys who are obviously repeat offenders, going back to court after serving time and getting out and committing the same damnable offenses again and again. I agree with people who argue that these guys can't be reformed. I mean, Jeffrey Dahmer even said he'd probably go back to practicing cannibalism on unsuspecting young men if he ever got out of jail. I hate these offenses as much as anyone; children don't ever deserve to be treated this way. But how do we justify going after this one guy and making sure everyone in the world knows all about his sins, when we don't do it for lots of others? What makes that right? If we made a consistent effort to warn people about every pervert who enters the court system facing charges like this, I might feel a little differently, but we don't." He saw a quizzical expression come over Lenhard's face, but he kept going.

"I guess when you boil it all down, I feel like we've abused our role in this case. I don't think we have the right to pick on people, no matter what they're accused of. If we really believe in the American system of justice, we should simply report the facts and let people draw their own conclusions and make their own decisions about what action needs to be taken. Do you know what I mean?"

Lenhard's face was paler than usual, and his smile had faded.

"Jed, if I hear you right, you're basically saying I made a mistake in how I wanted this story handled. Are you accusing me of some sort of tabloid journalism, of pumping this thing up just to get a reaction from viewers, maybe boost the ratings a little? Is that what you're trying to say?"

"I'm not accusing you of anything, John. I simply wonder if we don't have to be a little careful not to get carried away with the power that we have. I just want to be sure that when we bring down the hammer on someone we do it in a way that's justified and appropriate based on the circumstances." Lenhard's face showed no emotion at all.

"Jed, I think you need to spend some time getting a handle on what TV news is all about, especially these days. There was probably a time around here when our coverage of this case and the trial would have been really routine and boring, probably consisting of stories jam-packed with all sorts of arcane court language and little real feeling of what's involved here. What we did—what I helped you to do—was let people get close to the reality of this situation. More importantly, we helped raise the question of how creeps like Gilliam should be treated. Maybe we've influenced some lawmakers who will change the law so guys like this can't be out and about once we know they're perverts. Then they can't pose a threat to the children in our community. Don't you think those things are worth helping people think about? In fact," he warmed to the end of his oration, "don't we have an affirmative obligation to raise those issues, to help the people we serve think through dangerous situations so they're ready to respond to them, especially for the sake of the kids?" An expression of satisfaction had spread across Lenhard's face as he spoke. Berman regretted that his position seemed so far from Lenhard's. He was trying to convince himself that Lenhard was making a valid point when the news director threw down his final rationale. "And one more thing." He leaned forward and wagged his finger in Berman's face as he said, "Autry Domain has research showing that stations that push victims' rights hard can jump as much as five to eight ratings points between books. So, if we can be all these things to people, as the call I just received suggests we're starting to be, and end up getting our ratings up by doing it, then you can bet your ass we'll do it some more." He stopped and looked at Berman. He dropped his voice down and lowered the volume for his next comment.

"Jed, this is the way we're gonna do news around here now. As you found out, it takes a helluva lot of energy to stay on top of a story this way. I can promise you this won't be the last one we're gonna do like this. We probably won't do child molesting again any time soon. But there will be other cases that require us to swarm all over them to make our point. It's gonna mean working hard and sticking together. I'd like to know I can count on you to be part of the team, not someone standing off to the side undercutting our efforts. Can I count on you, Jed?"

Berman's emotions churned like the ocean waves during a storm, but he tried not to let any of them show on his face. If this was modern journalism, he wasn't sure he liked it. But he still wasn't ready to quit. For one thing, he didn't know what he could do if he left, and like most people, he couldn't afford to walk away. And, no matter the differences between his approach and Lenhard's, he still believed TV news could make a positive contribution to the community. His chin had sunk down toward his chest as he grappled with the feelings of the moment. At Lenhard's question, he raised his head and looked into Lenhard's steely, cold eyes, and lied.

"I'm with you, John. Our role in this community is too important and too meaningful to let a minor difference of opinion cloud our vision of the future. I guess I just wanted to share my reservations with someone, and your invitation to come in here made you the father confessor. Thanks for listening. I better get back to work."

Lenhard stood up with Berman and extended his hand. He gripped Berman's hand firmly and offered a benediction.

"You do a great job, Jed. Keep it up. We need you if we're gonna make it to number one. Hang in there." As Berman turned to leave, Lenhard walked around the desk and slapped him on the back. "Go get 'em, Tiger." The language and the physical contact made Berman shudder, but he kept it to himself. Instead, he managed a sort of growl as he walked out of the office. Lenhard heard it and smiled.

Nine

Under Advisement

The whole Gilliam affair left Berman feeling raw. Each day now he struggled with doubts about how TV 10 approached the news and the things he needed to do to be part of it. He decided to take some vacation time away from the newsroom to think it all over. As soon as the November ratings period ended, he slipped his notebook into his top desk drawer and headed out for a week of R-and-R. Jane shifted her schedule so she could be off during the same time. The book ended on Wednesday, and Thursday morning they boarded a plane for New Mexico. It seemed right to Berman to put some distance between himself and the root of his current pain, plus the weather had to be better than the cold, snowy grayness of Berrington and Pruitville in winter..

They checked into a quasi-dude ranch on the edge of Santa Fe. For the next four days they played tourist in the city, strolling slowly through its narrow, winding streets, sitting on the terrace of pizza shops designed to attract the upscale element that was fast becoming a major part of the ancient city. Jane loved the Southwest; she was happy strolling, hiking or just lounging at a cafe, taking in the scenery and enjoying the warm air that blew gently over their faces. Twice they drove their rented car south toward Albuquerque, to hike in the Sangria Mountains and sit along the banks of the Rio Grande in a state park named after the famous explorer Coronado. One afternoon they took a short ride on very old, very calm horses supplied by the ranch.

The dramatic change of scenery worked well for the first couple of days; Berman suddenly realized, on Saturday, that he hadn't thought about or talked about the station since they got to Santa Fe. Berman had told Jane that he wanted to get away from news for a while. As the vacation unfolded, she watched closely for signs that he wanted to take the topic out of its box and talk about it. She was pleased that he managed to keep it packed up those first couple of days, but she knew it was coming. Too many nights before they left she had worried about the change in Berman's attitude. The man who once strolled proudly about town, telling anyone who wanted to know that he was in the news business, now preferred to stay home or go someplace where the crowds were sparse, and better yet, far enough away that no one they ran into would recognize him from TV. He hadn't gone into a lot of detail since the days when Donnie Kurtz got the axe and Lenhard first arrived, but she could tell he was troubled, and she knew the best thing for it was to let it out in this brilliant New Mexican sunshine and give it a close going-over. They were sitting in a restaurant, enjoying an incredibly rich ice cream and quesadilla dessert favored by the locals, when she saw Berman's face cloud over. It was the same moment he realized how well he had succeeded, at least temporarily, in putting the problem out of his mind. When their eyes met, they knew it was time to talk. Berman's first words pierced Jane's heart.

"I think I may have made a big mistake." The glum look on his face told Jane this was going to be a painful conversation.

"What do you mean, a mistake, Jed?" She reached

across the table and put her hand on top of his.

"This TV stuff may not be for me. I mean, I was happy in newspaper work. I knew the ropes and I felt like the people I worked with respected me. My judgment counted."

Jane wanted to say something to ease the anguish she saw him going through, but she decided to let him get some of it out before she offered any advice. She tried to give Berman a smile that said, simply, I care that you hurt, but he saw something else and held up his hand like a traffic cop.

"Okay, stop right there, Jane. I don't want pity. If this is coming across as maudlin, maybe I should stop."

"Jed, it's not maudlin. All I meant to convey is that I'm sorry you're going through all of this. I've been watching you for weeks now, so I know things aren't going the way you'd hoped or the way you were used to. I don't feel sorry for you, I love you. Now go on talking."

Berman slipped his hand out from under hers and laid it on top and squeezed lightly as he looked deep into her eyes.

"I know you care, Jane. Believe me when I say that has helped keep me going these last few months. I didn't always want to come home and dump it all on you. It's not your fault I made the switch. I take responsibility for that. What I can't quite figure out is why I wasn't smart enough to see what I was getting into."

"Maybe you couldn't see it because it wasn't there. Did you have these feelings when Demarco was around?"

"No, of course not. Fred is one of the best newsmen I've ever worked with. He made me forget all the things we used to say about TV news when I was at *The Chronicle.*"

"So . . . " Jane stopped on an upward inflection, as though the single word, coming after what had already been said, should lead Berman to a conclusion. It didn't.

"So-o-o-o-o-o what? What do you think it is?"

"C'mon, Mr. Bright Reporter Guy. The process of deduction takes Demarco out of the picture. That's a change since you started, but not the biggest one. I think you know very well what the real problem is—or should I say who?"

Berman tried to wave her off.

"You mean Lenhard, don't you? I've tried thinking about that. He certainly has some ideas and approaches to news that don't come very naturally to me. But you know as well as I do that he's mostly left me alone to do my thing. So how can I blame him for the way I feel ?"

"You can't be serious, Jed. This guy has come in and upset the fruit basket. I'm just a viewer and I can see the difference. I can't believe you can sit here and defend him when he's obviously driving you nuts."

Berman slumped down in his chair. He heaved a sigh that seemed to start somewhere deep inside of him.

"Okay, okay," he said in a tired voice, " I didn't want to let Lenhard be the real focus of all this because he's the one thing I can't do a damn thing about. He holds all the cards, or at least the ones Autry Domain deals him. I told you what he said to me when I raised objections about our coverage of the Gilliam case, didn't I?"

Jane nodded.

"He's not about to tolerate any resistance, even from me. Which leaves me in a pretty tough position. I want to do news, but I can only do it here if I do what Lenhard wants, and a lot of what he wants I don't. Can you see what happens if I dwell on that for very long?"

"Sure, you become another Donnie Kurtz, committed to doing news the right way and increasingly frustrated about being forced to do it this other way. Eventually, unless you are a man of superhuman character, and I personally think you are, you self-destruct and find yourself working in a bookstore like Kurtz is."

"Damn it, Jane, I don't want to sell books. News is what I do. It's what I've done all my adult life, and I had intended to do it until I retire. How am I gonna do it if I can't stand the way it has to be done these days? There are lots of important stories to be told, important issues to raise. The frustrating thing is how often these new guys, like Lenhard and Domain, aren't interested in the issues I think we should be talking about. If they can't pump 'em up somehow and, more importantly, if their research tells them women twenty-five to fifty-four aren't going to pay attention to the topic, then it doesn't qualify. Sometimes I come away from the morning meetings so pissed off I could spit." He sat up and looked at Filips. "If you were me, which is asking you to deal with a painful hypothetical situation, would you stay in it and try to do something worthwhile?"

Filips had already thought about it. She had practiced the answer in her mind.

"Jed, only you can make the final decision about whether or not to stay with TV 10, but let me just say this: you are one helluva news guy. You care what happens to the people in our community. You have already done lots of good things and I know you can do lots more. Staying with Lenhard isn't going to be lots of fun; maybe the days of enjoying your job are gone. But the people are still out there, expecting you to tell them what's going on and why they should care about it. The Jed Berman I see sitting here right this minute still has a fire in his belly, he still gives a damn. And he's not likely to let a couple of assholes who care much more about building ratings and making money ruin it for him. Oh, sure, you may have to put up with some of their bullshit, maybe a lot of their bullshit. But along the way you will continue to make a difference and that's what

210

you have to continue to tell yourself. You can quit if you want and be about as happy out of the business as you are in it. Ask Donnie Kurtz about that. Maybe it's time to face the fact that adult life is not a joyous experience much of the time. Maybe you focus your attention on me and your other friends if you want a good laugh, and don't expect to feel much sense of identification with the people at work. Maybe it's come to that. What do you think?"

Tears welled up in Berman's eyes as he tried to respond. He took a deep breath and reached out to hold her hand again.

"I think I'm one of the luckiest men in the world to have met a human being as beautiful in every way as you are. Thank you for believing in me. I don't deserve it, but I'll damn sure take it and cherish it. You have to be right when you say it may not be much fun to hang in there, but if you believe I can still accomplish something worthwhile, in spite of the assholes who run the show, I'm willing to try. I admit I really thought this talk would end with you encouraging me to chuck it and do something else. Instead, you challenge me to grow up and realize life won't always be the party I used to have doing news. Your words felt like a verbal slap in the face and I needed that, and you and I both know it. Doesn't mean I won't get depressed once in a while and complain about the buttheads I work with. It does mean I'll try to focus on the good I can do as a journalist in spite of interference from Domain and Lenhard. And, I'll let them decide when it's time for me to go. How's that sound?"

Jane leaned across the table and kissed him on the lips.

"It sounds challenging but very grown up, Jed. And I promise to help you put up with the hassles and hang in there. I do love you, Jed Berman."

An idea suddenly popped into his head. It seemed

211

crazy but he decided to take a chance.

"How much do you love me, Jane Filips?"

"Tons, and you know it."

"Enough tons to drive over to Las Vegas and marry me?"

He expected to knock her off balance with the question, but that didn't happen. She responded as though she knew it was coming.

"Yep, even enough to do that." Her face lit up with a dazzling smile. He thought she had never seemed more beautiful than at this moment.

"Then what are we waiting for? We've got some driving to do." They stood up and moved around the edge of the table and embraced. Ten minutes later they pointed their rental car into the darkness toward Nevada.

*   *   *

When they returned to Berrington, they decided to give up Berman's apartment and move into Jane's larger, first floor apartment a couple of blocks down the street. It was no great sacrifice—the ancient heating system in his place clanked in winter and there was no air conditioning in summer—but Berman felt a twinge of nostalgia as he gazed out the front window for the last time and saw the perennial Christmas decorations strategically positioned by the Wise kids on their front porch and lawn. Crazy thing was, he'd never really talked to the Wises, never gotten to know them. Just by being there, day after day and year after year, they had come to occupy a certain place in his world. The children's innocence contrasted nicely against the sometimes harsh and ugly world he inhabited as a reporter. He thought about walking over to say goodbye, but decided not to. It would take longer to remind them who he was and how he knew them than it was worth. Their happy little family world would go on, the kids would get bigger and bigger and eventually head off on their own, without any memories of the guy who watched over their glowing pumpkins from his upstairs window. They weren't the first people he had knitted into his world without really getting attached to them, and they probably wouldn't be the last.

He sometimes wondered if he should worry about such parasocial relationships, giving someone a place in his life that they really didn't earn and might not even want. Did other people do the same thing? Notice someone on the way to work each day and maybe even get into the habit of waving hello, but never get out of the car at the same place and hold a real conversation—or find yourself shopping at the grocery story every week at nearly the same time and somehow feeling like you knew each other, when you'd never even exchanged names. Of course, since he started showing up on TV more people greeted him, often with the name of another reporter, but still thinking they had a connection to this guy they saw on the tube every night. That was okay, especially since they could only recognize him if they were watching, and viewers equalled ratings. But there were times when he grew tired of returning the wave and answering their frequently boring or rude questions.

The excitement of getting married stayed with him when he got back to the station, but he soon realized there were only a few people there with whom he felt like sharing his good news. The turnover in the newsroom had picked up significantly since Lenhard arrived. Some people departed for better opportunities elsewhere, some Lenhard invited to leave because they didn't seem to catch the spirit of news *à la* Autry. The hatchet work begun by Steve Kimmel before Lenhard arrived continued. A newsroom where most people once felt secure, assuming they did a decent job, now had an every-man-for-himself feel to it. Some of the veteran employees talked about the feeling of mutual commitment that once operated throughout the TV 10 building. Now, no one took anything for granted. There was less casual conversation, less water cooler chit-chat. People came in and did their job and left when their time was up. Berman felt little temptation to sully the joy he felt at being united with Jane Filips by exposing it to the grayness of the station surroundings. He told Carol, and called Dee Morgan at *The Chronicle*. Dee sounded very pleased to hear the news. Lenhard never asked about his vacation, and Berman felt no urge to tell him.

Three weeks after he got back, a cave-in put his new resolve to the test. It happened as some kids were walking to school in Pruitville. Three girls started across an old concrete bridge they had traversed a thousand times. This time, one of the girls stopped to lean over the low wall of the bridge to see if the stream running beneath it had frozen. As she leaned across the ancient molding, a chunk of concrete, roughly three feet square, suddenly gave way. The girl and the cement tumbled twenty feet down to the creek. They landed on the frozen water, with the girl under the concrete. It crushed her small skull, killing her instantly. The other two girls, peering anxiously through the unexpected hole in the bridge wall, could see their friend's legs extending out from under the artificial rock.

The ice had cracked, but the stream ran shallow beneath the bridge. The weight of the concrete had driven the girl's body through the frozen water and pinned it tightly against the mud beneath. The girls on the bridge started screaming and kept screaming until a passing motorist stopped to see what was wrong. When he took in the scope of the tragedy he pulled the girls away from the bridge wall and called police from the phone in his car.

The morning crew at TV 10 heard the first ambulance call go out over the scanners—LITTLE GIRL TRAPPED UNDER CONCRETE BOULDER AT FREESINGHAM AVENUE BRIDGE. The overnight producer called the early morning live crew to see if they'd heard the radio traffic. They had just gotten back in the truck to return to the station when it went out. They caught the end of it. The producer filled them in on the rest and told them to head for the bridge. By the time they arrived, emergency crews had managed to push the concrete off the girl's body and rush her up the embankment and past her wailing friends to a waiting ambulance. The live crew started shooting as police arrived to gather the details of what happened. Back at the station, the overnight producer confirmed with the hospital that the girl was dead in time to run a short reader in the 8:55 update. By the time Lenhard arrived for work, his news team already had shots of the scene, including the bridge, the boulder and the broken ice, and two interviews—one with a student who came on the bridge just as the wall gave way and another with an EMT who helped roll the concrete off the little girl's crumpled body.

Lenhard rubbed his hands as he waited for the morning meeting. Most of the staff had not yet heard about the accident. Lenhard's eyes shone as he broke the news.

"Boys and girls, we've got a good one today." He stopped to adjust his approach slightly, realizing that what he was about to say might sound ghoulishly insensitive in such a bright tone of voice. "A little girl died barely an hour ago at the Freesingham Avenue bridge. Seems she leaned on the wall of the bridge and a chunk of it came loose. She and the concrete fell to the stream below with the little girl ending up under the rock. She died instantly." He paused to let the revelation sink in. Several people shook their heads and grimaced at the thought of the youngster's final moments. Lenhard charged on. "Here's the deal. I know there isn't much else going on today, so we're gonna swarm all over this like flies on honey. Besides, it's a story made for TV news. People can't help but watch us to find out what we're going to show them and tell them about such an awful happening."

He pulled his white board beside him and uncapped the black marker he used to list story ideas.

"Okay, we're going to do the whole six o'clock show on this. We want at least two lives, maybe three packages and assorted vos and vo/sots. It's going to look like a fucking instant documentary and we're gonna win this day. Hell, I'll probably enter this six o'clock in the AP competition for best newscast. But first we gotta do it. Let's go. Who's doing what?"

Silence greeted his enthusiastic beginning. No one offered any suggestions at all. Lenhard had turned his back on the group to write down their ideas, but he slowly turned back to face them when no ideas were forthcoming. He scanned the faces before him intently.

"Hey, what gives? We've been doin' this together long enough now for you to know what we need to do. What are we gonna do?"

Most of the staff had never seen anyone wade into a tragedy like this one with such enthusiasm. They had all covered fatalities, including the truly awful ones involving children. But none of them had developed much of a stomach for it. Seeing Lenhard practically bouncing up and down with anticipation for reporting this sad story left them almost as shocked as the event itself. Without realizing what was happening, Lenhard prodded them to get on board.

"C'mon, people. Time is a-wasting. Maybe it's just a slow morning. I'll get it started." He turned back to the board and wrote "Nuts and Bolts." Returning his attention to the staff, he said, "There, that's the obvious one. What else should we be doing?"

Finally, another voice chimed in.

"Shouldn't someone be checking at the school for reaction from the little girl's classmates?"

Under "Nuts and Bolts," Lenhard wrote, "School Reax."

"That's good, I'd think between teachers and students that ought to be a package. Let's think about going live from there at six, but that could change."

"How about checking with the city on the status of that bridge?" someone else said. " Surely someone should have known the concrete was so worn out that it was about to fall apart."

Lenhard's earlier disapointment evaporated.

"Yeah, that's good. Not only the city but maybe find out who has ultimate responsibility for inspecting these things. Seems to me I've been reading that a lot of our bridges are shot and getting dangerous. Maybe this one was on a list of some kind calling for repairs."

At this point, contributions from the floor dried up. Berman hadn't offered any ideas because he was preoccupied with the mixed emotions triggered by Lenhard's excitement over sprucing up a slow day by inflating this one story to fill the whole newscast at six. Others who hadn't spoken felt much the same way. As Lenhard worked to fill his board, they avoided his glance, looking down at their notebooks or at their coffee cups. Lenhard couldn't wait; he started reeling off ideas and assignments and pointing to the people he wanted to do them.

"We're missing a couple of important ingredients. Who

is this little girl? What was she like? What did she want to be when she grew up? That's yours.

"How about the real eyewitnesses—the little girls who were on the bridge with the victim? Yeah, you can get that one. It may end up in the nuts and bolts part, or if it's really heart-rending it could be a stand-alone package. Let me know what you come up with."

The board was nearly full of ideas and Lenhard had not assigned any of them to Berman. Now he spun around and pointed at Jed.

"One more thing we gotta do, and you're the best man to do it: talk to the family. Get as many of them as you can and get pictures of her, too, while you're at it."

Berman knew he probably had as much chance of pulling it off as anyone, but the battle in his mind over what should and shouldn't be done had weakened his resolve to be a good soldier. Everyone looked up when they heard him question Lenhard's call.

"John, I'm not sure it's right to be all over those people in the first hours after they lose their daughter in such an awful way. Don't they deserve a little time to begin dealing with the tragedy of it all? They're probably in shock right now. I'm a little uncomfortable crashing in on them and shoving a microphone in their faces while they're still drying the first of what will be many tears."

Lenhard turned toward the board and wrote "Family Reax," slipped the cap back on the marker and laid it in the trough at the bottom of the board. Then he turned slowly around to face Berman.

"Jed, I hear what you're saying. Hell, I'm not an ogre or something; I have feelings. But this is news and people want to know how that family feels about this terrible thing. I believe we have an obligation to gather that information and share it with the public. If we start flinching every time something painful happens, we'll be out of business."

Berman stiffened at the tone and substance of Lenhard's remarks. He never liked to be talked down to and that's how Lenhard's comments came across. He tried not to let Lenhard read the emotions on his face.

"John, I hear what you're saying. It's just that when we go roaring in there before the body is even cold, I feel a little inhumane. I know we have to try for some reaction from them, but can't we give them a little time to mourn before we do it?"

Lenhard's eyes narrowed. He didn't like to have his judgment questioned, especially in front of the entire newsroom. He walked toward Berman and towered over him as he sat at his desk.

"Here's the deal, Jed. I want to be understanding in situations like this, but I also want to be the best. If we don't get over there and talk to that family, you can bet your ass the other guys will and I don't want that to happen. Which means we have to get going right now. Can you do it? Will you do it?" He added a touch of mock politeness. Berman felt the urge to stand up and punch Lenhard in the face, but he swallowed it. He forced all emotion out of his voice as he answered.

"I was just raising a question, John. Of course, you're the boss. If you want family reaction, you'll get it. That's assuming they'll talk to us. I'll keep you posted." He grabbed his notebook and coat and headed for the assignment editor's desk to find out which photog he would be working with.

Lenhard slid the assignment board to its normal position, just outside his office. He felt a little irritated. Berman's question had taken some of the shine off what he hoped would be his best day as news director, but he still had pride in his ability to deploy his troops for maximum results. Autry Domain called in the early afternoon. He had seen the story of the bridge mishap on the wire. He congratulated Lenhard on his plan of action. He felt a certain pride, too. John Lenhard was proving to be a very good student of news in the nineties.

Berman managed to find the little girl's family and, despite their initial reluctance, they talked on camera, standing on the front porch of their home. In Berman's story, viewers saw a woman, probably in her thirties, clinging to a man of similar age, and sobbing uncontrollably. The girl's father answered Berman's questions in a quavering voice. Both parents looked dazed. The father kept repeating, "She was such a little thing. We loved her so much." Knowing Lenhard expected it, Berman posed the ultimate TV news question.

"How do you feel right now?"

The father managed to say something about deep, deep pain and knowing how much they would miss their daughter. Then, he, too, broke down. The man and woman clung to each other as though the earth were tilting and they feared they would fall off. Berman thanked them for the interview and motioned to the photographer that it was time to leave. Lenhard was pleased with what they brought back. He made sure the producer put Berman's story right after the brief nuts and bolts piece. He had Berman introduce it live from in front of the little girl's house.

By the time Berman got back to the station, Lenhard had gone home. The reporters and photographers who were still hanging around told him Lenhard had loved his piece. They also mentioned that TV 10 had spent at least ten more minutes on the freak happening than either of the other two stations. When he heard that, Berman thought to himself, "That's because they don't have John Lenhard calling the shots." Along with the boss' second-hand appreciation of his effort, Berman took home a sick feeling in his stomach. He wondered, for the umpteenth time in recent months, if he was losing it. The people calling the shots loved what he was doing. They demanded more and more of it, and he felt like giving them less and less.

*   *   *

Three months later, when the TV 10 news team arrived for work, they were greeted by a mail message in the computer. Lenhard had stayed late the night before to compose it and send it flashing through the computerways to each of their terminals. It was brief and to the point. It was also the next logical step in Lenhard's efforts to follow Autry Domain's advice for making TV 10 a news team for the nineties. In its entirety it read:

TO: News staff
FR: Lenhard
RE: Stories after week night prime time

Just a small suggestion for coming up with story ideas for the late show, especially Monday through Friday. Keep in mind we're shooting for 18- to 49-year-old women, primarily. The stories we do must leave viewers with a deep emotional response that will keep them coming back for more night after night. The actual topic isn't as important as the impact the story will have on viewers. We want to maintain the emotional level they're coming out of network programming with. So let's get our heads together and come up with some good gut-wrenching tear-jerkers. I know you can do it. Feel free to submit ideas to me or any of the producers.

Berman couldn't believe what he was reading. Since the days of Fred Demarco he had tried to accept the crass pandering to ratings that permeated so much of TV programming in general, and more recently, TV news in particular. But Lenhard's memo went too far. In fact, this bit of advice brought the news process 180 degrees around from where Berman had started. In the old days, the idea was to be in touch with the community so you could report on important events and issues that people would or should want to know about. The finished product was, in a sense, a snapshot of that day in the community. It kept people up to date on developments that would affect their lives and explained happenings they might hear about but would not be able to witness for themselves. It was reporting, the modern day equivalent of the old town crier. And some days people could tell not much had happened because even the top story didn't have much pizzazz. Those days weren't much fun for reporters either, but if that's the way the day went, it seemed only right to let people know it. It didn't mean you couldn't develop enterprise or feature stories that people would find interesting. But you started with the event or issue and made a story out of it. And, if you did it well, people liked it or disliked it, felt happy or sad about it. It became part of the day's news.

This memo from Lenhard was the exact opposite. In this demographically massaged new world, you started with the emotional reaction you wanted people to have after they saw the story and worked backward until you could come up with something, anything, that you knew would trigger the right response. The concept of news hardly applied. This was entertainment, like the movies. He knew movie makers were into testing their films, nearly minute by minute to see how people reacted to them. If a scene left people flat, it was likely to wind up on the cutting room floor, or reshot for the right effect. He also knew, because Demarco had told him and Lenhard wouldn't let him forget, that Autry Domain and his buddies were compiling a stack of research on TV news that would allow news directors to do basically the same thing—tailor the news "product," as they liked to call it, to the emotional tastes of the viewer. Never mind trying to give them an accurate accounting of the day's happenings. The goal was to grab them by the emotions and never let go. The concept left such a bad taste in Berman's mouth that he nearly spat on his computer screen. Instead, he reread Lenhard's memo six or seven times and sat silently in his chair, waiting for Lenhard to arrive.

For some reason, Lenhard was late. While everyone else sat around waiting for the morning meeting, Berman walked to Lenhard's office door, which Lenhard normally locked overnight. Today it stood wide open. Berman reached in and switched on the light. It was a small office, with barely enough room for a chair in front of the desk and Lenhard's chair, the one Domain liked to lounge in, behind the desk. Without thinking about it, Berman scanned the papers lying on top of the desk, reading them upside down as he had often done in other offices when he was working on a story, especially when someone wasn't being very cooperative. A couple of memos lay on the left side of the desk calendar that occupied the center of Lenhard's work space. The surface of the calendar was clear, but a thick stack of papers, stapled in the top corner, lay just to the right. The top page bore a title in large black type: Mangold & Foreman Series Catalogue. Although he was adept at snooping upside down, Berman never actually lifted a paper from anyone's desk without being invited to. This morning he granted himself a special dispensation. If the catalogue contained what he thought it did, it would only add to his aggravation. It would also be more proof of the incredible manipulation taking the place of news judgment in the broadcasting industry.

He picked up the publication and opened it to the first page. At the top was a paragraph explaining how to use the catalogue. It reminded Berman of a book he'd used to identify trees. The instructions referred to a list of demographic categories at the bottom of the page: age ranges, gender, educational background, profession, income level, and others. Each category had a number in front of it. Catalogue users were advised to select the demographic characteristics that fit the audience they wanted to attract, then add up the numbers in front of those categories. Next, they matched that total to a list of numbers on the next page. Those numbers referred catalogue users to ideas for special reports a station could do during the four ratings periods each year. Mangold & Foreman had tested the topics to make sure they would attract the desired audience, assuming they were properly promoted. As he paged through the sections, Berman came across the exact titles of most of the series TV 10 had done since John Lenhard arrived. For the first time he knew where Lenhard got most of his ideas, and he understood why Lenhard insisted those ideas were better than the suggestions from anyone else in the newsroom. Chances were, if you traveled across the country to markets where Mangold & Foreman had clients, and tuned in during a ratings period, you would see the same series TV 10 had done—or would do in the not too distant future. It was news by formula, a formula not based on serving the public but on generating ratings. Berman threw the catalogue back onto the desk in disgust. Just as it landed, Lenhard spoke from behind him.

"You need to see me, Jed?"

Berman jumped. He hadn't heard Lenhard coming.

He moved aside to let Lenhard enter his office. For an instant, he was tempted to abandon this confrontation. In many ways, it would be easier to just let it ride. Do what he was told and not make waves. But somewhere in the back of his mind a small voice urged him to get on with it. Someone had to speak up, whatever it might cost to do it.

"Yes, I do need to see you, John," he said.

"Then c'mon in and have a seat. What's on your mind?" Lenhard asked as he walked into the room.

Berman sat down on the front edge of the chair in front of Lenhard's desk, but it seemed too close, considering what he had come to say. He slid back and trained his eyes directly on Lenhard, who was busy taking some papers out of his briefcase. He dropped the papers onto the desk and looked up at Berman.

"You were about to say, Jed?"

Berman shifted a little in his chair and cleared his throat. Despite the fact that he was sitting within three feet of another human being, he felt terribly alone.

"John, I got your mail message this morning about story ideas for the late show."

Lenhard brightened, pleased to have his star reporter's response to the memo so quickly. Autry Domain had urged him to write it, hoping his staff could generate the ideas that would bring in the right audience. If not, Domain had also offered to provide a list of story ideas himself. Lenhard was eager to hear some of Berman's suggestions.

"So, what ideas do you have?"

"That's just it, John. I don't have any. I can't do news that way. It's backward from everything I've ever known or believed in."

Lenhard flinched. His cheeks grew red with irritation.

"What are you saying, Jed? I thought you told me I

could count on you to have the right attitude about how we do news around here."

"I intended to. But this is more than I can swallow. This isn't news, it's manipulating viewers so we can count them in the ratings book."

Lenhard held up his hand to stop Berman's recitation. He leaned across the desk and spoke in an ominously quiet voice.

"Stop right there and think about what you're saying, Jed. As the news director, it's my job to make this newsroom work. The best way to measure our success is the numbers. If they go up, we win. If they go down, we lose. The memo I sent you is based on the best research Mangold & Foreman can get their hands on; much of it they did themselves. They charge us a lot of money for their services each year. In exchange, they promise to help us win. We can only benefit from their advice if we follow it, and Autry Domain says choosing stories based on the emotional response they generate works. Now, what part of that can't you understand?" He stayed bent over the desk, waiting for Berman to answer. It reminded Berman of when Lenhard had stood over him during their conversation about how to cover the story of the little girl who fell off the bridge, and he resented Lenhard's attempts to intimidate him. Anger welled up and flooded over the irritation that led him into this room this morning.

"John, I understand it all very well. My concern is that what you want us to do has little or nothing to do with covering the news. It's a fabrication. We don't make the news, even though people have accused us of that. Real journalists report the news, based on what's happening in the community, and let the ratings fall where they may. What you want to do is take us down the same road as the tabloid newspapers and their modern-day cousins—the tabloid TV shows, the ones that masquerade as news magazines. It's all calculated to get a reaction, usually pandering to fairly base instincts, and the saddest thing is, if that's all we give people, and if we promote it as news, they begin to believe it. Or else they forget what real news is because it's been so long since they saw or heard any. That kind of crap may generate numbers and give you and the consultant boys a chance to gloat, but I for one think it sucks. The community deserves better than that. The community deserves decent coverage of the serious issues that affect their lives. If there are some stories or even whole days when that coverage seems a little boring, so be it. Life isn't one big orgasm after another. It has ups and downs and the news ought to reflect that. Purposely choosing our stories so we can sustain some sort of perpetual high for viewers is not honest news coverage, and I don't want to do it."

Lenhard's face was crimson. He sat back and glared at Berman. Berman's eyes blazed with heat of their own. Finally, Lenhard broke the silence. His voice was strangely flat and lifeless.

"Berman, get out."

"What?"

"I said, get out. I will no longer tolerate your insubordination, not to mention a list of insults too long to mention. You have rendered yourself useless to what we're trying to do here. I want you out of here before the morning meeting starts. That gives you about five minutes because I'm already running a little late. Now, get out."

Berman made no effort to dispute the order. The longer he talked to this man the more convinced he became that he wanted nothing to do with what was going on here. In the heat of the moment, he doubted if he wanted anything to do with TV news at all. He stood up and walked out of Lenhard's office. He found an empty computer paper box next to the newsroom printer and dumped the contents of his desk drawer into it. He carefully placed Jane's picture on top. He picked up the box and walked over to Carol, who was waiting for the morning meeting to start. She looked at him quizzically as he extended his hand. No one in the newsroom had heard his conversation with Lenhard.

"See ya, kiddo. Lenhard just threw me out."

Carol nearly choked on her coffee.

"What are you talking about, Jed? He wouldn't do that."

"Oh, yes, he would and he did. Let's just say he and I have a serious difference of opinion over how to cover the news," he said with a wry smile. "Hell, Carol, I'm not even sure he knows what news is. Doesn't matter. He's the boss and I'm fired. It's been great working with you. I'm sure I'll see you around."

"Hey, c'mon, you're not really serious are you?"

"'Fraid so, my friend. I'll tell you about it sometime, if we get the chance."

He saw the other reporters and photographers moving toward Lenhard's office for the morning meeting.

"I better go. He wants me out of here before the meeting." He extended his hand again. This time Carol took it and gave him a hug.

"Take care, Jed. We'll miss you."

"You, too. I'll see ya around." Clutching his box, Berman turned and walked through the double doors, down the front hallway, across the shiny floor of the lobby and into the parking lot. He followed the sidewalk around the side of the building to the back lot where his car was parked with the rest of the TV 10 team. He slid the box into the back seat and climbed in the front. He eased the car out of the lot and turned left and headed back to Berrington. It was a few minutes past nine.

*　　*　　*

By the time Jane arrived home that night, four empty beer cans stood on the end table beside the living room couch and Berman was pouring number five into a glass. The sight immediately triggered two thoughts for Jane: Jed normally drank wine, not beer, and considering it was just a little after five, he should have been at the station. She tossed her coat over a chair and walked over to the couch.

"Jed, what are you doing home? Are you sick?"

Berman looked up at her through bloodshot eyes. He tried to smile but it came out lopsided.

"Hi to you, too. I'm not sick. I'm home because this is where I want to be right at this particular moment."

Berman seldom drank to excess. It was clear to Jane that he was a bit over his limit tonight. She had only seen him close to this state a couple of times after weekend parties. She sat down on the couch and put her arm around him.

"You look like a whipped puppy, Jed." She kissed him lightly on the cheek. "What's going on? Why are you here?" She had a bad feeling about what he was likely to say. Even with the resolve he had brought back from vacation, she had worried about how well he would hold up in the shifting environment of the TV 10 newsroom. "Something happened at the station, didn't it?"

Berman wanted to capture Jane's loving concern and store it up. This woman made even the darkest times bearable. In this dark moment, despite the alcoholic haze clouding parts of his brain, he knew he shouldn't make her wait for an explanation. He turned to look into her eyes.

"Jane, I am officially unemployed."

She wiped her hand across her forehead in a gesture of relief.

"Thank God, that's all it is. I thought maybe you killed Lenhard."

"No, it was the other way around. The bastard killed me."

"How did it happen?"

"It's not a very long story. I finally went in and told him exactly what I think of his bullshit approach to news and he told me what he thought of my attitude to his bullshit approach."

"How did he do it?"

"Pretty simple, really. He let me dig a really deep hole and then he kicked the dirt in on top of my head."

"What do you mean? When did it happen?"

Berman laughed and his sour breath wafted over her face.

"Say, why was I trying to be in the news business? You ask all the questions." He laughed again and leaned his head against the back of the couch. "You know, I'm feeling a little dizzy here. Can't remember the last time I put away this many cans of beer."

Jane ran her fingers through his hair and kissed him again, on the forehead.

"Listen here, superman," she told him gently, "I want to know the whole story so I can hate this guy as much as you do. How did he get around to actually firing you? What did you say that made him do that?"

"He sent out this memo that basically said the actual news isn't important, it's just making sure our stories have the right ingredients to give viewers an emotional reaction. It's all about ratings, not about information or what's important to people."

"And you told him what you thought of that?"

Berman grinned again. "Yeah, I told him it sucks."

"And what did he say?"

"Well, first he told me off and said I had insulted him and then he leaned real close to me and lowered his voice like a big important man and said, 'Berman, get out.' The son-of-a-bitch actually gave me five minutes to get out of the building." Tears welled up in his eyes and rolled down his cheeks as he remembered the encounter. Jane pulled him close to her.

"Jed, I'm so sorry. I know how hard you tried to make it work, how much you wanted to do something worthwhile. It's John Lenhard's loss, not yours."

Berman wiped the tears from his face.

"Well, it's our loss, too. I don't have a job and we can't live on just what you make."

"We can until you find something else. Don't worry about that. I keep the books and I say we can make it as long as we have to."

"You're just trying to make me feel better, and I love you for that. But I also have a plan."

"Can you share it with your partner?"

"Sure. I cut my teeth in print and I don't have any qualms about going back there where I know I can still do news the right way."

"Are you thinking about going back to *The Chronicle*?"

Berman pointed his finger at her.

"Bang! You got it. I was the best thing they had a couple of years ago, I don't see what's changed since then. I'm gonna call Dee first thing in the morning and scope things out. I may be back in action before the end of the week. Why wouldn't they want their ace reporter back? I haven't noticed too many big scoops in the old *Chronicle* since I left."

"Did they replace you?"

"I don't really know, but even if they did, I'm guessing

they know enough not to let me walk away again."

"You know I'm your biggest fan, but didn't you tell me they hardly put up a fight when you jumped ship for TV 10?"

"Yeah, but I think I took 'em by surprise that day. I've got a strong hunch they'll see it differently when I give them a second shot at it."

"How confident are you?"

He looked startled by her question.

"What do you mean by that? Don't you have faith in me?"

"Sure I do. I just don't want to see you march in there full of expectations only to get hurt again right after today's whipping."

"Jane, I don't really have much confidence at all. I'm trying to put up a good front and hoping it'll work out. If there's any justice in this fucked-up world, they'll take me back."

She held him close and gazed across the living room as dusk slid into darkness.

"You're right, Jed. If there's any justice, they will."

*   *   *

Berman had stopped at five beers the night before, but that was enough to leave his brain a little tender the next morning. He forced himself to get up and join Jane at the breakfast table, although he had no appetite. He sipped on black coffee while she ate her usual cereal and toast. The sun's rays sparkled on the silverware lying on the table, but it did little to brighten the gloom he had descended into the night before.

After Jane left he put in a call to Dee Morgan. A voice he didn't recognize picked up the phone.

"*Chronicle.* Newsroom. This is Phil Herrold."

"Hello. May I speak with Dee Morgan, please?"

Berman heard the new voice yell across the newsroom.

"Hey, Dee, somebody for you on the phone. Line two."

A moment later, Berman heard Morgan's familiar tone.

"Good morning, this is Dee Morgan."

"Dee, Jed Berman here. How are you?"

"Jed, what a surprise. How's married life? I've been waiting to hear how you like it, 'cause if you say it's okay, I might pick up some guy somewhere and try it myself."

"Dee, it's the best thing that ever happened to me. I definitely recommend it. It's tons better than playing computer solitaire every night."

"Hey," Morgan objected, "Who told you that's all I've been doing?"

"Just kidding, Dee. How are you?"

"I'm okay, things don't change that much around here from day to day. You know, you really haven't been very good about keeping in touch, Jed. Remember all that crap about working on stories together? When is that gonna happen?"

"Well, Dee, not to get too serious on you, it may happen sooner than you think."

Morgan's curiosity was piqued.

"What do you mean by that?"

"Not exactly what you have in mind, I'm afraid."

"Which means what?"

Berman had to force himself to say the words. He paused a long while before he responded. Morgan thought the line had gone dead.

"Hey, Berman, you still there? What's up?"

"Dee, I got fired yesterday."

"You got what? Jed Berman, ace investigative reporter, local news hero, got fired?" Berman's departure from the paper had not detracted from Morgan's respect for his abilities. She was honestly shocked by the thought that anyone would intentionally let him go. "Who would be stupid enough to can you?"

"It was the new guy in charge of TV 10 news, John Lenhard. Have you met him?"

"No, but I've heard the name. What the hell did you do to get fired?"

"I guess I was too honest. I told him what I thought of some of the stuff he had us doing over there to boost ratings. It's been coming for a while; yesterday it happened."

"So what are you gonna do now?"

"Well, that's what I wanted to talk to you about. What's the situation there in the newsroom? Got room for another pair of hands to help fill your news hole?"

"Geez, I don't know, Jed. We aren't advertising for anyone right now. But considering it's you, maybe the big guy would consider expanding the staff a little."

"Did they replace me when I left?"

"Not right away. But I think the head count is probably about the same by now as it was when you were here."

"Is the big guy there this morning?"

"Yeah, wanna talk to him?"

"I guess that's the only way I'm going to find out."

"Okay, hang on, I'll transfer you in there. And, Jed," she paused, "Good luck."

The line went silent for a moment as Morgan put him on hold, then Berman heard the familiar voice of the managing editor, the man who had not fought to keep him when he walked away before. They ran through the mandatory chitchat for a couple of minutes before Berman raised the job issue. The editor said he didn't like discussing personnel questions over the phone. His voice betrayed no reaction to Berman's renewed interest in working for *The*

234

Evening Chronicle. He invited Berman to stop in after lunch, around two.

Berman's hangover still throbbed slightly as he mounted the steps to his old newsroom. He was wearing one of the expensive suits Demarco had helped him pick out when he first arrived at TV 10. As he reached the top of the stairs he looked across the room to his old desk, hoping to see it unoccupied, perhaps piled up with old editions of the paper and assorted junk nobody wanted on their own desks. Instead he saw a young woman, no more than twenty-five, with a phone cradled against her shoulder, pounding away on the computer while she talked. Seeing her there in his space, looking so settled in, sapped some of the confidence Berman had mustered up on the way over. He turned to find Dee Morgan, who still sat at the same desk as before. She spotted him and called him over.

"Hey, stranger, welcome home." She stood up and gave him a hug and a kiss on the cheek. "What did the big guy have to say on the phone? Must have been something positive or you wouldn't be here, right?"

Berman looked toward the closed door of the managing editor's office and back toward Morgan.

"He didn't commit himself one way or the other. Said he didn't like to talk about job stuff over the phone and I should come in this afternoon. So, here I am. I better get in there and see what he has in mind. Wish me luck."

Morgan patted him on the arm.

"Good luck. It would be great working with you again."

Berman walked slowly to the editor's door and knocked three times. From her desk, Morgan heard her boss invite him in. Berman stepped inside and closed the door. He reached out his hand to the editor who remained seated behind his desk as they shook hands. Berman waited a moment in silence, then sat down in a chair by the desk. He felt embarrassed and humiliated, but he had to give it a shot.

"So, Ed, what's your personnel situation? Got room for an ace reporter who's a self-starter and needs little supervision?" He tried to sound light-hearted and relaxed, but he suspected that the pain he felt showed on his face and in his voice. The editor waited a long moment and then looked straight at Berman.

"Jed, no one can argue with the quality of work you did when you worked here. I used to call you our secret weapon, not that I ever let you know that. I also called you one of us. Until the day you walked in here and gave your notice, I'd have bet anything you would never chuck print reporting for that electronic crap." He paused again, then waved his hand in the air as if to disperse the thoughts he'd just expressed. "Thing is, Jed, you did leave. I guess it was for the money, right? 'Cause I haven't seen much else from you in the rare moments when I've caught your act on television that impressed me very much. You may be the once-great Jed Berman, but you do the same superficial stuff the rest of those cute people do. So my respect for you is, to say the leas. li.. nished. All of which means I haven't been sitting here just waiting for the moment when you came back to us, older but wiser. And, if I understand this right, the only reason you're here now is because you somehow managed to get canned by a TV news director. How in the hell did you manage that?"

Berman felt a little raw listening to this lecture, but he answered the question. "You'll be pleased to know I objected to the shallowness of what we were doing over there and the hotshot young news director got pissed and showed me the door."

"That's tough luck, Jed," the editor said. "I'm tempted

to think maybe there's a little bit of the old Jed Berman left, after all. But it doesn't make a whole lot of difference." He took a sip of coffee from the Styrofoam cup on his desk. "Let's cut to the chase. I guess I'm a little flattered you could bring yourself to crawl back in here when you're in trouble, but I don't have anything for you, for two reasons. One, I'm feeling a little vindictive after the way you dropped us before, but two, and more importantly, management slapped a hiring freeze on us about six months ago. Circulation is still going the wrong direction, so I couldn't hire you even if I wanted to." He stood up and extended his hand to Berman. "Good luck, Jed. Life's a bitch and then you die. Hope you find something." He shook Berman's hand and sat down again. Berman said nothing. As he turned to leave, the editor scrutinized a story on his computer screen.

In less than fifteen minutes, Berman was back in the newsroom. He walked toward Morgan's desk, but she wasn't there. The guy at the next desk said he thought she had run over to city hall. Berman sat down and wrote a short note on a pink phone message pad:

"Dee, good to see you. Big guy says no good. No room plus he has some feelings about my walking out before. Doesn't expect to have a place for me in the foreseeable future. Take care, Jed." He ripped a piece of Scotch tape from the dispenser on Morgan's desk and attached the message to the top edge of her computer screen. As he stood up, several people noticed him and waved or called out a greeting. He waved back and smiled, then headed down the stairs and out the front doors.

Jane was already home when he arrived. She greeted him with a warm hug and a long kiss. She didn't like the look on Berman's face. She suggested they take a walk and talk things over. The sky was a radiant blue, the sun felt warm, even on a mid-winter day. Jane took Berman's hand as they stepped outside.

"So how did it go?"

Berman didn't look at her as he answered.

"It didn't go. The big guy gave me about half as much time in his office as Lenhard gave me to get out of his, and he used more than half of that to tell me off for running out on them before. He said he doesn't have any jobs right now and he doesn't sound like he'll ever have one for me again."

"Wow! Was he really that rough about it?"

"Yeah, he was. This has not been a great day for me." Berman's voice shook as he spoke. Neither of them knew what to say next. They walked in silence for several blocks, past Brady's restaurant, past the *Chronicle* building, past Berman's old apartment, past the Wises' home, and eventually past the driveway to Charlotte Spanner's house. The Spanner house, where he'd taken on the Child Welfare department, triggered good memories for Berman. His spirits rose slightly. He pointed down the driveway.

"Charlotte Spanner would tell you I'm worth having around. That's an example of the work I can do. I felt really good about getting her kids back for her. Why couldn't *The Chronicle* remember that?"

"That's right," Jane agreed. "You did a lot of good things while you were with the paper. Even some great things. I'm sorry they can't see the value of giving you another chance."

Berman tried to climb above the gloom. It seemed like ages since he had driven down Charlotte Spanner's driveway. So much had changed, and yet, he didn't feel that much different. He shook his head, trying to clear away some of the confusion of the past couple of days. He squeezed Jane's hand and took a deep breath. She looked up at him, squinting a little in the bright sunlight.

"Are you okay, Jed? Do you have a plan for what comes next?"

"Oh, I'm okay," he answered, trying to sound more confident than he felt. "No, I don't have a plan, but I know there's something out there." He repeated it, almost to himself, "I know there's something out there." Not far beyond the grain elevators they turned around and started back to their apartment.